Girlfriend of the Corpse

I scurried after Carrie, catching the door as she passed into the corridor.

"Who else was Bobby hanging out with back then?" I asked. "Just give me a couple of names. I gotta have something to go on."

She paused, glancing back at me. "Try a kid named Gus. I don't know his last name, but he works at the skate-rental place down at the beach. He's an old high-school buddy and I think Bobby trusted him."

"What were the other things? You said you got pregnant 'among other things.'"

Her smile was tense. "God, you are so persistent. Bobby was in love with someone else. I have no idea who, so don't bother to ask. If I'd known about the other woman I'd have broken off our relationship long before. As it was, I didn't hear about her until I told him I was pregnant. I thought at first he might marry me, but when he told me he was seriously involved with someone else, I knew what I had to do. To his credit, he did feel terrible about the bind I was in and he did as much as he could. There was nothing cheap about Bobby and he really was a sweet guy at heart."

She started to move away and I caught her by the arm, thinking rapidly. "Carrie, I don't suppose he gave you a little red address book, did he?"

"All he gave me was a heartache," she said and walked off without looking back.

"C"
is for
CORPSE

A Kinsey Millhone Mystery

SUE GRAFTON

BANTAM BOOKS
TORONTO · NEW YORK · LONDON · SYDNEY · AUCKLAND

"C" IS FOR CORPSE

A Bantam Book / published by arrangement with
Henry Holt and Company

PRINTING HISTORY
Henry Holt edition published May 1986
Bantam edition / May 1987

ISBN 0-553-26468-0

Published simultaneously in the United States and Canada

Bantam Books are published by Bantam Books, Inc. Its trademark, consisting of the words "Bantam Books" and the por-
trayal of a rooster, is registered in U.S. Patent and Trademark
Office and in other countries. Marca Registrada. Bantam
Books, Inc., 666 Fifth Avenue, New York, New York 10103.

For the children who chose me:
Leslie, Jay, and Jamie

The author wishes to acknowledge the invaluable assistance of the following people: Steven Humphrey; Sam Chirman, M.D., and Betty Johnson of the Rehabilitation Group of Santa Barbara; David Dallmeyer, R.P.T.; Deputies Tom Nelson and Juan Tejeda of the Santa Barbara County Sheriff's Department; C. Robert Dambacher, Chief of Investigations, Los Angeles County Medical Examiner–Coroner; Andrew H. Bliss, Director of Medical Records, LAC-USC Medical Center; Delbert Dickson, M.D.; R. W. Olson, M.D.; Peg Ortigiesen; Barbara Stephans; Billie Moore Squires; H. F. Richards; Michael Burridge; Midge Hayes and Adelaide Gest of the Santa Barbara Public Library; and Michael Fitzmorris of Security Services Unlimited, Inc.

1

I met Bobby Callahan on Monday of that week. By Thursday, he was dead. He was convinced someone was trying to kill him and it turned out to be true, but none of us figured it out in time to save him. I've never worked for a dead man before and I hope I won't have to do it again. This report is for him, for whatever it's worth.

My name is Kinsey Millhone. I'm a licensed private investigator, doing business in Santa Teresa, California, which is ninety-five miles north of Los Angeles. I'm thirty-two years old, twice divorced. I like being alone and I suspect my independence suits me better than it should. Bobby challenged that. I don't know quite how or why. He was only twenty-three years old. I wasn't romantically involved with him in any sense of the word, but I did care and his death served to remind me, like a custard pie in the face, that life is sometimes one big savage joke. Not funny "ha ha," but cruel, like those gags sixth-graders have been telling since the world began.

It was August and I'd been working out at Santa Teresa Fitness, trying to remedy the residual effects of a broken left arm. The days were hot, filled with relentless sunshine and clear skies. I was feeling cranky and bored, doing pushdowns and curls and wrist rolls. I'd just worked two cases back-to-back and I'd sustained more damage than a fractured humerus. I was feeling emotionally battered and I needed a rest. Fortunately, my bank account was fat and I knew I could afford to take two months off. At the same time, the idleness was making me restless and the physical-therapy regimen was driving me nuts.

Santa Teresa Fitness is a real no-nonsense place: the brand X of health clubs. No Jacuzzi, no sauna, no music

piped in. Just mirrored walls, body-building equipment,
and industrial-grade carpeting the color of asphalt. The
whole twenty-eight-hundred square feet of space smells
like men's jockstraps.

I'd arrive at eight in the morning, three days a week, and
warm up for fifteen minutes, then launch into a series of
exercises designed to strengthen and condition my left del-
toid, pectoralis major, biceps, triceps, and anything else
that had gone awry since I'd had the snot beaten out of me
and had intersected the flight path of a .22 slug. The
orthopedist had prescribed six weeks of physical therapy
and so far, I'd done three. There was nothing for it but to
work my way patiently from one machine to the next. I was
usually the only woman in the place at that hour and I
tended to distract myself from the pain, sweat, and nausea
by checking out men's bodies while they were checking out
mine.

Bobby Callahan came in at the same time I did. I wasn't
sure what had happened to him, but whatever it was, it had
hurt. He was probably just short of six feet tall, with a foot-
ball player's physique: big head, thick neck, brawny shoulders, heavy legs. Now the shaggy blond head was held to
one side, the left half of his face pulled down in a permanent grimace. His mouth leaked saliva as though he'd just
been shot up with Novocain and couldn't quite feel his own
lips. He tended to hold his left arm up against his waist and
he usually carried a folded white handkerchief that he used
to mop up his chin. There was a terrible welt of dark red
across the bridge of his nose, a second across his chest, and
his knees were crisscrossed with scars as though a swords-
man had slashed at him. He walked with a lilting gait, his
left Achilles tendon apparently shortened, pulling his left
heel up. Working out must have cost him everything he
had, yet he never failed to appear. There was a doggedness
about him that I admired. I watched him with interest,
ashamed of my own interior complaints. Clearly, I could
recover from my injuries while he could not. I didn't feel
sorry for him, but I did feel curious.

That Monday morning was the first time we'd been alone
together in the gym. He was doing leg curls, facedown on
the bench next to mine, his attention turned inward. I had

shifted over to the leg-press machine, just for variety. I weigh 118 and I only have so much upper body I can rehabilitate. I hadn't gotten back into jogging since the injury, so I figured a few leg presses would serve me right. I was only doing 120 pounds, but it hurt anyway. To distract myself, I was playing a little game wherein I tried to determine which apparatus I hated most. The leg-curl machine he was using was a good candidate. I watched him do a set of twelve repetitions and then start all over again.

"I hear you're a private detective," he said without missing a beat. "That true?" There was a slight drag to his voice, but he covered it pretty well.

"Yes. Are you in the market for one?"

"Matter of fact, I am. Somebody tried to kill me."

"Looks like they didn't miss by much. When was this?"

"Nine months ago."

"Why you?"

"Don't know."

The backs of his thighs were bulging, his hamstrings taut as guy wires. Sweat poured off his face. Without even thinking about it, I counted reps with him. Six, seven, eight.

"I hate that machine," I remarked.

He smiled. "Hurts like a son of a bitch, doesn't it?"

"How'd it happen?"

"I was driving up the pass with a buddy of mine late at night. Some car came up and started ramming us from behind. When we got to the bridge just over the crest of the hill, I lost it and we went off. Rick was killed. He bailed out and the car rolled over on him. I should have been killed too. Longest ten seconds of my life, you know?"

"I bet." The bridge he'd soared off spanned a rocky, scrub-choked canyon, four hundred feet deep, a favorite jumping-off spot for suicide attempts. Actually, I'd never heard of anyone surviving that drop. "You're doing great," I said. "You've been working your butt off."

"What else can I do? Just after the accident, they told me I'd never walk. Said I'd never do anything."

"Who said?"

"Family doctor. Some old hack. My mom fired him on the spot and called in an orthopedic specialist. He brought me

back. I was out at Rehab for eight months and now I'm
doing this. What happened to you?"

"Some asshole shot me in the arm."

Bobby laughed. It was a wonderful snuffling sound. He
finished the last rep and propped himself up on his elbows.

He said, "I got four machines to go and then let's bug out.
By the way, I'm Bobby Callahan."

"Kinsey Millhone."

He held his hand out and we shook, sealing an unspoken
bargain. I knew even then I'd work for him whatever the
circumstances.

We ate lunch in a health-food café, one of those places
specializing in cunning imitation meat patties that never
fool anyone. I don't understand the point myself. It seems
to me a vegetarian would be just as repelled by something
that *looked* like minced cow parts. Bobby ordered a bean-
and-cheese burrito the size of a rolled-up gym towel,
smothered in guacamole and sour cream. I opted for stir-
fried veggies and brown rice with a glass of white wine of
some indeterminate jug sort.

Eating, for Bobby, was the same laborious process as
working out, but his single-minded attention to the task allowed me to study him at close range. His hair was sun-
bleached and coarse, his eyes brown with the kind of lashes
most women have to buy in a box. The left half of his face
was inanimate, but he had a strong chin, accentuated by a
scar like a rising moon. My guess was that his teeth had
been driven through his lower lip at some point during the
punishing descent into that ravine. How he'd lived through
it all was anybody's guess.

He glanced up. He knew I'd been staring, but he didn't
object.

"You're lucky to be alive," I said.

"I'll tell you the worst of it. Big hunks of my brain are
gone, you know?" The drag in his speech was back, as
though the very subject affected his voice. "I was in a coma
for two weeks, and when I came out, I didn't know what the
fuck was going on. I still don't. But I can remember how I
used to be and that's what hurts. I was smart, Kinsey. I
knew a lot. I could concentrate and I used to have ideas. My

mind would make these magic little leaps. You know what I mean?"

I nodded. I knew about minds making magic little leaps.

He went on. "Now I got gaps and spaces. Holes. I've lost big pieces of my past. They don't exist anymore." He paused to dab impatiently at his chin, then shot a bitter glance at the handkerchief. "Jesus, bad enough that I drool. If I'd always been like this, I wouldn't know the difference and it wouldn't bug me so much. I'd assume everybody had a brain that felt like mine. But I was quick once. I know that. I was an A student, on my way to medical school. Now all I do is work out. I'm just trying to regain enough coordination so I can go to the fuckin' toilet by myself. When I'm not in the gym, I see this shrink named Kleinert and try to come to terms with the rest of it."

There were sudden tears in his eyes and he paused, fighting for control. He took a deep breath and shook his head abruptly. When he spoke again, his voice was full of self-loathing.

"So. That's how I spent my summer vacation. How about you?"

"You're convinced it was a murder attempt? Why couldn't it have been some prankster or a drunk?"

He thought for a moment. "I knew the car. At least I think I did. Obviously, I don't anymore, but it seems like . . . at the time, I recognized the vehicle."

"But not the driver?"

He shook his head. "Couldn't tell you now. Maybe I knew then, maybe not."

"Male? Female?" I asked.

"Nuh-un. That's gone, too."

"How do you know Rick wasn't meant to be the victim instead of you?"

He pushed his plate away and signaled for coffee. He was struggling. "I knew something. Something had happened and I figured it out. I remember that much. I can even remember knowing I was in trouble. I was scared. I just don't remember why."

"What about Rick? Was he part of it?"

"I don't think it had anything to do with him. I couldn't swear to it, but I'm almost positive."

"What about your destination that night? Does that tie in somehow?"

Bobby glanced up. The waitress was standing at his elbow with a coffeepot. He waited until she'd poured coffee for both of us. She departed and he smiled uneasily. "I don't know who my enemies are, you know? I don't know if people around me know this 'thing' I've forgotten about. I don't want anyone to overhear what I say . . . just in case. I know I'm paranoid, but I can't help it."

His gaze followed the waitress as she moved back toward the kitchen. She put the coffeepot back on the unit and picked up an order at the window, glancing back at him. She was young and she seemed to know we were talking about her. Bobby dabbed at his chin again as an after-thought. "We were on our way up to Stage Coach Tavern. There's usually a bluegrass band up there and Rick and I wanted to hear them." He shrugged. "There might have been more to it, but I don't think so."

"What was going on in your life at that point?"

"I'd just graduated from UC Santa Teresa. I had this part-time job at St. Terry's, waiting to hear if I was accepted for med school."

Santa Teresa Hospital had been called St. Terry's ever since I could remember. "Wasn't it late in the year for that? I thought med-school candidates applied during the winter and got replies back by spring."

"Well, actually I *had* applied and didn't get in, so I was trying again."

"What kind of work were you doing at St. Terry's?"

"I was a 'floater,' really. I did all kinds of things. For a while, I worked Admissions, typing up papers before patients came in. I'd call and get preliminary data, insurance coverage, stuff like that. Then for a while, I worked in Medical Records filing charts until I got bored. Last job I had was clerk-typist in Pathology. Worked for Dr. Fraker. He was neat. He let me do lab tests sometimes. You know, just simple stuff."

"It doesn't sound like hazardous work," I said. "What about the university? Could the jeopardy you were in be traced back to the school somehow? Faculty? Studies?

Some kind of extracurricular activity you'd been involved in?"

He was shaking his head, apparently drawing a blank. "I don't see how. I'd been out since June. Accident was November."

"But your feeling is that you were the only one who knew this piece of information, whatever it was."

His gaze traveled around the café and then came back to me. "I guess. Me and whoever tried to kill me to shut me up."

I sat and stared at him for a while, trying to get a fix on the situation. I stirred what was probably raw milk into my coffee. Health-food enthusiasts like eating microbes and things like that. "Do you have any sense at all of how long you'd known this thing? Because I'm wondering . . . if it was potentially so dangerous . . . why you didn't spill the beans right away."

He was looking at me with interest. "Like what? To the cops or something like that?"

"Sure. If you stumbled across a theft of some kind, or you found out someone was a Russian spy . . ." I was rattling off possibilities as they occurred to me. "Or you uncovered a plot to assassinate the President . . ."

"Why wouldn't I have picked up the first telephone I came to and called for help?"

"Right."

He was quiet. "Maybe I did that. Maybe . . . shit, Kinsey, I don't know. You don't know how frustrated I get. Early on, those first two, three months in the hospital, all I could think about was the pain. It took everything I had to stay alive. I didn't think about the accident at all. But little by little, as I got better, I started going back to it, trying to remember what happened. Especially when they told me Rick was dead. I didn't find out about that for weeks. I guess they were worried I'd blame myself and it would slow my recovery. I did feel sick about it once I heard. What if I was drunk and just ran us off the road? I had to find out what went on or I knew I'd go crazy on top of everything else. Anyway, that's when I began to piece together this other stuff."

"Maybe the rest of it will come back to you if you've re-membered this much."

"But that's just it," he said. "What if it does come back? I figure the only thing keeping me alive right now is the fact that I can't remember any more of it."

His voice had risen and he paused, gaze flicking off to one side. His anxiety was infectious and I felt myself glancing around as he had, wanting to keep my voice low so our conversation couldn't be overheard.

"Have you actually been threatened since this whole thing came up?" I asked.

"No. Un-un."

"No anonymous letters or strange phone calls?"

He was shaking his head. "But I *am* in danger. I know I am. I've been feeling this way for weeks. I need help."

"Have you tried the cops?"

"Sure, I've tried. As far as they're concerned, it was an accident. They have no evidence a crime was committed. Well, hit-and-run. They know somebody rear-ended me and forced me off the bridge, but premeditated murder? Come on. And even if they believed me, they don't have manpower to assign. I'm just an ordinary citizen. I'm not entitled to police protection twenty-four hours a day."

"Maybe you should hire a bodyguard—"

"Screw that! It's you I want."

"Bobby, I'm not saying I won't help you. Of course I will. I'm just talking about your options. It sounds like you need more than me."

He leaned forward, his manner intense. "Just get to the bottom of this. Tell me what's going on. I want to know why somebody's after me and I want them stopped. Then I won't need the cops or a bodyguard or anything else." He clamped his mouth shut, agitated. He rocked back.

"Fuck it," he said. He shifted restlessly and got up. He pulled a twenty out of his wallet and tossed it on the table. He started for the door with that lilting gait, his limp more pronounced than I'd seen it. I grabbed my handbag and caught up with him.

"God, slow down. Let's go back to my office and we'll type up a contract."

He held the door open for me and I went out.

"I hope you can afford my services," I said back over my shoulder.

He smiled faintly. "Don't sweat it."

We turned left, moving toward the parking lot.

"Sorry I lost my temper," he murmured.

"Quit that. I don't give a shit."

"I wasn't sure you'd take me seriously," he said.

"Why wouldn't I?"

"My family thinks I've got a screw loose."

"Yeah, well that's why you hired me instead of them."

"Thanks," he whispered. He tucked his hand through my arm and I glanced over at him. His face was suffused with pink and there were tears in his eyes. He dashed at them carelessly, not looking at me. For the first time, I realized how young he was. God, he was just a kid, banged up, bewildered, scared to death.

We walked back to my car slowly and I was conscious of the stares of the curious, faces averted with pity and uneasiness. It made me want to punch somebody out.

2

By two o'clock that afternoon, the contract was signed,
Bobby had given me a two-thousand-dollar advance against
fees, and I was dropping him off outside the gym, where
he'd left his BMW before lunch. His disability entitled him
to the handicapped slot, but I noticed he hadn't used it.
Maybe someone else was parked there when he arrived, or
maybe, obstinately, he preferred to walk the extra twenty
yards.

I leaned across the front seat as he got out. "Who's your
attorney?" I asked. He held the door open on the passenger
side, his head tilted so he could look in at me.

"Varden Talbot of Talbot and Smith. Why? You want to
talk to him?"

"Ask him if he'd have copies of the police reports released
to me. It would save me a lot of time."

"O.K. I'll do that."

"Oh, and I should probably start with your immediate
family. They might have a theory or two about what's going
on. Why don't I give you a call later and find out when
people are free?"

Bobby made a face. On the way to my office, he'd told me
his disabilities had forced him to move back into the family
home temporarily, which didn't sit well with him. His parents had divorced some years ago and his mother had re-
married, in fact, this was marriage number three.
Apparently, Bobby didn't get along with his current stepfather, but he had a seventeen-year-old stepsister named
Kitty whom he seemed to like. I wanted to talk to all three.
Most of my investigations start with paperwork, but this
one felt different from the outset.

10

"I have a better idea," Bobby said. "Stop by the house this afternoon. Mom's having some people in for drinks around five. My stepfather's birthday. It'll give you a chance to meet everyone."

I hesitated. "You sure it'll be all right? She might not want me barging in on a special occasion like that."

"It's fine. I'll tell her you're coming. She won't care. Got a pencil? I'll give you directions."

I rooted through my handbag for a pen and my notebook and jotted down the details. "I'll be there about six," I said.

"Great." He slammed the car door and moved off.

I watched him hobble as far as his car and then I headed for home.

I live in what was once a single-car garage, converted now to a two-hundred-dollar-a-month studio apartment maybe fifteen feet square, which serves as living room, bedroom, kitchen, bathroom, closet, and laundry room. All of my possessions are multipurpose and petite. I have a combination refrigerator, sink, and stovette, a doll-sized stacking washer/dryer unit, a sofa that becomes a bed (though I seldom bother to unfold it), and a desk that I sometimes use as a dining-room table. I tend to be work-oriented and my living quarters seem to have shrunk, year by year, to this miniature state. For a while, I lived in a trailer, but that began to feel too opulent. I'm often out of town and I object to spending money for space I don't use. It's possible that one day I'll reduce my personal requirements to a sleeping bag that I can toss in the backseat of my car, thus eliminating altogether the need for paying rent. As it is, my wants are few. I don't have pets or houseplants. I do have friends, but I don't entertain. If I have any hobbies at all, they consist of cleaning my little semi-automatic and reading up on evidential documents. I'm not exactly a bundle of laughs, but I do pay my bills, keep a little money tucked away, and provide myself with medical insurance to cover the hazards of my trade. I like my life as it is, though I try not to boast overmuch about the fact. About every six or eight months, I run into a man who astounds me sexually, but between escapades, I'm celibate, which I don't think is any big deal. After two unsuccessful marriages, I find myself keeping my guard up, along with my underpants.

My apartment is located on a modest palm-lined street a block from the beach and it's owned by a man named Henry Pitts, who lives in the main house on the property. Henry is eighty-one years old, a retired baker who supplements his income now by turning out breads and pastries that he trades with local merchants for goods and services. He caters tea parties for the little old ladies in the neighborhood, and in his spare time, he writes crossword puzzles that are a bitch to figure out. He's a very handsome man: tall, lean, and tanned, with shocking-white hair that looks as soft as baby fuzz, a thin aristocratic face. His eyes are a violet-blue, the color of ground morning glories, and they radiate intelligence. He's caring, compassionate, and sweet. It shouldn't have surprised me, therefore, to find him in the company of the "babe" who was having mint juleps with him in the garden when I got home.

I had parked my car out front as usual, and I was heading around to the back, where my entrance is located. My apartment faces the rear and looks out onto a picturesque little bit of scenery. Henry has a patch of grass back there, a weeping willow, rosebushes, two dwarf citrus trees, and a small flagstone patio. He was just coming out of his own back door with a serving tray when he caught sight of me.

"Oh, Kinsey. Well, good. Come on over here. There's someone I want you to meet," he said.

My glance followed his and I saw a woman stretched out on one of the lounge chairs. She must have been in her sixties, plump, with a crown of dyed brown curls. Her face was as lined as soft leather and she used makeup skillfully. It was her eyes that bothered me: a velvety brown, quite large, and, just for a moment, poisonous.

Henry set the tray down on a round metal table between the chairs. "This is Lila Sams," he said, then nodded at me. "My tenant, Kinsey Millhone. Lila's just moved to Santa Teresa. She's renting a room from Mrs. Lowenstein down the street."

She held out a hand with a clatter of red plastic bracelets, moving as though she meant to struggle to her feet.

I crossed the patio. "Don't get up," I said. "Welcome to the neighborhood." I shook hands with her, smiling sociably. Her return smile erased the chill from her gaze and I found myself doing a mental doubletake, wondering if I'd misinterpreted. "What part of the country are you from?"

"Here, there, and everywhere," she said, glancing slyly at Henry. "I wasn't sure how long I'd stay, but Henry makes it seem veerry niiice."

She wore a low-cut cotton sundress, a bright green-and-yellow geometric print on a white background. Her breasts looked like two five-pound flour sacks from which some of the contents had spilled. Her excess weight was carried in her chest and waist, her hefty hips and thighs tapering to a decent set of calves and quite dainty feet. She wore red canvas wedgies and fat red plastic button earrings. As with a painting, I found my gaze traveling right back around to the place where it began. I wanted to make eye contact again, but she was surveying the tray Henry held out to her.

"Oh my. Well, what's all this? Aren't you a sweetie pie!"

Henry had prepared a plate of canapés. He's one of those people who can whip into the kitchen and create a gourmet snack out of canned goods from the back of the cupboard. All I have at the back of my kitchen cupboard is an old box of cornmeal with bugs.

Lila's red fingernails formed a tiny crane. She lifted a canapé and conveyed it to her mouth. It looked like a toast round with a bite of smoked salmon and a dab of dilled mayonnaise. "Mmm, that's *wonderful*," she said, mouth full, and then licked her fingertips, one by one. She wore several crusty diamond rings, the stones clotted together with rubies, and a square-cut emerald the size of a postage stamp, with diamonds on either side. Henry offered me the plate of canapés. "Why don't you try one of these while I fix you a mint julep?"

I shook my head. "I better not. I may try to jog and then I have work to do."

"Kinsey's a private detective," he said to her.

Lila's eyes got big and she blinked in wonderment. "Oh my goodness. Well, how interesting!" She spoke effusively, implying more enthusiasm than etiquette required. I wasn't nearly that thrilled with her and I'm sure she sensed it. I like older women as a rule. I like almost all women, as a matter of fact. I find them open and confiding by nature, amusingly candid when it comes to talk of men. This one was of the old school: giddy and flirtatious. She'd despised me on sight.

She looked at Henry and patted the chaise pad. "Now, you sit down here, you bad boy. I won't have you waiting on me hand and foot. Can you believe it, Kinsey? All he's done this afternoon is fetch me this, fetch me that." She bent over the canapé plate, enthralled. "Now, what is this one?"

I glanced at Henry, half expecting him to shoot me a pained look, but he had settled on the chaise as commanded, peering over at the plate. "That's smoked oyster. And that's a little cream cheese and chutney. You'll like that one. Here."

He was apparently about to hand-feed her, but she smacked at him ineffectually.

"Quit that. You take one for yourself. You are spoiling the life out of me, and what's more, you're going to make me get fat!"

I could feel my face set with discomfort, watching their two heads bent together. Henry is fifty years older than I am and our relationship has always been completely decorous, but I wondered if this was how he felt on those rare occasions in the past when he'd spotted some guy rolling out of my place at six A.M.

"Talk to you later, Henry," I said, moving toward my front door. I don't even think he heard me.

I changed into a tank top and a pair of cutoffs, laced up my running shoes, and then slipped out again without calling attention to myself. I walked briskly one block over to Cabana, the wide boulevard that parallels the beach, and broke into a trot. The day was hot and there was no cloud cover at all. It was now three o'clock and even the surf seemed sluggish. The breeze fanning in off the ocean was dense with brine and the beach was littered with debris. I don't even know why I was bothering to run. I was out of shape, huffing and puffing, my lungs on fire within the first quarter-mile. My left arm ached and my legs felt like wood. I always run when I'm working and I guess that's why I did it that day. I ran because it was time to run and because I needed to shake the rust and stiffness from my joints. As dutiful as I am about jogging, I've never been a big fan of exercise. I just can't think of any other way to feel good.

The first mile was pure pain and I hated every minute of it. Mile two, I could feel the endorphins kick in, and by mile three, I'd found my pace and might have gone on forever. I checked my running watch. It was 3:33. I never said I was swift. I slowed to a walk, pouring sweat. I would pay for this on the morrow, I was relatively sure, but for the moment, I felt loose, my muscles soft and warm. I used the walk home to cool down.

By the time I reached my place again, evaporating sweat had left me chilled and I was looking forward to a hot shower. The patio was deserted, empty mint-julep glasses sitting side by side. Henry's back door was closed and the window shades were drawn. I let myself into my place with the key I carry tied to my shoelace.

I washed my hair and shaved my legs, slipped into a robe, and puttered around for a while, tidying up the kitchen, cleaning off my desk. Finally, I donned a pair of pants, tunic top, sandals, and cologne. At 5:45, I grabbed my big leather handbag and went out again, locking up.

I checked the directions to Bobby's house and turned left on Cabana toward the bird refuge, following the road as it wound into Montebello, which is rumored to have more millionaires per square mile than any other community in the country. I don't know if that's true or not. The residents of Montebello are a mixed lot. Though the big estates are interspersed now with middle-class homes, the overall impression is of money, carefully cultivated and preserved, vintage elegance harking back to a time when wealth was handled with discretion and material display reserved for one's financial peers. The rich, these days, are merely gaudy imitators of their early California counterparts. Montebello does have its "slums," a curious string of clapboard shacks that sell for $140,000 apiece.

The address Bobby'd given me was off West Glen, a narrow road shaded by eucalyptus and sycamore, lined with low walls of hand-hewn stone that curve back toward mansions too remote to be seen by passing motorists. An occasional gatehouse hints at the stately digs beyond, but for the most part West Glen seems to wander through groves of live oak with nothing more on its mind than dappled sunshine, the scent of French lavender, and bumblebees droning

among hot-pink geraniums. It was six now and wouldn't get
dark for another two hours or so.

I spotted the number I was looking for and turned into a
driveway, slowing. To my right were three white stucco cottages, looking like something the three little pigs might
have built. I peered through the windshield, but couldn't
see a parking place. I rolled forward, hoping there would be
a parking pad somewhere around the bend coming up. I
glanced back over my shoulder, wondering why there
weren't any other cars in sight, and wondering which of the
little bungalows belonged to Bobby's folks. I felt a brief moment of uneasiness. He *had* said this afternoon, hadn't
he? I could just picture myself arriving on the wrong
day. I shrugged. Oh, well. I'd suffered worse embarrass-
ments in my life, though for the moment, I couldn't think of
one. I rounded the curve, looking for a place to pull in.
Involuntarily, I slammed on the brakes, skidding to a stop.
"Holy shit!" I whispered.

The lane had opened out into a large paved courtyard.
Just ahead I saw a house. Somehow, in my gut, I knew
Bobby Callahan lived here, not in one of those homey little
snuggeries up front. Those were probably servants' quarters. This was the real thing.

The house was the size of the junior high school I'd at-
tended and had probably been designed by the same architect, a man named Dwight Costigan, dead now, who had
revitalized Santa Teresa single-handedly during the forty-
odd years he worked. The style, if I'm not mistaken, is
Spanish Revival. I have tended, I confess, to sneer at white
stucco walls and red tile roofs. I've been contemptuous of
arches and bougainvillea, distressed beams and balconies,
but I had never seen them put together quite like this.

The central portion of the house was two stories high,
flanked by two cloistered arcades. Arch after arch after
arch, supported by graceful columns. There were clusters
of airy palms, sculptured portals, tracery windows. There
was even a bell tower, like an old mission church. Hadn't
Kim Novak been pushed out of something similar? The
place looked like a cross between a monastery and a movie
set. Four Mercedes were parked in the courtyard like a

glossy ad campaign, and a fountain in the center shot a stream of water fifteen feet high.

I pulled in as far to the right as I could get and parked, then looked down at what I had on. The pants, I saw now, had a stain on one knee that I could only conceal if I held myself in a continual crouch so the tunic would hang down that far. The tunic itself wasn't bad: black gauzy stuff with a low square neck, long sleeves, and a matching tie belt. For a moment, I considered driving home again to change clothes. Then, it occurred to me that I didn't have anything at home that looked any better than this. I torqued myself around to the backseat, sorting through the incredible collection of odds and ends I keep back there. I drive a VW, one of those nondescript beige sedans, great for surveillance work in most neighborhoods. Around here, I could see I'd need to hire a stretch limo. The gardeners probably drove Volvos.

I pushed aside the law books, file boxes, tool kit, the briefcase where I keep my gun locked. Ah, just what I was looking for: an old pair of pantyhose, useful as a filter in an emergency. On the floor, I found a pair of black spike heels I'd bought when I'd intended to pass myself off as a hooker in a tacky part of Los Angeles. When I'd gotten there, of course, I'd discovered that all the whores looked like college girls, so I'd abandoned the disguise.

I tossed the sandals I was wearing into the backseat and hunched my long pants off. I wiggled into the pantyhose, did a spit polish on the pumps, and slipped into those. I took the self-belt off the tunic and tied it around my neck in an exotic knot. In the bottom of my handbag, I found an eyeliner pencil and some blusher and I did a quick makeover, tilting the rearview mirror so I could see myself. I thought I looked weird, but how would they know? Except for Bobby, none of them had ever seen me before. I hoped.

I got out of the car and steadied myself. I hadn't worn heels this high since I'd played dress-up in my aunt's cast-offs when I was in first grade. Beltless, the tunic hit me midthigh, the lightweight fabric clinging to my hips. If I walked in front of a light, they'd see my bikini underpants, but so what? If I couldn't afford to dress well, at least I could provide a distraction from the fact. I took a deep breath and clattered my way toward the door.

3

I rang the bell. I could hear it echo through the house. In due course, the door was opened by a black maid in a white uniform like a nurse's aide's. I wanted to fall into her arms and be dragged off to the infirmary, my feet hurt so bad, but I mentioned my name instead and murmured that Bobby Callahan expected me.

"Yes, Miss Millhone. Won't you come in, please?"

She stepped aside and I moved into the hallway. The ceiling in the entryway was two stories high, light filtering down through a series of windows that followed the line of the wide stone stairs curving up to the left. The floor was tile, a soft red, polished to a satiny sheen. There were runners of Persian carpeting in faded patterns. Tapestries hung from ornamental wrought-iron rods that looked like antique weaponry. The air temperature was perfect, cool and still, scented by a massive floral arrangement on a heavy side table to my right. I felt like I was in a museum.

The maid led me down the hallway to a living room so large the group of people at the far end seemed constructed on a smaller scale than I. The stone fireplace must have been ten feet wide and a good twelve feet high, with an opening big enough to roast an ox in. The furniture looked comfortable; nothing fussy or small. The couches, four of them, seemed substantial, and the chairs were large and overstuffed, with wide arms, reminding me somehow of first-class seats on an airplane. There was no particular color scheme and I wondered if it was only the middle class that ran out and hired someone to make everything match.

I caught sight of Bobby and, mercifully, he lumbered in my direction. He had apparently divined from my expression that I was ill-prepared for this whole pageant.

"I should have warned you. I'm sorry," he said. "Let me get you a drink. What would you like? We've got white wine, but if I tell you what it is, you'll think we're showing off."

"Wine is perfect," I said. "I'm crazy about the show-off kind."

Another maid, not the one who opened the door, but one especially trained for living rooms, anticipated Bobby's needs, approaching with glasses of wine already poured. I was really hoping I wouldn't disgrace myself by spilling a drink down my front or catching a heel on the rug. He handed me a glass of wine and I took a sip.

"Did you grow up in this place?" I asked. It was difficult to picture binkies, Johnny-Jump-Ups, and Tonka trucks in a room that looked like the nave of a church. I suddenly tuned in to what was happening in my mouth. This wine was going to ruin me for the stuff in a cardboard box, which is what I usually drink.

"Actually, I did," he said, looking around with interest now, as though the incongruity had just occurred to him. "I had a nanny, of course."

"Oh sure, why not? What do your parents do? Or should I guess."

Bobby gave me a lopsided smile and dabbed at his chin, almost sheepishly, I thought. "My grandfather, my mother's father, founded a big chemical company at the turn of the century. I guess they ended up patenting half the products essential to civilization. Douches and mouthwashes and birth-control devices. A lot of over-the-counter drugs, too. Solvents, alloys, industrial products. The list goes on for a bit."

"Brothers? Sisters?"

"Just me."

"Where's your father at this point?"

"Tibet. He's taken to mountain climbing of late. Last year, he lived in an ashram in India. His soul is evolving at a pace with his VISA bill."

I cupped a hand to my ear. "Do I detect some hostility?"

Bobby shrugged. "He can afford to dabble in the Great Mysteries because of the settlement he got from my mother when they divorced. He pretends it's a great spiritual jour-

ney when he's really just indulging himself. Actually, I felt
O.K. about him until he came back just after the accident.
He used to sit by my bedside and smile at me benevolently,
explaining that being crippled must be something I was
having to sort through in this life." He looked at me with an
odd smile. "Know what he said when he heard Rick was
dead? 'That's nice. That means he's finished his work.' I got
so upset Dr. Kleinert refused to let him visit anymore, so he
went off to hike the Himalayas. We don't hear from him
much, but it's just as well, I guess."

Bobby broke off. For a moment, tears swam in his eyes
and he fought for control. He stared off toward a cluster of
people near the fireplace and I followed his gaze. There
were only ten or so on a quick count.

"Which one is your mother?"

"The woman in the cream-colored outfit. The guy standing just behind her is my stepfather, Derek. They've been
married three years, but I don't think it's working out."

"How come?"

Bobby seemed to consider several replies, but he finally
settled for a slight head shake and silence. He looked back
at me. "You ready to meet them?"

"Tell me about the other people first." I was stalling, but I
couldn't help myself.

He surveyed the group. "Some, I forget. That woman in
blue I don't know at all. The tall fellow with gray hair is Dr.
Fraker. He's the pathologist I was working for before the
accident. He's married to the redhead talking to my mom.
My mother's on the board of trustees for St. Terry's so she
knows all these medical types. The balding, heavyset man
is Dr. Metcalf and the guy he's talking to is Dr. Kleinert."

"Your psychiatrist?"

"Right. He thinks I'm crazy, but that's all right because he
thinks he can fix me." Bitterness had crept into his voice
and I was acutely aware of the level of rage he must be
dealing with day by day.

As though on cue, Dr. Kleinert turned and stared at us
and then his eyes slid away. He looked like he was in his
early forties with thin, wavy gray hair and a sorrowful expression.

Bobby smirked. "I told him I was hiring a private detective, but I don't think he's figured out yet that it's you or he'd have come down here to have a little chat to straighten us out."

"What about your stepsister? Where is she?"

"Probably in her room. She's not very sociable."

"And who's the little blonde?"

"My mother's best friend. She's a surgical nurse. Come on," he said impatiently. "You might as well take the plunge."

I followed Bobby, keeping pace with him as he hobbled down the room toward the fireplace, where people had congregated. His mother watched us approach, the two women with her pausing in the middle of their conversation to see what had engaged her attention.

She looked young to be the mother of a twenty-three-year-old, lean, with narrow hips and long legs. Her hair was a thick glossy bush of pale fawn brown, not quite shoulder-length. Her eyes were small and deep-set, her face narrow, mouth wide. Her hands were elegant, her fingers long and thin. She wore a cream-colored silk blouse and a full linen skirt nipped in at the waist. Her jewelry was gold, delicate chains at her wrist and throat. The gaze she turned on Bobby was intense and I thought I could feel the pain with which she regarded his crippled form. She looked from him to me, smiling politely.

She moved forward, holding out her hand. "I'm Glen Callahan. You must be Kinsey Millhone. Bobby said you'd be stopping by." Her voice was low and throaty. "I'll give you a chance to enjoy yourself. We'll talk in a bit."

I shook hands with her, startled how bony and warm her hand felt in mine. Her grip was iron.

She glanced at the woman to her right, introducing me. "This is Nola Fraker."

"Hi, how are you?" I said as we shook hands.

"And Sufi Daniels."

Murmured pleasantries were exchanged. Nola was a redhead, with clear, fine-textured skin, and luminous blue eyes, wearing a dark red jumpsuit that left her arms bare and a deep V of naked flesh visible from throat to waist. Already, I didn't want her to bend down or make any sud-

den moves. I had the feeling I knew her from somewhere.
Possibly I'd seen her picture in the society section or something of that sort. Reminder bells went off, at any rate, and I
wondered what the story was.

The other woman, Sufi, was small and somewhat misshapen, thick through the trunk, her back hunched. She
wore a mauve velour sweatsuit that looked like she'd never
sweated in it. Her blond hair was thin and fine, worn too
long, I thought, to be flattering.

After a decent interval, the three of them resumed their
conversation, much to my relief. I hadn't the faintest idea
what to say to them. Nola was talking about a thirty-dol-
lar fabric remnant she was whipping up to wear to a wine-
tasting down in Los Angeles. "I checked all the shops in
Montebello, but it was ridiculous! I wouldn't pay four bills
for an outfit. I wouldn't even pay *two*," she said with energy.

That surprised me. She looked like a woman who enjoyed
extravagance. Unless I just make up things like that. My
notion of women with money is that they drive to Beverly
Hills to have their legs waxed, charge a bauble or two on
Rodeo Drive, and then go to charity luncheons at $1,500 a
plate. I couldn't picture Nola Fraker pawing through the
bargain bin at our local Stretch N' Sew. Maybe she'd been
poor as a young girl and couldn't get used to being a doctor's
wife.

Bobby took my arm and steered me toward the men. He
introduced me to his stepfather, Derek Wenner, and then in
quick succession to Drs. Fraker, Metcalf, and Kleinert. Before I knew what to think, he was hustling me toward the
hallway. "Let's go upstairs. We'll find Kitty and then I'll
show you the rest of the house."

"Bobby, I want to talk to those people!" I said.

"No, you don't. They're dull and they don't know anything."

As we passed a side table, I started to set my wineglass
down, but he shook his head. "Bring it with you."

He grabbed a full bottle of wine out of a silver cooler and
tucked it under his arm. He was really moving at a fair clip,
limp and all, and I could hear my high heels clip-clopping
along inelegantly as we moved toward the foyer. I paused for
a moment to slip my shoes off, and then I caught up with

him. Something about Bobby's attitude made me want to laugh. He was accustomed to doing exactly as he pleased among people I'd been taught to respect. My aunt would have been impressed by the company, but Bobby didn't seem to be.

We went up the stairs, Bobby pulling himself along by the smooth stone banister.

"Your mother doesn't use the name Wenner?" I asked, as I followed him.

"Nope. Callahan is her maiden name as a matter of fact. I changed mine to Callahan when she and my father divorced."

"That's unusual, isn't it?"

"Doesn't seem that way to me. He's a jerk. This way, I don't have to be connected to him any more than she does."

The gallery at the top formed a semicircle with wings branching out on either side. We passed through an archway to the right and into a wide corridor with rooms opening off at intervals. Most of the doors were closed. Daylight was beginning to fade and the upstairs was gloomy. I once conducted a homicide investigation at an exclusive girls' school that had this same air to it. The house felt as if it had been converted to institutional use, someplace impersonal and chill. Bobby knocked at the third door down on the right.

"Kitty?"

"Just a minute," she called.

He flashed me a smile. "She'll be stoned."

Hey, why not? I thought with a shrug. Seventeen.

The door opened and she looked out, gaze shifting from Bobby to me with suspicion. "Who's this?"

"Come on, Kitty. Would you knock that shit off?"

She moved away from the door indifferently. Bobby and I went in and he closed the door behind us. She was anoretic; tall and painfully thin, with knees and elbow joints standing out like Tinkertoys. Her face was gaunt. She was barefoot, wearing shorts and a white tube top that looked about as big as a man's crew sock, one size fits all.

"What are *you* looking at?" she said. She didn't seem to expect an answer so I didn't bother with one. She flopped down on an unmade king-sized bed, staring at me as she

took up a cigarette and lit it. Her nails were bitten to the
quick. The room had been painted black and looked like a
parody of an adolescent girl's room. There were lots of
posters and stuffed animals but all of them had a nightmare
quality. The posters were of rock groups in tartish makeup,
sinister and sneering, depicted in vignettes largely hostile
toward women. The stuffed animals ran more to satyrs than
Winnie-the-Pooh. The air was scented with eau de dope
and my guess was she'd smoked so much grass in there, you
could bury your nose in the bedcovers and get high.

Bobby apparently enjoyed her antagonism. He pulled a
chair over for me, dumping clothes on the floor uncer-
emoniously. I sat down and he stretched out on the foot of
the bed, circling her left ankle with one hand. His fingers
overlapped as if he were holding her wrist instead. It reminded me of Hansel and Gretel. Maybe Kitty was worried
that if she got fat, they'd put her in the cooking pot. I
thought they'd put her in a grave long before that point and
it was frightening. She leaned back on both elbows, smiling
at me faintly down the length of her long, frail legs. All the
veins were visible, like an anatomical diagram with a cel-
luloid overlay. I could see how the bones were strung together in her feet, her toes looking almost prehensile.

"So what's going on downstairs?" she said to Bobby, her
gaze still pinned on me. Her speech was ever so slightly
slurred and her eyes seemed to swim in and out of focus. I
wondered if she was drunk or had just popped some pills.

"They're standing around sucking up booze as usual.
Speaking of which, I brought us wine," he said. "Got a
glass?"

She leaned over to her bed-table and sorted through the
mess, coming up with a tumbler with something sticky and
green in the bottom: absinthe or crème de menthe. She
held the glass out to him. The wine he poured into it be-
came tainted with the remnants of liqueur.

"So, who's the chick?"

I loathe being called a chick.

Bobby laughed. "Oh God, I'm sorry. This is Kinsey. She's
the private detective I told you about."

"I should've figured as much." Her eyes came back to
mine, her pupils so dilated I couldn't tell what color the

irises were. "So how do you like our little sideshow? Bobby and I are the family freaks. What a pair, right?"

This child was getting on my nerves. She wasn't smart enough or quick enough to pull off the tough air she was affecting, and the strain was evident, like watching a stand-up comic with second-rate gags.

Bobby cut in smoothly. "Dr. Kleinert's downstairs."

"Ah, Dr. Destructo. What did you think of him?" She took a drag of her cigarette, feigning nonchalance, but I sensed that she was genuinely curious about my response.

"I didn't talk to him," I said. "Bobby wanted me to meet you first."

She stared at me and I stared back. I remembered doing this sort of stuff in sixth grade with my mortal enemy, Tommy Jancko. I forget now why we disliked each other, but stare contests were definitely the weapons of choice.

She looked back at Bobby. "He wants me hospitalized. D'I tell you that?"

"You going?"

"Hey, no *way*! Get all those needles stuck in me? Uh-un, no thanks. I'm not interested." She swung her long legs over the side of the bed and got up. She crossed the room to a low dressing table with a gilt-edged mirror above it. She studied her face, glancing back at me. "You think I look thin?"

"Very."

"Really?" She seemed fascinated by the notion, turning slightly so she could see her own flat behind. She studied her face again, watching herself take a drag of her cigarette. She did a quick shrug. Everything looked fine to her.

"Could we talk about this murder attempt?" I said.

She padded back to the bed and flopped down again. "Somebody's after him. Definitely," she said. She stubbed out her cigarette, with a yawn.

"What makes you say that?"

"The vibes."

"Aside from the vibes," I said.

"Oh balls, you don't believe us either," she said. She turned sideways and settled against the pillows, folding an arm under her head.

"Is someone after you too?"

"Nun-un. I don't think so. Just him."

"But why would someone do that? I'm not saying I don't believe you. I'm looking for a place to start and I want to hear what you have to say."

"I'd have to think about it some," she said and then she was quiet.

It took me a few minutes to realize she'd passed out. Jesus, what was she on?

4

I waited in the hallway, shoes in hand, while Bobby covered her with a blanket and tiptoed out of the room, closing the door gently.

"What's the story?" I said.

"She's O.K. She was just up late last night."

"What are you talking about? She's half dead!"

He shifted uneasily. "You really think so?"

"Bobby, would you *look* at her? She's a skeleton. She's doing drugs, alcohol, cigarettes. You know she's smoking dope on top of that. How's she going to survive?"

"I don't know. I guess I didn't think she was that bad off," he said. He was not only young, he was *naïve*, or maybe she'd been going under so gradually that he couldn't see the shape she was in.

"How long has she been anoretic?"

"Since Rick died, I guess. Maybe some before that. He was her boyfriend and she took it pretty hard."

"Is that what Kleinert's seeing her for? The anorexia?"

"I guess. I never really asked. She was a patient of his before I started seeing him."

A voice cut in. "Is there some problem?"

Derek Wenner was approaching from the gallery, highball in hand. He was a man who'd been good-looking once. Of medium height, fair-haired, his gray eyes magnified by glasses with steel-blue frames. He was in his late forties now, by a charitable estimate, a solid thirty pounds overweight. He had the puffy, florid complexion of a man who drinks too much and his hairline had receded in a wide U that left a runner of thinning hair down the center, clipped short and brushed to one side. The excess pounds had given him a double chin and a wide neck that made the collar of

his dress shirt seem tight. His pleated gabardine pants
looked expensive and so did his loafers, which were tan and
white, with vents cut into the leather. He'd been wearing a
sport coat earlier, but he'd taken it off, along with his tie.
He unbuttoned his collar with relief.

"What's going on? Where's Kitty? Your mother wants to
know why she hasn't joined us."

Bobby seemed embarrassed. "I don't know. She was talking to us and she fell asleep."

"Fell asleep" seemed a bit understated to me. Kitty's face
had been the color of a plastic ring I sent away for once as a
kid. The ring was white, but if you held it to the light for a
while and then cupped your hand over it, it glowed faintly
green. This, to me, did not connote good health.

"Hell, I better talk to her," he said. I had to guess he'd
had his hands full with her. He opened the door and went
into Kitty's room.

Bobby gave me a look that was part dismay and part anxiety. I glanced in through the open door. Derek put his
drink on the table and sat down on Kitty's bed.

"Kitty?"

He put a hand on her shoulder and shook her gently.
There was no response. "Hey, come on, honey. Wake up."

He shot me a worried look.

He gave Kitty a rough shake. "Hey, come on. Wake up."

"You want me to get one of the doctors from downstairs?"
I said. He shook her again. I didn't wait for a response.

I slipped my shoes on and left my handbag by the door,
heading for the stairs.

When I reached the living room, Glen Callahan glanced
over at me, apparently sensing that something was wrong.

She moved forward. "Where's Bobby?"

"Upstairs with Kitty. I think it might be smart to have
somebody take a look at her. She passed out and your husband's having trouble rousing her."

"I'll get Leo."

I watched while she approached Dr. Kleinert, murmuring to him. He glanced over at me and then he excused
himself from his conversation. The three of us went upstairs.

Bobby had joined Derek at Kitty's bedside, his face creased with concern. Derek was trying to pull Kitty into a sitting position, but she slumped to one side. Dr. Kleinert moved forward swiftly and pushed both men out of the way. He did a quick check of her vital signs, pulling a penlight out of the inside breast pocket of his suit. Her pupils had contracted down to pinpoints, and from where I stood, the green eyes looked milky and lifeless, apparently responding little to the light he flashed first in one, then the other. Her breathing was slow and shallow, her muscles flaccid. Dr. Kleinert reached for the telephone, which was sitting on the floor near the bed, and dialed 911.

Glen remained in the doorway. "What is it?"

Kleinert ignored her, apparently talking to the emergency dispatcher.

"This is Dr. Leo Kleinert. I'm going to need an ambulance out on West Glen Road in Montebello. I've got a patient suffering from barbiturate poisoning." He gave the address and a brief set of instructions about how to reach the place. He hung up and looked at Bobby. "You have any idea what she took?"

Bobby shook his head.

Derek responded, addressing the remark to Glen. "She was fine half an hour ago. I talked to her myself."

"Oh Derek. For God's sake," she said with annoyance.

Kleinert reached over and opened the bed-table drawer. He sorted through some junk and then hesitated, pulling out a stash of pills that would have felled an elephant. They were in a Ziploc bag, maybe two hundred capsules: Nembutals, Seconals, blue-and-orange Tuinals, Placidyls, Quaaludes, like colorful supplies for some exotic cottage industry.

Kleinert's expression was despairing. He looked up at Derek, holding the bag by one corner. Exhibit A in a trial that had been going on for some time by my guess.

"What are those things?" Derek said. "How'd she get them?"

Kleinert shook her head. "Let's get people out of here and then we'll worry about that."

Glen Callahan had already turned and left the room and I could hear her heels clipping purposefully toward the stairs. Bobby took my arm and the two of us moved out into the hallway.

Derek was apparently still having trouble believing this was happening. "Is she going to be O.K.?"

Dr. Kleinert murmured a reply, but I couldn't hear what it was.

Bobby steered me into a room across the hall and closed the door. "Let's stay out of the way. We'll go downstairs in a bit." He rubbed at the fingers of his bad hand as if it were a talisman. The drag in his voice was back.

The room was large, with deep-set windows looking out onto the rear of the property. The wall-to-wall carpeting was white, a dense cut-pile so recently vacuumed that I could see Bobby's footprints in places. His double bed seemed diminutive in a room that was probably thirty feet square, with a large dressing room opening off to the left and what was apparently a bathroom beyond that. A television set rested on an antique pine blanket-chest at the foot of the bed. On the wall to my right was a long built-in desk with a white Formica surface. An IBM Selectric II and the keyboard, monitor, and printer for a home computer were lined up along its length. The bookshelves were white Formica too, filled almost exclusively with medical texts. There was a sitting area in the far corner: two overstuffed chairs and an ottoman covered in a plaid fabric of rust, white, and slate blue. The coffee table, reading lamp, books and magazines stacked nearby suggested that this was where Bobby spent his leisure time.

He went to an intercom on the wall and pressed a button. "Callie, we're starving up here. Could you send us a tray? There are two of us and we'll need some white wine too."

I could hear a hollow clattering in the background: dishes being loaded into the dishwasher. "Yes, Mr. Bobby. I'll have Alicia bring something up."

"Thank you."

He limped over to one of the chairs and sat down. "I eat when I'm anxious. I've always done that. Come sit down. Shit, I hate this house. I used to love it. When I was a kid, it was great. Places to run. Places to hide. A yard that went on forever. Now it feels like a cocoon. Insulated. But it doesn't keep bad stuff out. It feels cold. Are you cold?"

"I'm fine," I said.

I sat down in the other chair. He pushed the ottoman over and I put my feet up. I wondered what it must be like to live in a house like this where all of your needs were tended to, where someone else was responsible for grocery shopping and food preparation, cleaning, trash removal, landscape maintenance. What did it leave you free to do?

"What's it like coming from money like this? I can't even imagine it."

He hesitated, lifting his head.

In the distance, we could hear the ambulance approach, the siren reaching a crescendo and then winding down abruptly with a whine of regret. He glanced at me, dabbing self-consciously at his chin. "You think we're spoiled?" The two halves of his face seemed to give contradictory messages: one animated, one dead.

"How do I know? You live a lot better than most," I said.

"Hey, we do our share. My mother does a lot of fund raising for local charities and she's on the board for the art museum and the historical society. I don't know about Derek. He plays golf and hangs out at the club. Well, that's not fair. He has some investments he looks after, which is how they met. He was the executor for the trust my grandfather left me. Once he and Mom got married, he left the bank. Anyway, they support a lot of causes so it's not like they're just self-indulgent, grinding the poor underfoot. My mother launched the Santa Teresa Girls' Club just about single-handedly. The Rape Crisis Center too."

"What about Kitty? What does she do with herself besides get loaded?"

He looked at me carefully. "Don't make judgments. You don't know what any of us has been through."

"You're right. I'm sorry. I didn't mean to sound quite so righteous. Is she in private school?"

He shook his head. "Not anymore. They moved her over to Santa Teresa High School this year. Anything to try to get her straightened out."

He stared at the door uneasily. The house was so solidly constructed there was no way to tell if the paramedics had come upstairs yet.

I crossed the room and opened the door a crack. They were just coming out of Kitty's room with the portable gurney, its wheels swiveling like a grocery cart's as they angled her into the hall. She was covered with a blanket, so frail that she scarcely formed a mound. One thin arm was extended outside the covers. They'd started an I.V., a plastic bag of some clear solution held aloft by one of the paramedics. Oxygen was being administered through a nose cone. Dr. Kleinert moved toward the stairs ahead of them and Derek brought up the rear, hands shoved awkwardly in his pockets, his face pale. He seemed out of place and ineffectual, pausing when he caught sight of me.

"I'm going to follow in my car," he said, though no one had asked. "Tell Bobby we'll be at St. Terry's."

I felt sorry for him. The scene was like something out of a TV series, the medical personnel very deadpan and businesslike. This was his daughter being taken away and she might actually die, but no one seemed to be addressing the possibility. There was no sign of Bobby's mother, no sign of the people who'd come for drinks. Everything felt ill-planned somehow, like an elaborate entertainment that was falling flat. "You want us to come, too?" I asked.

Derek shook his head. "Let my wife know where I am," he said. "I'll call as soon as I know what's going on."

"Good luck," I said, and he flashed me a weak smile as if good luck was not something he'd had much experience with.

I watched the procession disappear down the stairs. I closed the door to Bobby's room. I started to say something, but Bobby cut me off.

"I heard," he said.

"Why isn't your mother involved in this? Are she and Kitty on the outs or what?"

"Jesus, it's all too complicated to explain. Mom washed her hands of Kitty after the last incident, which isn't as heartless as it sounds. Early on, she did what she could, but I guess it was just one crisis after another. That's part of the reason she and Derek are having such a tough time."

"What's the other part?"

His look was bleak. Clearly, he felt he was equally to blame.

There was a tap at the door and a Chicano woman with her hair in a braid appeared with a tray. Her face was expressionless and she made no eye contact. If she knew what was happening, she gave no indication of it. She fussed around for a bit with cloth napkins and cutlery. I almost expected her to present a room-service check to be signed off with a tip added in.

"Thanks, Alicia," Bobby said.

She murmured something and departed. I felt uncomfortable that it was all so impersonal. I wanted to ask her if her feet hurt like mine, or if she had a family we could talk about. I wanted her to voice curiosity or dismay about the people she worked for, carted away on stretchers at odd hours of the day. Instead, Bobby poured the wine and we ate.

The meal was like something out of a magazine. Plump quartered chicken served cold with a mustard sauce, tiny flaky tarts filled with spinach and a smoky cheddar cheese, clusters of grapes and sprigs of parsley tucked here and there. Two small china bowls with lids held an icy tomato soup with fresh dill clipped across the surface and a little dollop of crème fraîche. We finished with a plate of tiny decorated cookies. Did these people eat like this every day? Bobby never batted an eye. I don't know what I expected him to do. He couldn't squeal with excitement every time a supper tray showed up, but I was impressed and I guess I wanted him to marvel, as I did, so I wouldn't feel like such a rube.

By the time we went downstairs, it was nearly eight and the guests were gone. The house seemed deserted, except for the two maids who were tidying up the living room in silence as we passed. Bobby led us to a heavy oak-paneled door across the wide hall. He knocked and there was a murmured response. We went into a small den, where Glen Callahan was seated with a book, a wineglass on the end table at her right hand. She'd changed into chocolate-brown wool slacks and a matching cashmere pullover. A fire burned in a copper grate. The walls were painted tomato red, with matching red drapes drawn against the chill dusk. In Santa Teresa, most nights are cold regardless of the month. This room felt cozy, an intimate retreat from the rest of the house with its high ceilings and chalk-white stucco walls.

Bobby sat down in the chair across from his mother. "Has Derek called yet?"

She closed her book and set it aside. "A few minutes ago. She's pulled out of it. She had her stomach pumped and they'll be admitting her as soon as she's out of emergency. Derek will stay until the papers have been signed."

I glanced at Bobby. He lowered his face into his hands and sighed once with relief, a sound like a low note on a bagpipe. He shook his head, staring down at the floor.

Glen studied him. "You're exhausted. Why don't you go on to bed? I'll want to talk to Kinsey alone anyway."

"All right. I might as well," he said. The slur in his voice had become pronounced and I could see now that the fine muscles near his eyes were being tugged, as though stimulated electrically. Fatigue apparently exacerbated his disability. He got up and crossed to her chair. Glen took his face in her hands and stared at him intently.

"I'll let you know if there's any change in Kitty's condition," she murmured. "I don't want you to worry. Sleep well."

He nodded, laying the good side of his face near hers. He moved toward the door. "I'll call you in the morning," he said to me, then let himself out. I could hear his dragging gait for a moment in the hallway and then it faded from hearing.

5

I sat in the chair Bobby had vacated. The down-filled cushion was still warm, contoured to the shape of his body. Glen was watching me, formulating, I gathered, an opinion of me. By lamplight, I could see that her hair color was the handiwork of an expert who'd matched it almost exactly to the mild brown of her eyes. Everything about her was beautifully coordinated: makeup, clothing, accessories. She was apparently a person who paid attention to detail and her taste was impeccable.

"I'm sorry you had to see us like this."

"I'm not sure I ever see people at their best," I said. "It gives me a rather skewed impression of humankind. Will he be paying my bills or will you?"

The question caused her to focus on me with interest and I guessed that she brought a considerable intelligence to any matter involving money. She raised an eyebrow ever so slightly.

"He will. He came into his trust when he was twenty-one. Why do you ask?"

"I like to know who I'm reporting to," I said. "What's your feeling about his claim that someone's trying to kill him?"

She took a moment to respond, shrugging delicately. "It's possible. The police seem convinced that someone forced him off that bridge. Whether it was premeditated, I have no idea." Her voice was distinct, low, and intense.

"From what Bobby says, it's been a long nine months."

She ran a thumbnail along her pantleg, directing her comments to the crease. "I don't know how we survived it. He's my only child, the light of my life."

She paused, smiling slightly to herself, and then looked up at me with an unexpected shyness. "I know all mothers must talk like this, but he was special. He really was. Even from infancy. Smart, alert, sociable, quick. And gorgeous. Such a beautiful little boy, easygoing and affectionate, funny. He was magical.

"The night of the accident, the police came to the house. They weren't able to notify us until four in the morning because the car wasn't discovered for a while and then it took hours to get the two boys up the side of the mountain. Rick died instantly, of course."

She broke off and I thought at first she'd lost her train of thought. "Anyway. The doorbell rang. Derek went down, and when he didn't come back, I grabbed a robe and went down myself. I saw two policemen in the foyer. I thought they'd come to tell us there was a burglary in the neighborhood or an accident on the road out front. Derek turned around and he had this awful look on his face. He said, 'Glen, it's Bobby.' I thought my heart had stopped."

She looked up at me and her eyes were luminous with tears. She laced her fingers together, making a steeple of her two index fingers, which she rested against her lips. "I thought he was dead. I thought they'd come to tell me he'd died. I felt a spurt of ice, like I'd been stabbed. It started in my heart and spread through my body 'til my teeth chattered. He was at St. Terry's by then. All we knew at that point was he was still alive, but barely. When we got to the hospital, the doctor didn't give us any hope at all. None. They told us there were extensive injuries. Brain damage and so many broken bones. They said he'd never recover, that he'd be a vegetable if he survived. I was dying. I died because Bobby was dying and it went on for days. I never left his side. I was crazy, screaming at everyone, nurses, doctors . . ."

Her gaze flattened and she lifted an index finger, like a teacher who wants to make a point very clear. "I'll tell you what I learned," she said carefully. "I understood I couldn't buy Bobby's life. Money can't buy life, but it can buy anything else you want. I'd never used money that way, which seems odd to me now. My parents had money. My parents' parents had money. I've always understood the power of money, but I'd never wielded it with quite such effect. He had the best of everything. The best! Nothing was spared.

And he pulled out of it. Having endured so much, I'd hate
to think someone did it deliberately. To all intents and pur-
poses, Bobby's life is ruined. He'll be all right and we'll find
a way for him to live productively, but only because we're in
a position to make that happen. The losses are incalculable.
It's miraculous he's come this far."

"You have any theories about why someone might try to
kill him?"

She shook her head.

"You said Bobby has his own money. Who benefits if he
dies?"

"You'd have to ask him that. He has a will, I'm sure, and
we've discussed his leaving his money to various charities
. . . unless of course, he marries and has legitimate heirs of
his own. You think money might be the motive?"

I shrugged. "I tend to look at that first, especially in a
situation like this when it sounds like there's a lot."

"What else could it be? What could anyone have against
him?"

"People murder for absurd reasons. Someone gets into a
rage over something and retaliates. People get jealous or
want to defend themselves from a real or imagined attack.
Or they've done something wrong and they kill to cover it
up. Sometimes it doesn't even make that much sense.
Maybe Bobby cut someone off in a lane change that night
and the driver followed him all the way up the pass. People
go nuts in cars. I take it he wasn't in the middle of a hassle
with anyone?"

"Not that I was aware of."

"Nobody mad at him? A girl friend maybe?"

"I doubt it. He was going with someone at the time, but
it was a fairly casual relationship from what I could tell.
Once this happened, we didn't see much of her. Of course,
Bobby changed. You don't come that close to death without
paying a penalty. Violent death is like a monster. The closer
you get to it, the more damage you sustain . . . if you survive at all. Bobby's had to pull himself out of the grave, step
by step. He's different now. He's looked into the monster's
face. You can see the claw marks on his body everywhere."

I glanced away from her. It was true. Bobby looked like
he had been attacked: torn and broken and mauled. Violent

death leaves an aura, like an energy field that repels the
observer. I've never looked at a homicide victim yet without
a quick recoil. Even photographs of the dead chill and re-
pulse me.

I shifted back to the matter at hand. "Bobby said he was
working for Dr. Fraker at the time."

"That's right. Jim Fraker's been a friend of mine for years.
That's why Bobby was hired at St. Terry's, as a matter of fact.
As a favor to me."

"How long had he worked there?"

"At the hospital itself, maybe four months. He'd been
working for Jim in Pathology for two months, I think."

"And what did he actually do?"

"Cleaned equipment, ran errands, answered the phone.
It was all routine. They'd taught him to do a few lab tests
and sometimes he monitored machinery, but I can't imagine his job entailed anything that would endanger his life."

"He had his degree from UCST by then, I gather," I said,
repeating what Bobby'd told me.

"That's right. He was working temporarily, hoping to get
accepted to med school. His first applications had been
turned down."

"How come?"

"Oh, he got cocky and only applied to about five schools.
He'd always been an excellent student and he'd never failed
at anything in his life. He miscalculated. Med schools are
ferociously competitive and he simply didn't get accepted
to the ones he tried for. It set him back on his heels for a
time, but he'd rallied, I think. I know he felt the job with
Dr. Fraker was valuable, because it gave him some ex-
posure to disciplines he wouldn't otherwise have known
about until much later in the game."

"What else was going on in his life at that point?"

"Not a lot. He went to work. He dated. He did some
weight lifting, surfed now and then. He went to movies,
went out to dinner with us. It all seemed very ordinary at
the time and it seems very ordinary looking back."

There was another avenue I needed to explore and I wondered how she would react. "Were he and Kitty involved
with one another sexually?"

"Ah. Well, I can't really answer that. I have no idea."

"But it's possible."

"I suppose so, though I don't think it's likely. Derek and I have been together since she was thirteen. Bobby was eighteen, nineteen, something like that. Out of the house at any rate. I do think Kitty was smitten with him. I don't know how he felt about her, but I can't believe a thirteen-year-old would interest him in the least."

"She's grown up pretty fast from what I've seen."

She crossed her legs restlessly, wrapping one around the other. "I don't understand why you're pursuing this point."

"I need to know what was going on. He was anxious about her tonight and more than relieved when he found out she was all right. I wondered how deep the connections ran."

"Oh. I see. A lot of his emotionalism is the aftermath of the accident. From what I'm told, it's not uncommon for people who've suffered head injury. He's moody now. Impatient. And he overreacts. He weeps easily and he gets very frustrated with himself."

"Is part of that the memory loss?"

"Yes," she said. "What makes it hard is he can never predict where the losses will occur. Sometimes he can remember the most inconsequential things, then he'll turn around and forget his own birthdate. Or he'll blank out on someone altogether, maybe someone he's known all his life. That's one of the reasons he's seeing Leo Kleinert. To help him cope with the personality changes."

"He told me Kitty was seeing Dr. Kleinert, too. Was that for the anorexia?"

"Kitty's been impossible from the first."

"Well, I gathered that much. What was it about?"

"Ask Derek. I'm the wrong person to consult about her. I did try, but I don't give a damn anymore. Even this business tonight. I know it sounds cruel, but I can't take it seriously. She does it to herself. It's her life. Let her do anything she wants as long as it doesn't affect the rest of us. She can drop dead for all I care."

"It looks like her behavior affects you whether you like it or not," I ventured carefully. This was clearly touchy stuff and I didn't want to antagonize her.

"I'm afraid that's true, but I've had it. Something's got to change. I'm tired of playing games and I'm sick of watching her manipulate Derek."

I shifted the subject slightly, probing a question I'd been curious about. "You think the drugs were actually hers?"

"Of course. She's been stoned since she walked in my front door. It's been such a bone of contention between Derek and me I can hardly speak of it. She's ruining our relationship." She closed her mouth and composed herself, then said, "What makes you put it that way?"

"About the drugs? It seems odd to me, that's all," I said. "I can't believe she'd leave them in her bed-table drawer in a Ziploc bag for starters and I can't believe she'd have pills in that quantity. Do you know what that stuff is worth?"

"She has an allowance of two hundred dollars a month," Glen said crisply. "I've argued and cajoled until I'm blue in the face, but what's the point? Derek insists. The money comes out of his own account."

"Even so, it's pretty high-level stuff. She'd have to have an incredible connection somewhere."

"I'm sure Kitty has her little ways."

I let the subject pass and made a mental note for myself. I'd recently made the acquaintance of one of Santa Teresa High School's more enterprising drug dealers and he might be able to identify her source. He might even *be* her source, for all I knew. He'd promised me he'd shut down his operation, but that was like a wino promising to buy a sandwich with the dollar you'd donated in good faith. Who were we trying to kid here?

"Maybe we should let it go for now," I said. "I'm sure this day has seemed long enough. I'd like to have the name and telephone number of Bobby's old girl friend if you have it, and I'll probably want to talk to Rick's parents, too. Can you tell me how to get in touch with them?"

"I'll give you both numbers," she said. She got up and crossed to a little antique rosewood desk with pigeonholes and tiny drawers along the top. She opened one of the large drawers below and took out a monogrammed leather address book.

"Beautiful desk," I murmured. This was like telling the Queen of England she has nice jewels.

"Thank you," Glen said idly, while she leafed through the address book. "I bought it at an auction in London last year. I'd hesitate to tell you how much I paid for it."

"Oh, give it a whirl," I said, fascinated. I was getting giddy hanging out with these people.

"Twenty-six thousand dollars," she murmured, running a finger down the page.

I could feel myself shrug philosophically. Hey, big deal. Twenty-six grand was as nothing to her. I wondered what she paid for underwear. I wondered what she paid for *cars*.

"Here it is." She scribbled the information on a scratch pad and tore off a leaf, which she passed to me.

"You'll find Rick's parents rather difficult, I suspect," she said.

"How so?"

"Because they blame Bobby for his death."

"How does he handle that?"

"Not well. Sometimes I think he believes it himself, which is all the more reason to get to the bottom of this."

"Can I ask you one more thing?"

"Of course."

"Is it 'Glen' as in 'West Glen'?"

"The other way around," she said. "I wasn't named for the road. The road was named for me."

By the time I got back in my car, I had a lot of information to digest. It was 9:30, fully dark, and too chilly for a black gauze tunic that ended six inches above my knees. I took a few minutes to wiggle out of my pantyhose and hunch into my long pants. I dropped the high heels into the backseat and pulled on my sandals again, then started the car and put it in reverse. I backed around in a semicircle, looking for a way out. I spotted the second arm of the drive and followed it, catching a glimpse of the rear of the house. There were four illuminated terraces, each with a reflecting pool, shimmering black by night, probably giving back sequential images of the mountains by day, like a series of overlapping photographs.

I reached West Glen and turned left, heading toward town. There'd been no indication that Derek had gotten home and I thought I'd try to catch him at St. Terry's before he left. Idly, I wondered what it'd be like to have a city street named after me. Kinsey Avenue. Kinsey Road. Not bad. I figured I could learn to live with the tribute if it came my way.

6

Santa Teresa Hospital, by night, looks like an enormous art deco wedding cake, iced with exterior lights: three tiers of creamy white, with a square piece missing in front where the entranceway has been cut out. Visiting hours must have been over because I found a parking space right across the street. I locked my car, crossed, and headed up the circular driveway. There was a large portico and covered walk leading up to double doors that shushed open as I approached. Inside, the lobby lights had been dimmed like the interior of an airplane on a night flight. To my left was the deserted coffee shop, one waitress still at work, dressed in a white uniform almost like a nurse's. To my right was the gift shop with a window display done up with the hospital equivalent of naughty lingerie. The whole place smelled like cold carnations in a florist's refrigerated case.

The decor had been designed to soothe and pacify, especially over in the area marked "cashier." I moved to the information desk, where a woman who resembled my old third-grade teacher sat in a pink-striped pinafore with an expectant look on her face.

"Hi," said I. "Can you tell me if Kitty Wenner's been admitted? She was brought into the emergency room a little while ago."

"Well, now let me just check," she said.

I noticed that her name tag read "Roberta Choat, Volunteer." It sounded like one of a series of novels for young girls that was now sorely out of date. Roberta must have been in her sixties and she had all sorts of good-conduct medals pinned to her bib.

"Here it is. That's Katherine Wenner. She's on Three South. You just walk down this corridor and around these elevators to the bank on the far side. Third floor, and you'll be turning to your left. But now, that's a locked psychiatric ward and I don't know that you'll be able to see her. Visiting hours are over, you know. Are you family?"

"I'm her sister," I said easily.

"Well now, dear, why don't you repeat that to the charge nurse up on the floor and maybe she'll believe you," Roberta Choat said just as easily.

"I hope so," I said. It was actually Derek I wanted to see.

I moved down the corridor, as instructed, and rounded the elevators to the bank on the far side. Sure enough, there was a sign that read SOUTH WING, which I found reassuring. I punched the "up" button and the doors opened instantly. A man entered the elevator behind me and then hesitated, eyeing me as if I were the kind of person he'd read about in a rape-prevention pamphlet. He punched "2" and then stayed close to the control panel until he reached his floor and exited.

The south wing looked better than most of the hotels where I've stayed. Of course, it was also more expensive and offered many personal services that didn't interest me, autopsy being one. The lights were all on and the carpet was a blaze of burnt orange, the walls hung with Van Gogh reproductions; a curious choice for the psycho ward, if you ask me.

Derek Wenner was sitting in a visitors' lounge just outside a set of double doors that had small windows embedded with chicken wire and a sign reading PLEASE RING FOR ADMITTANCE with a buzzer underneath.

He was smoking a cigarette, an issue of *National Geographic* open on his lap. He glanced at me blankly when I sat down next to him.

"How's Kitty?" I said.

He started slightly. "Oh. Sorry. I didn't recognize you when you came around the corner. She's better. They just brought her up and they're getting her settled. I'll have a chance to see her in a bit." His glance strayed toward the elevators. "Glen didn't come down with you by any chance, did she?"

I shook my head, watching a mixture of relief and momentary hope fade out of his face.

"Don't tell her you caught me with a cigarette," he said, sheepishly. "She made me quit last March. I'll toss these out before I go home tonight. It's just with Kitty so sick and then all this stuff—" He broke off with a shrug.

I didn't have the heart to tell him he reeked of tobacco. Glen would have to be comatose not to notice it.

"What brings you down here?" he asked.

"I don't know. Bobby went off to bed and I talked to Glen for a while. I just thought I'd stop by and see what was happening with Kitty."

He smiled, not quite sure what to make of it. "I was just sitting here thinking how much this felt like the night she was born. Waiting out in the lounge for hours, wondering how it was all going to come out. They didn't let fathers in the delivery room in those days, you know. Now, I understand, they practically insist."

"What happened to her mother?"

"She drank herself to death when Kitty was five."

He lapsed into silence. I couldn't think of a comment that didn't seem either trivial or beside the point. I watched him put out his cigarette. He worked the hot ember loose, leaving an empty socket like a pulled tooth.

Finally, I said, "Is she being admitted to Detox?"

"Actually, this is the psychiatric ward. I think the detoxification unit is separate. Leo wants to get her stabilized and then do an evaluation before he does anything. Right now, she's a little bit out of control."

He shook his head, pulling at his double chin. "God, I don't know what to do with her. Glen's probably told you what a source of friction it's been."

"Her drug use?"

"Oh, that and her grades, her hours, the drop in her weight. That's been a nightmare. I think she's down to ninety-seven pounds at this point."

"So maybe this is where she needs to be," I said.

One of the double doors opened and a nurse peered out. She wore jeans and a T-shirt. No cap, but she did wear a nursing pin and a name tag that I couldn't read from where I sat. Her hair was ill-dyed, a stade of orange I'd only seen before in marigolds, but her smile was quick and pleasant.

"Mr. Wenner? Would you like to follow me, please?"

Derek got up with a glance at me. "You want to wait? It won't be long. Leo said five minutes was all he'd permit, given the shape she's in. I could buy you a cup of coffee or a drink as soon as I'm done."

"All right. That's nice. I'll be out here."

He nodded and moved off with the nurse. For one brief moment, as they passed into the ward, I could hear Kitty delivering some high-decibel curses of a quite imaginative sort. Then the door closed and the key turned resoundingly in the lock. No one on 3 South was going to sleep tonight. I picked up the *National Geographic* magazine and stared at a series of time-lapse photographs of a blowhole in Yosemite.

Fifteen minutes later, Derek and I were seated in a motel bar half a block away from the hospital. The Plantación is a rogue of a drinking establishment that looks as if it's crept to its present location from some other part of town. The motel itself was apparently built with an eye to sheltering the relatives of the ill and infirm who come to St. Terry's for treatment from small towns nearby. The bar was added as an afterthought, in violation of God knows what city codes, as it is smack in the middle of the residential neighborhood. Of course, the area by now has been infiltrated by medical buildings, clinics, convalescent homes, pharmacies, and various other suppliers to the health-care industry, including a mortuary two blocks away to service folk when all else fails. Maybe the city planning commission decided, at some point, to help ease the pain by making eighty-six-proof alcohol available along with the other kind.

The interior is narrow and dark, with a diorama of a banana plantation that extends behind the bar in the space that usually supports a long mirror, liquor bottles, and a neon beer sign. Instead, arranged as though on a small lighted stage, scale-model banana palms are laid out in orderly rows and tiny mechanized laborers go about the business of harvesting fruit in a series of vignettes. All of the workers appear to be Mexican, including the tiny carved woman who arrives with a water barrel and a dipper just as the noon whistle blows. One man waves from a treetop while a wee wooden dog barks and wags its tail.

Derek and I sat at the bar for a while, scarcely speaking, we were so taken by the scene. Even the bartender, who must have seen it hundreds of times, paused to watch while the mechanical mule pulled a load of bananas around the bend and another cart took its place. Not surprisingly, the house specialties run to cuba libres and banana daiquiris, but no one cares if you order something adult. Derek had a Beefeater martini and I had a glass of white wine that made my lips pull together like a drawstring purse. I'd watched the bartender pour it from a gallon jug that ran about three bucks at any Stop N' Go. The label was from one of those wineries the grape pickers are always striking and I pondered the possibility that they'd peed on the crop to retaliate for unfair labor practices.

"What do you think about this business with Bobby?" I said to Derek when I finally got my mouth unpuckered.

"His claim about a murder attempt? God, I don't know. It sounds pretty farfetched to me. He and his mother seem to believe it, but I can't figure out why anybody'd do such a thing."

"What about money?"

"Money?"

"I've been wondering who benefits financially if Bobby dies. I asked Glen the same thing."

Derek began to stroke his double chin. The excess weight made him look as if he had one normal-sized face superimposed on a much larger one. The jowls were just leftover flesh hanging out the sides. "It'd be a fairly conspicuous motive, I should think," he said. He wore the skeptical look of a man in a stage play: an exaggerated effect for the audience twenty-five rows back.

"Yeah, well forcing him off the bridge was conspicuous too. Of course, if he'd died in the wreck, nobody would have known the difference," I said. "Cars go off the pass every six months or so anyway because people take the curves too fast, so it could have been passed off as a single-car accident. There might have been some damage to the rear bumper where the other driver made contact, but by the time they'd hauled Bobby's car up the mountain, I don't think anybody would have suspected what really occurred. I take it there weren't any witnesses."

"No, and I'm not sure you can count on what Bobby says."

"Meaning what?"

"Well, he obviously has a vested interest in having someone else to blame. The kid doesn't want to own up to the fact that he'd been drinking. He always drove too fast anyway. His best friend gets killed. Rick was Kitty's boyfriend, you know, and his death threw her for a loop. I don't mean to cast doubt on Bobby's version of the story, but it's always struck me as self-serving to some extent."

I studied Derek's face, wondering at the change in his tone of voice. It was an interesting theory and I got the impression that he'd been thinking about it for some time. He seemed uncomfortable, though, pretending to be casual and objective when, in fact, he was undermining Bobby's credibility. I was sure he hadn't dared mention his idea to Glen. "You're saying Bobby made it up?"

"I didn't say *that*," he replied evasively. "I think *he* believes it, but then it gets him off the hook, doesn't it?" His eyes slid away from mine and he signaled to the bartender for a repeat, then glanced back at me. "You ready for another one?"

"Sure, why not?" I hadn't actually finished the wine I had, but I hoped he'd be more at ease if he thought I was matching him drink for drink. Martinis will make you say anything and I was curious what might come out once his tongue was loosened. I could already see that look in his eyes, something slithery and pink that hints of alcoholic tendencies. He fumbled in his shirt pocket and took out the pack of cigarettes, his gaze riveted to the diorama. A tiny mechanical Mexican with a machete was climbing up the tree again. Derek lit a cigarette without looking at it and the gesture took on a curious air, as if it couldn't count against him if he ignored it himself. He was probably the kind of person who eats while watching TV and tops off his Scotch so it will always look as though he is only having one.

"How was Kitty when you saw her? You haven't said."

"She was . . . you know, she was upset, I guess, to find herself hospitalized, but I told her . . . I said, 'Now look, kid. You're just going to have to shape up.'" Derek had shifted into his parental persona and he seemed uncomfortable with that, too. I could just imagine how effective he'd been to date.

"Glen didn't seem very sympathetic," I said.

"Well, no. I can't blame her for that, but then Kitty's had it rough and I don't think Glen understands the toll it can take on a kid like her. Bobby's had every advantage money could buy. Why shouldn't he have it made? I tell you what bothers me. I mean, anything Bobby does is excused. Anything Kitty does is the crime of the century. Bobby's screwed up. Don't kid yourself. But when he fouls up, Glen can always find a way to rationalize what he's done. Know what I mean?"

I shrugged noncommittally. "I don't know what he's done."

The drinks arrived and Derek took a sip from his as though he tasted martinis for a living. He nodded judiciously and set the glass down with care in the center of his cocktail napkin. He touched a knuckle to the corners of his mouth. His movements were becoming liquid and his eyes were beginning to slide around in their sockets like marbles in oil. Kitty had apparently gotten crocked in exactly the same way, only on downers instead of gin.

The bartender took a couple of beers out of the cooler and moved down to the other end of the bar to serve a customer.

Derek's voice dropped. "This is just between you and me and the lamppost," he said. "But the kid's been cited twice on drunk-driving raps and he got some little gal knocked up over a year ago. Glen wants to treat it like youthful hijinks—boys will be boys and all that sort of crap—but let Kitty cross the line once and all hell breaks loose."

I was beginning to see why Bobby thought their marriage wouldn't last. We were playing hardball here, parent vs. parent in the semifinals. Derek tried on a smile that was meant to charm, shifting over to neutral ground.

"So where do you start on a thing like this?" he asked.

"I don't know yet. Usually I nose around, do a background check, uncover a thread, and follow where it leads." I looked at him, watching while he nodded as though I'd actually said something significant.

"Well, I wish you luck. Bobby's a good kid, but there's a lot going on. More to that kid than meets the eye," he said with a knowing look. His speech wasn't slurred, but the consonants were getting soft. The winsome smile flickered back with its sly message. His whole manner implied that he could have said plenty, but discretion held him back. I didn't take him seriously. He was doing some kind of maneuvering, apparently unaware of how transparent he was. I took a sip of wine, wondering if there was anything else I might learn from him.

Derek glanced at his watch. "I better get home. Face the music." He tossed the rest of his martini back and eased himself off the barstool. He pulled out his wallet and sorted through several layers of bills until he found a five and a ten, which he placed on the bar.

"Will Glen be mad?"

He smiled to himself as if he were considering a number of replies. "Glen is always mad these days. It's been a hell of a birthday, I can tell you that."

"Maybe next year will be better. Thanks for the drinks."

"Thanks for coming down here. I appreciate your concern. If I can do anything to help you, you just let me know."

We walked the half-block to my car and then parted company. I watched him in my rearview mirror as he ambled toward the visitors' parking lot on the far side of the hospital. I suspected he was pretending more motor control than he actually had. We'd only been in the Plantación for thirty minutes and I'd watched him down two martinis. I started my car and did a U-turn, pulling up next to him. I leaned across the seat and opened the door on the passenger side. "Why don't I give you a lift?"

"Oh no, I'm fine," he said. He stood for a moment, his body swaying slightly. I could see the message being relayed through his central nervous system. He cocked his head, frowning, and then he got into my car and pulled the door shut. "I got problems enough, right?"

"Right," I said.

7

By the time I got into the office the next morning at nine,
Bobby's attorney had forwarded copies of the initial accident report, along with notes from the follow-up investigation and numerous eight-by-ten color photographs that
showed in glossy detail just how thoroughly demolished
Bobby's car had been and just how dead Rick Bergen had
become as a result. His body had been found, crushed and
mangled, halfway down the slope. I recoiled from the sight
as though a bright light had been flashed in my face, a shock
of revulsion running down my frame. I had to steel myself
to look again so that I could study the details dispas-
sionately. There was something about the way the police
photographer's lights had been rigged against the harsh
dark of night that made the death seem garish, like a low-
budget horror move that was real short on plot. I shuffled
through the series until I found photographs of the accident
scene itself.

Bobby's Porsche had taken out a big section of guardrail,
had sheared off a scrub oak at its base, scarred boulders,
and dug a long trench through the underbrush, apparently
flipping over five or six times before it came to rest at the
bottom of the ravine in a crumpled mass of twisted metal
and shattered glass. There were several views of the car,
front and rear, showing its position relative to various landmarks in the terrain and then the close-ups of Bobby before
the ambulance crew had removed him from the wreckage.
"Oh shit," I breathed. I put the whole stack down for a moment and put a hand across my eyes. I hadn't even had my
coffee yet and there I was looking at human bodies turned
inside out on impact.

I opened the French doors and went out on the balcony and sucked in some fresh air. Below me, State Street was orderly and quiet. Traffic was light and pedestrians obeyed the signals as if they were appearing in an educational film instructing grade-school kids how to conduct themselves on city streets. I watched all the healthy people walk up and down with their limbs intact and the flesh still covering their bones. The sun was shining and the palm trees weren't even stirred by a breeze. Everything looked so ordinary, but only for the moment and only as far as I could see. Death could pop up anytime, a jarring jack-in-the-box with a fixed, bloody grin.

I went back inside and made a pot of coffee and then sat down at my desk, going through the photographs again and taking time now to study the police reports. A copy of the postmortem examination on Rick Bergen had been included and I noticed that it had been conducted by Jim Fraker, whose responsibilities at St. Terry's apparently extended to such services. Santa Teresa is too small a town to pay for its own police morgue and its own medical examiner, so the work is contracted out.

The report Dr. Fraker had dictated effectively reduced Rick's death to observations about the craniocerebral trauma he'd sustained, with a catalogue of abrasions, contusions, small-intestine avulsions, mesenteric lacerations, and sufficient skeletal damage to certify Rick's crossing of the River Styx.

I hauled out my typewriter and opened a file for Bobby Callahan, feeling soothed and comforted as I translated all the unsettling facts into a terse account of events to date. I logged in his check, made a note of the receipt number, and filed the copy of the contract he'd signed. I typed in the names and addresses of Rick Bergen's parents and Bobby's ex–girl friend, along with a list of those present at Glen Callahan's house the night before. I didn't speculate. I didn't editorialize. I just typed it all out and used my two-hole punch at the top of the paper, which I then clamped into a folder and placed in my file cabinet.

That done, I glanced at my watch. Ten-twenty. Bobby's physical-therapy regimen was parceled out into daily stints, while mine was set up for Mondays, Wednesdays, and Fridays. It was possible he was still at the gym. I closed up the office and went down the back steps to the lot, where I keep my car parked. I headed toward Santa Teresa Fitness, gassing up on the way, and caught Bobby just as he was coming out of the building. His hair was still damp from the shower and the scent of Coast soap radiated from his skin. Despite the facial paralysis, the crippled left arm, and the limp, something of the original Bobby Callahan shone through, young and strong, with the blond good looks of a California surfer. I'd seen pictures of him broken, and by comparison, he now seemed miraculously whole, even with the scars still etched on his face like tattoos done by an amateur. When he saw me, he smiled crookedly, dabbing automatically at his chin. "I didn't expect to see you here this morning," he said.

"How was your workout?"

He tilted from side to side, indicating so-so. I tucked my arm through his.

"I have a request, but you don't have to agree," I said.

"What's that?"

I hesitated for a moment. "I want you to go up the pass with me and show me where the car went off."

The smile faded. He glanced away from me and launched into motion again, moving toward his car with that lilting gait. "All right, but I want to stop by and see Kitty first."

"Is she allowed to have visitors?"

"I can talk my way in," he said. "People don't like to deal with cripples, so I can usually get anything I want."

"Spoiled," I said.

"Take any advantage you can," he replied sheepishly. "You want to drive?"

He shook his head. "Let's drop my car off at the house and take yours."

I parked in the visitor's lot at St. Terry's and waited in the car while he went in to see Kitty. I imagined she'd be back on her feet by now, still pissed off, and raising hell on the ward. Not anything I wanted to face. I hope to talk to her again in a couple of days, but I preferred to give her time to settle down. I flipped on the car radio, tapping on the steering wheel in time to the music. Two nurses passed through the parking lot in white uniforms, white shoes and hose, with dark blue capes that looked like something left over from World War I. In due course, Bobby emerged from the building and hobbled across the parking lot, his expression preoccupied. He got into the car. I flipped the radio off and started the engine, backing out of the slot.

"Everything okay?"

"Yeah, sure."

He was quiet as I headed across town and turned left onto the secondary road that cuts along the back side of Santa Teresa at the base of the foothills. The sky was a flat blue and cloudless, looking like semigloss paint that had been applied with a roller. It was hot, and the hills were brown and dry, laid out like a pile of kindling. The long grasses near the road had bleached out to a pale gold, and once in a while, I caught sight of lizards perched up on big rocks, looking as gray and still as twigs.

The road twisted, two lanes of blacktop angling back and forth up the side of the mountain. I downshifted twice and my little VW still complained of the climb.

"I thought I remembered something," Bobby said after a while. "But I can't seem to pin it down. That's why I had to see Kitty."

"What kind of thing?"

"I had an address book. One of those small leather-bound types about the size of a playing card. Cheap. Red. I gave it to someone for safekeeping and now I have no idea who." He paused, shaking his head with puzzlement.

"You don't remember why it was important?"

"No. I remember feeling anxious about it, thinking I better not have it in my possession because it was dangerous to me, so I passed it on. At the time—and I remember this part clearly—I figured I could retrieve it later." He shrugged, snorting derisively. "So much for that."

"Was this before the accident or afterwards?"

"Don't know. I just remember giving it to someone."

"Wouldn't it be dangerous to whoever you gave it to?"

"I don't think so. God." He slid down on his spine so he could rest his head on the back of the seat. He peered through the windshield, following the line of gray hills up to the left where the pass cuts through at the crest. "I *hate* this

feeling. I hate knowing I once knew something and having
no access to it. It's just an image with nothing attached to it.
There aren't any memory cues so I have no way to place it in
time. It's like pieces of a jigsaw puzzle with a whole hunk
knocked off on the floor."

"But how does it work when you forget like that? Is there
any retrieving the information or is it just gone?"

"Oh, sometimes it'll come back, but usually it's blank . . .
like a hole in the bottom of a box. Whatever used to be
there has spilled out along the way."

"What made you think of it in the first place?"

"I don't know. I was looking through a desk drawer and
came across the red leather memo pad that was part of the
same set. Suddenly, I got this flash." He fell silent. I
glanced over at him and realized how tense he was. He was
massaging his bad hand, milking the fingers as if they were
long rubber teats.

"Kitty didn't know anything about it?"

He shook his head.

"How's she doing?"

"She's up and around. I guess Derek's going over to see
her later on. . . ." He paused. We were reaching the crest
of the hill and a muscle near his left eye had started to
jump.

"Are you going to be all right with this?" I asked.

He was staring intently at the side of the road. "Just up
here. Slow down and pull over if you can."

I checked my rearview mirror. There were three cars behind me, but the road was narrowing from three lanes to
two. I eased over to the right and found a gravel shoulder
where I could park. The bridge, with its low concrete
guardrails, was about ten yards ahead. Bobby sat there,
staring to his right.

Where the road descends from the summit, the whole
valley opens out, hills sweeping back as far as the eye can
see to a range of lavender mountains pasted against the rim
of the sky. The August heat shimmered in silence. The land
seemed vast and primitive, looking as it must have looked
for thousands of years. In the distance, live oaks dotted the
landscape, as shaggy and dark and hunched as buffalo.

There'd been no rain for months and the vista seemed chalky and pale, the color washed out.

Closer to us, the roadside dropped away into the treacherous canyon that had nearly marked Bobby's death nine months ago. A length of metal railing had been replaced, but where the bridge began, there was still a chunk of concrete missing.

"The other car started ramming us from behind just as we came over the rim of the hill," he said. I thought he meant to continue, so I waited.

He walked forward a few feet, gravel crunching under his shoes. He was clearly uneasy as he peered down the rocky slope. I looked back over my shoulder at the few cars passing. No one paid the slightest attention to us.

I studied the scene, picking out one of the scarred boulders I'd seen in the photograph, and farther down, the raw, jagged stump where a scrub oak had been snapped off at the base. I knew the Santa Teresa police had swept the area clean of debris from the accident, so there was no need to whip out a magnifying glass or creep around picking fibers from the underbrush.

Bobby turned to me. "Have you ever been close to death?"

"Yes."

"I remember thinking, 'This is it. I'm gone.' I disconnected. I felt like a plant ripped up by the roots. Airborne." He stopped. "And then I was cold and everything hurt and people were talking to me and I couldn't understand a word they said. That was in the hospital and two weeks had passed. I've wondered since then if that's how newborn babies feel. Bewildered like that and disoriented. Helpless. It was such a struggle to stay in touch with the world. Sending down new roots. I knew I could choose. I was barely attached, barely tethered, and I could feel how easy it'd be just to let go like a balloon and sail away."

"But you hung on."

"Hey, my mother willed it. Every time I opened my eyes, I saw her face. And when I closed my eyes, I heard her voice. She'd say, 'We're going to make it, Bobby. We're going to do this, you and I.'"

He was silent again. I thought, Jesus, what must it be like to have a mother who could love you that way? My parents had died when I was five, in a freak car accident. We'd been on a Sunday outing, driving up to Lompoc, when a huge boulder tumbled down the mountain and smashed through the windshield. My father had died instantly and we'd crashed. I'd been in the backseat, thrust down against the floorboards on impact, wedged in by the crushed frame. My mother had lingered, moaning and crying, sinking into a silence finally that I sensed was ominous and forever. It had taken them hours to extract me from the wreckage, trapped there with the dead whom I loved who had left me for all time. After that, I was raised by a no-nonsense aunt who had done her best, who had loved me deeply, but with a matter-of-factness that had failed to nourish some part of me.

Bobby had been infused with a love of such magnitude that it had brought him back from the grave. It was odd, when he was so broken, that I experienced an envy that made tears well up in my eyes. I felt a laugh burble and he turned a puzzled glance on me.

I took out a Kleenex and blew my nose. "I just realized how much I envy you," I said.

He smiled ruefully. "That's a first."

We got back in the car. There'd been no blinding recall, no sudden recollection of forgotten facts, but I'd seen the miry pit into which he had been flung and I'd felt the bond between us strengthened.

"Have you been up here since the accident?"

"No. I never had the nerve and no one ever suggested it. Made me sweat."

I started the car. "How about a beer?"

"How about a bourbon on the rocks?"

We went to the Stage Coach Tavern, just off the main road, and talked for the rest of the afternoon.

8

When I dropped him off at his house at five, he hesitated as he got out of the car, pausing as he'd done before with his hand on the door, peering back in at me.

"Know what I like about you?" he said.

"What," I said.

"When I'm with you, I don't feel self-conscious or like I'm crippled or ugly. I don't know how you do that, but it's nice."

I looked at him for a moment, feeling oddly self-conscious myself. "I'll tell you. You remind me of a birthday present somebody's sent through the mail. The paper's torn and the box is damaged, but there's still something terrific in there. I enjoy your company."

A half-smile formed and disappeared. He glanced over at the house and then back to me. He had something else on his mind, but he seemed embarrassed to admit to it.

"What," I coaxed.

He tilted his head and the look in his eyes was one I knew. "If I were O.K. . . . . if I'd been whole, would you have thought about having a relationship with me? I mean, boy-girl type?"

"You want the truth?"

"Only if it's flattering."

I laughed. "The truth is if I'd run into you before the accident, I'd have been intimidated. You're too good-looking, too rich, and too young. So I gotta say no. If you were 'whole,' as you put it, I probably wouldn't have known you at all. You're really not my type, you know?"

"What is your type?"

"I haven't figured that out yet."

57

He looked at me for a minute with a quizzical smile forming.

"Would you just say what's on your mind?" I said.

"How can you turn it around and make me feel good that I'm deformed?"

"Oh God, you're not deformed. Now, quit that! I'll talk to you later."

He smiled and slammed the car door, moving back then so I could make the turn-around and head out the far side of the driveway.

I drove back to my place. It was only 5:15. I still had time to get a run in, though I wondered at the wisdom of it. Bobby and I had spent the better part of the day drinking beer and bourbon and bad Chablis, gnawing barbecued spareribs and sourdough bread tough enough to tug your dentures out. I was really more in the mood for a nap than a run, but I thought the self-discipline would serve me right.

I changed into my running clothes and did three miles while I went through the mental gymnastics of getting the case organized. It felt like iffy stuff and I wasn't quite sure where to start. I thought I better check with Dr. Fraker in the Pathology Department at St. Terry's first, maybe pop in and see Kitty at the same time, and then try the newspaper morgue and go through the tedious business of checking back through local news prior to the accident just to see what was going on at the time. Maybe some event then current would shed light on Bobby's claim that someone had tried to murder him.

I went over to Rosie's at seven for a glass of wine. I was feeling restless and I wondered if Bobby hadn't set something in motion somehow. It was nice having someone to pal around with, nice to while away an afternoon in good company, nice to have someone whose face I looked forward to seeing. I wasn't sure how to categorize our relationship. My affection for him wasn't maternal in any way. Sisterly, perhaps. He seemed like a good friend and I felt for him all the admiration one feels for a good friend. He was fun, and being with him was peaceful. I'd been alone for so long that a relationship of any kind seemed like seductive stuff.

I snagged a glass of wine at the bar and then I sat in the back booth and surveyed the place. For a Tuesday night, there was a lively crowd, which is to say, two guys arguing nasally at the bar, and an old couple from the neighborhood sharing a big plate of pancakes layered with ham. Rosie remained at the bar with a cigarette, smoke drifting up around her head in a halo of nicotine and hair spray. She's in her sixties, Hungarian and bossy, a creature of muumuus and dyed auburn tresses, which she wears parted down the center and plastered into place with sprays that have sat on the grocery-store shelves since the beehive hairdo bumbled out of fashion in 1966. Rosie has a long nose, a short upper lip, eyes that she pencils into narrow, suspicious-looking slits. She's short, top-heavy, and opinionated. Also she pouts, which in a woman her age is ludicrous, but effective. Half the time, I don't like her much, but she never ceases to fascinate.

Her establishment has the same crude but cranky appeal. The bar extends along the left wall with a stuffed marlin arched above it that I suspect was never really alive. A big color TV sits on the far end of the bar, sound off, images dancing about like transmissions from another planet where life is vibrant and lunatic. The place always smells of beer, cigarette smoke, and cooking grease that should have been thrown out last week. There are six or seven tables in the center of the room surrounded by chrome-and-plastic chairs out of somebody's 1940s dinette set. The eight booths along the right wall have been fashioned out of plywood and stained the color of walnut, complete with tasteless suggestions carved in by ruffians who apparently had had a go at the ladies' room, too. It's possible that Rosie doesn't read English well enough to divine the true meaning of these primitive slogans. It's also possible that they express her sentiments exactly. Hard to know with her.

I glanced over at her and discovered that she was sitting bolt upright and very still, squinting narrowly at the front door. I followed her gaze. Henry had just come in with his new lady friend, Lila Sams. Rosie's antennae had apparently gone up automatically, like My Favorite Martian in drag. Henry found a table that seemed reasonably clean and pulled out a chair. Lila sat down and settled her big plastic bag on her lap like a small dog. She was wearing a bright cotton dress in a snazzy print, bold red poppies on a ground of blue, and her hair looked as if it had been poufed at the beauty parlor that very afternoon. Henry sat down, glancing back at the booth, where he knows I usually sit. I gave a little finger wave and he waved back. Lila's head swiveled in my direction and her smile took on a look of false delight.

Rosie, meanwhile, had set her evening paper aside and had left her stool, gliding through the bar like a shark. I could only surmise that she and Lila had met before. I looked on with interest. This might be almost as entertaining as *Godzilla Meets Bambi,* at my local cinema. From my vantage point, of course, the whole encounter took place in pantomime.

Rosie had her order pad out. She stood and stared at Henry, behaving as though he were alone, which is exactly how she treats me when I come in with a friend. Rosie doesn't speak to strangers. She doesn't make eye contact with anyone she hasn't known for some time. This is especially true when the "anyones" are women. Lila was all aflutter. Henry conferred with her and ordered for them both. Much discussion ensued. I gathered that Lila had made some request that didn't suit Rosie's notion of gourmet Hungarian cuisine. Maybe Lila wanted the peppers left out or something roasted instead of fried. Lila looked like the sort of woman who'd have lots of dietary taboos. Rosie only had the one. You ate it the say she served it or you went somewhere else. Lila apparently couldn't believe that she couldn't be catered to. Shrill and quarrelsome noises arose, all Lila's. Rosie didn't say a word. It was her place. She could do anything she wanted to. The two men at the bar who'd been arguing about politics turned to watch the show. The couple eating the sonkás palacsinta paused simultaneously, forks in midair.

Lila flounced her chair back. I thought for a minute she meant to hit Rosie with her purse. Instead, she delivered what looked like a scathing remark and marched toward the door with Henry scrambling after her. Rosie remained unruffled, smiling secretly as cats do in the midst of mouse dreams. The customers in the place, all five of us, got very quiet, tending studiously to our own private thoughts lest Rosie turn on us inexplicably and eighty-six us for life.

Twenty minutes passed before Rosie found an excuse to head my way. My wineglass was empty and she was bringing me a refill with unheard-of good grace. She set the second glass on the table and then folded her hands in front of her, wiggling slightly in place. She does this when she wants your attention or feels you haven't lauded her with quite enough praise for some culinary accomplishment.

"Looks like you took care of *her*," I remarked.

"Is vulgar woman. Terrible creature. She was in once before and I don't like her a bit. Henry must be crazy nuts to come in my place with a hussy like that. Who is she?"

I shrugged. "Listen, all I know is her name is Lila Sams. She's renting a room from Mrs. Lowenstein and Henry seems to be smitten."

"I'm gonna smitten her if she comes in here again! She got something funny with her eyes." Rosie screwed her face up and did an imitation of Lila that made me laugh. Rosie's generally a humorless person and I had no idea her powers of observation were so keen, let alone her ability to mimic. She was dead serious, of course. She drew herself together. "What's she want with him anyway?"

"What makes you think she wants anything? Maybe the two of them are just interested in a little companionship. Henry's very handsome, if you ask me."

"I didn't ask you! He's very handsome. He's good fellow too. So why does he need companionship with that little snake?"

"Like they say, Rosie, there's no accounting for taste. Maybe she has redeeming qualities that aren't immediately evident."

"Oh no. Not her. She's up to something no good. I'm gonna talk to Mrs. Lowenstein. What's the matter with her, renting to a woman like that?"

I rather wondered about that myself, walking the half-block home. Mrs. Lowenstein is a widow who owns considerable property in the neighborhood. I couldn't believe she needed the money and I was curious how Lila Sams had arrived at her doorstep.

When I got back to my place, Henry's kitchen light was on and I could hear the muffled sounds of Lila's voice, shrill and inconsolable. The encounter with Rosie had apparently

upset her thoroughly and all of Henry's murmured reas-
surances were doing no good. I unlocked my door and let
myself in, effectively shutting out the noise.

I read for an hour—six thrilling chapters from a book on
burglary and theft—and went to bed early, wrapping myself
up in my quilt. I turned off the light and lay there for a
while in the dark. I could have sworn I still heard the faint
rise and fall of Lila's wine, circling my ear like a mosquito. I
couldn't distinguish the words, but the tone was clear . . .
contentious and ill-humored. Maybe Henry would realize
she was not as nice as she pretended to be. Maybe not,
though. I'm always startled at what fools men and women
make of themselves in the pursuit of sex.

I woke at seven, had a cup of coffee while I read the paper, and then headed over to Santa Teresa Fitness for my
Wednesday workout. I was feeling stronger and the two
days of jogging had left my legs aching pleasantly. The
morning was clear, not yet not, the sky as blank as a canvas
being prepared for paint. The parking lot at the gym was
almost full and I snagged the one empty space. I spotted
Bobby's car two slots over and I smiled, looking forward to
seeing him.

The gym was surprisingly populated for the middle of the
week, with five or six two-hundred-and-eighty-pound guys
lifting weights, two women in tights on the Nautilus equipment, and a trainer supervising the workout of a young
actress whose rear end was spreading out like slowly melt-
ing candle wax. I caught sight of Bobby doing bench presses
on a Universal machine near the far wall. He'd apparently
been there for a while because his T-shirt was ringed with
sweat and his blond hair had separated into damp strands. I
didn't want to interrupt him so I simply stashed my gym
bag and and got down to business myself.

I started my workout with some bicep curls, using dumb-
bells with hardly any weight, beginning to concentrate as I
warmed up. By now, I knew my routine and I had to fight a
certain mounting impatience. I'm not a process person. I
like goals and closure, the arrival instead of the journey itself. Repetition makes me rebellious. How I manage to jog
from day to day I'm never sure. I proceeded to wrist curls,
mentally leaping ahead through my routine, wishing I was

at the end of it instead of two exercises in. Maybe Bobby and I could have lunch again if he was free.

I heard a clatter and then a thump and looked up in time to see that he'd lost his balance and stumbled against a stack of five-pound plates. It was clear he hadn't hurt himself, but he seemed to catch sight of me for the first time and his embarrassment was acute. He flushed, trying to scramble to his feet again. One of the guys at the next machine leaned over casually and gave him an assist. He steadied himself self-consciously, waving aside any further help. He limped over to the leg-press machine, his air brusque and withdrawn. I went on working out as though I hadn't seen anything, but I kept a discreet eye on him. Even at that distance, I could see that his mood was dark, his face tense. A couple of people sent looks in his direction that spoke of pity, veiled as concern. He mopped at his chin, his attention turned inward. His left leg was going into muscle spasms of some sort and he clutched at his knee with frustration. The leg was like a separate creature, jumping fitfully, defying containment or control. Bobby groaned, pounding angrily at his own flesh as though he might subdue it with his fist. I struggled with an impulse to cross the room, but I knew it would only make things worse. He'd been pushing himself and his body was vibrating with fatigue. Just as suddenly as it had begun, the spasm seemed to fade. He dashed at his eyes, keeping his head low. As soon as he was able to walk again, he snatched up a towel and headed for the locker room, abandoning the rest of his regimen.

I hurried through the rest of my workout and showered as quickly as I could. I expected to find his car gone, but it was still parked in the slot where I'd seen it. Bobby sat with his arms encircling the steering wheel, his head resting on his arms, his shoulders convulsing with dry, hacking sobs. I hesitated for a moment and then approached the car on the passenger side. I got in and closed the door and sat there with him until he was done. I didn't have any comfort for him. There wasn't anything I could do. I had no way to address his pain or his despair and my only hope was to let him know by my presence that I did feel for him and I did care.

It passed by degrees, and when it was over, he dried his eyes with a towel and blew his nose, keeping his face averted.

"You want to go have some coffee?"

He shook his head. "Just leave me alone, O.K.?" he said.

"I got time," I said.

"Maybe I'll call you later."

"All right. I'll go ahead and take care of some business and maybe we can connect up this afternoon. You need anything in the meantime?"

"No." The tone was dull, his manner listless now.

"Bobby—"

"No! Just get the fuck away from me and leave me alone. I don't need your help."

I opened the car door. "I'll check back with you," I said. "Take care."

He reached over and grabbed the door handle, slamming it shut. He started the engine with a roar, and I stepped aside, as he backed out of the slot with a squeal of tires and shot out of the parking lot without a backward glance.

That was the last I ever saw of him.

9

The Pathology Department at St. Terry's is located below ground in the heart of a maze of small offices. Miles of corridors branch out in all directions, connecting the nonmedical departments charged with the actual running of the facility: maintenance, housekeeping, engineering, plant operations. Where the floors above are renovated and tastefully done, the decor down here runs to brown vinyl tile and glossy paint the color of vanished bones. The air smells hot and dry and certain open doorways reveal glimpses of ominous machinery and electrical ducts as big as sewer pipes.

There was a steady flow of pedestrian traffic that day, people in hospital uniforms, as pale and expressionless as residents of an underground city, starved for sunlight. The Pathology Department itself was a pleasant contrast: spacious, well lighted, handsomely appointed in royal blue and gray, with fifty to sixty lab technicians working to accommodate the blood, bone, and tissue specimens that filtered down from above. The computerized equipment seemed to click, hum, and whir: efficiency augmented by an army of experts. Noise was muted, telephones pinging daintily against the artificial air. Even the typewriters seemed to be muffled, recording discreetly the secrets of the human condition. There was order, proficiency, and calm, the sense that here, at least, the pain and indignation of illness was under control. Death was being held at bay, measured, calibrated, and analyzed. Where it had claimed a victory, the same crew of specialists dissected the results and fed them into the machinery. Paper poured out in a long road, paved with hieroglyphics. I stood in the doorway for a moment, struck by the scene. These were microscope detectives, pursuing killers of another order than those I hunted down.

"May I help you?"

I glanced over at the receptionist, who was watching me.

"I'm looking for Dr. Fraker. Do you know if he's here?"

"Should be. Down this aisle to the first left, then left again and you can ask somebody back there."

I found him in a modular compartment lined with bookshelves, furnished with a desk, a swivel chair, plants, and graphic art. He was tipped back in his chair, his feet propped up on the edge of his deck, leafing through a medical book the size of the *Oxford English Dictionary*. He had a pair of rimless bifocals in one hand, chewing on one of the stems as he read. He was substantially built—wide shoulders, heavy thighs. His hair was a thick, silvery white, his skin the warm tone of a flesh-colored crayon. Age had given his face a softly crumpled look, like a freshly laundered cotton sheet that needs to be starched and ironed. He wore surgical greens with matching booties.

"Dr. Fraker?"

He glanced up at me and his gray eyes registered recognition. He pointed a finger. "Bobby Callahan's friend."

"That's right. I wondered if I could talk to you."

"Sure, absolutely. Come on in."

He got to his feet and we shook hands. He indicated the chair near his desk and I sat down.

"We can make an appointment to talk later if I've caught you at a bad time," I said.

"Not at all. What can I do for you? Glen told me Bobby hired someone to look into the accident."

"He's convinced it was a murder attempt. Hit and run. Has he talked to you about that?"

Dr. Fraker shook his head. "I haven't seen him for months except for Monday night. Murder. Do the police agree?"

"I don't know yet. I've got a copy of the accident report and as nearly as I can tell, they don't have much to go on. There weren't any witnesses and I don't think they found much evidence at the scene."

"That's unusual, isn't it?"

"Well, there's usually *something* to go on. Broken glass, skid marks, transfer traces on the victim's vehicle. Maybe the guy jumped out of his car and swept up all the soil and paint flecks, I don't know. I do trust Bobby's intuition on this. He says he was in danger. He just can't remember why."

Dr. Fraker seemed to consider that briefly and then shifted in his seat. "I'd be inclined to believe him myself. He's a bright boy. He was a gifted student, too. It's a damn shame there's so little left of that. What's he think is going on?"

"He hasn't any idea and, as he points out, the minute he remembers, he's in more trouble than he is now. He suspects somebody's still after him."

He cleaned his glasses with a handkerchief, contemplating the matter. He was a man apparently accustomed to dealing with puzzles, but I imagined his solutions were derived from symptoms instead of circumstances. Diseases don't require an underlying motivation in the same way homicide does.

He shook his head slightly, his eyes meeting mine. "Odd. The whole thing's a little bit out of my range." He put his glasses on, turning businesslike. "Well. We better figure out what's going on, then. What do you need from me?"

I shrugged. "All I know to do is start back at square one and see if I can determine what kind of trouble he was in. He'd worked for you for what? Two months?"

"About that. He started in September, I believe. I can have Marcy look that up if you want exact dates."

"I gather he was hired here because of your relationship with his mother."

"Well, yes and no. We generally have a slot available for a premed student. It just happened that Bobby filled the bill in this case. Glen Callahan's a very big cheese around here, but we wouldn't have hired him if he'd been a dud. Can I get you some coffee? I'm about to have some."

"All right, sure."

He leaned sideways slightly, calling to the secretary, whose desk was in his line of sight. "Marcy? Can we get some coffee in here, please?"

To me, he said, "You take cream and sugar?"

"Black is fine."

"Both black," he called out.

There was no reply, but I assumed it was being taken care of. He turned his attention back to me. "Sorry to interrupt."

"That's all right. Did he have desk space down here?"

"He had a desk up front, but that was cleared out, oh, I'd say within a day of the accident. Nobody thought he'd survive, you know, and we had to bring somebody else in pretty quickly. This place is a madhouse most of the time."

"What happened to his things?"

"I dropped them by the house myself. There wasn't much, but we put what we came across in a cardboard box and I passed it on to Derek. I don't know what he did with it, if anything. Glen was at the hospital twenty-four hours a day at that point."

"Do you remember what was in it?"

"His desk? Odds and ends. Office things."

I made a note to myself to check for the box. I supposed there was a chance it was still at the house somewhere. "Can you walk me through Bobby's day and show me what sorts of things he did?"

"Sure. Actually, he divided his time between the lab and the morgue out in the old county medical facility on Frontage Road. I've got to make a run out there anyway and you can ride along if you like, or follow in your car if that's easier."

"I thought the morgue was here."

"We've got a small one here, just off the autopsy room. We've got another morgue out there."

"I didn't realize there was more than one."

"We needed the added space for the contract work we do. St. Terry's maintains a few offices out there, too."

"Really. I didn't think that old county building was still in use."

"Oh yes. There's a private radiology group that works out there, and we've got storage rooms for medical records. It's a bit of a hodgepodge, but I don't know what we'd do without it."

He glanced over as Marcy came in with two mugs, her gaze carefully affixed to the surface of the coffee, which was threatening to slop over the sides. She was young, dark-haired, no makeup. She looked like the sort of person you'd want holding your hand if the lab techs did something excruciating.

"Thank you, Marcy. Just on the edge of the desk here is fine."

She set the mugs down and gave me a quick smile on her way out.

Dr. Fraker and I discussed the office procedures while we drank the coffee and then he took me on a tour of the lab, explaining Bobby's various responsibilities, all of which seemed routine and not very important at that. I made a note of the names of a couple of his co-workers, thinking I might talk to them at a later date.

I waited while he took care of a few details and signed out, telling Marcy where he'd be.

I followed him to the freeway in my car, heading toward the former county hospital. The complex was visible from the highway: a sprawling labyrinth of yellowing stucco and red tile roofs that had turned nearly rust-brown with age. We passed it, took the next off-ramp, and circled back along Frontage Road, turning left into the main driveway.

County General had once been a flourishing medical facility, designed to serve the entire Santa Teresa community. It was secondarily earmarked as the treatment center for the indigent, funded through various social-service agencies. As the years passed, it came to be associated with the underprivileged: welfare recipients, illegal aliens, and all the unfortunate victims of Saturday-night crime sprees. Gradually, County General was shunned by both the middle class and the well-to-do. Once MediCal and Medicare came into effect, even the poor opted for St. Terry's and other local private hospitals, turning this place into a ghost town.

There was a sprinkling of cars in the parking lot. Temporary wooden signs shaped like arrows directed the visitor to Medical Records, nursing offices, Radiology, the morgue, and departments representing obscure branches of medicine.

Dr. Fraker parked his car and I pulled into the slot next to his. He got out, locked up, and waited while I did the same. A modest attempt was being made to maintain the grounds, but the driveway itself was cracked, coarse weeds beginning to sprout through the asphalt. The two of us headed toward the main entrance without saying much. He seemed to take the place for granted, but I found it all vaguely unsettling. The architecture was, of coarse, of the usual Spanish styling: wide porches along the front, deeply recessed windows faced with wrought-iron bars.

We went in, pausing in a spacious lobby. It was clear that over the years some attempt had been made to "modernize" the place. Fluorescent lighting was now tucked up against the high ceilings, throwing down illumination too diffuse to satisfy. Once-grand anterooms had been partitioned off. Counters had been built across two of the interior arches but there was no furniture in the reception area and no one awaiting admission. The very air was permeated with the smell of abandonment and neglect. From the far end of the dim hallway to our right, I could hear a typewriter clacking, but it sounded like an old manual, operated by an amateur. There was no other indication of occupancy.

Dr. Fraker gave me a perfunctory tour. According to him, Bobby had made the round-trip as needed between this place and St. Terry's, picking up inactive files for patients readmitted to the hospital after an interval of years, hand-delivering X rays and autopsy reports. Old charts were automatically retired to the storage facilities out here. Of course, most data was kept on computer now, but there was still a backlog of paper that had to be warehoused somewhere. Bobby apparently also did some moonlighting out here, taking the graveyard shift for morgue attendants who were out sick or on vacation. Dr. Fraker indicated that this was largely a babysitting function, but that Bobby had put in a considerable number of hours during the two months he was on the job.

We were on our way downstairs by then, descending a wide staircase of red Spanish tile, our footsteps resounding at a hollow, mismatched pace. Because the hospital is constructed against a hillside, the rear of the building is below ground, while the front portion looks out onto paths partially overgrown with shrubs. It was darker down here, as though the utilities had been cut back for the sake of economy. The temperature was cool and the air was scented with formaldehyde, that acrid deodorant for the deceased. An arrow on the wall pointed us to Autopsy. I began to armor myself against the images my senses were conjuring up.

Dr. Fraker opened the door with its frosted-glass panel. I didn't actually hesitate before entering, but I did do a quick visual scan to assure myself that we weren't interrupting some guy with a boning knife filleting a corpse. Dr. Fraker seemed to sense my apprehension and he touched at my elbow briefly.

"There's nothing scheduled," he said and led the way.

I smiled uneasily and followed. At first glance, the place seemed deserted. I noted walls of apple-green ceramic tile, long stainless-steel counters with lots of drawer space. This was like a high-tech kitchen in a decorator magazine, complete with a stainless-steel island in the middle that sported its own wide sink, tall crook-necked faucets, a hanging scale, and drainboard. I felt my mouth set in distaste. I knew what was prepared here and it wasn't food.

A swinging door on the far side of the room was pushed open and a young man in surgical greens backed in, pulling a gurney after him. The body on the cart was wrapped in a dense, tawny plastic that obscured age and sex. A toe tag was visible and I could see a portion of the dark head, blank face swaddled in plastic like a mummy's. It reminded me vaguely of the caution spelled out now on dry cleaners' bags: "WARNING: To avoid danger of suffocation, keep away from babies and children. Do not use in cribs, beds, carriages, or playpens. This bag is not a toy." I averted my gaze, taking in a deep breath then just to prove I could.

Dr. Fraker introduced me to the attendant, whose name was Kelly Borden. He was in his thirties, big and soft-bodied, with fuzzy, prematurely graying hair pulled back in a fat braid that extended halfway down his back. He had a beard, a handlebar mustache, mild eyes, and a wristwatch that looked like it would keep time on the ocean floor.

"Kinsey's a private investigator looking into Bobby Callahan's accident," Dr. Fraker said.

Kelly nodded, his expression neutral. He rolled the gurney over to what looked like a big refrigerator case and eased it in beside a second gurney, also occupied. Roommates, I guessed.

Dr. Fraker looked back at me. "I've got some things to take care of upstairs. Why don't I leave you two alone and you can ask him anything you want. Kelly worked with him. Maybe he can fill you in and then we can talk again, when you see what's what."

"Great," I said.

10

Once Dr. Fraker left, Kelly Borden got out a spray bottle of disinfectant that he began to squirt on the stainless-steel counters, wiping everything down methodically. I wasn't sure he really needed to do it, but it allowed him to keep his eyes averted. It was a polite way of ignoring me, but I didn't object. I used the time to circle the room, peering into glass-fronted cabinets filled with scalpels, forceps, and grim little hacksaws.

"I thought there'd be more bodies," I said.

"In there."

I glanced over at the door he'd come through. "Can I look?"

He shrugged.

I crossed and opened the door, which had a temperature gauge beside it reading forty degrees. The room, about the size of my apartment, was lined with fiberglass pallets arranged in tiers like bizarre bunk beds. There were eight bodies in evidence, most wrapped in the same yellowing plastic, through which I could discern, in some cases, arms and legs and seeping injuries, blood and body fluids condensing on the surface of the plastic wrap. Two bodies were covered with sheets. An old woman, lying on the pallet nearest me, was naked, as still as wood and looking faintly dehydrated. A dramatic Y-shaped cut had been made down the middle of her body, sewn back in big clumsy stitches, like a chicken, stuffed and trussed. Her breasts were splayed outward like old beanbags and her pubic area was almost as hairless as a young girl's. I wanted to cover her, but what was the point? She was beyond cold, beyond pain, modesty, or sex. I watched her chest, but there was no reassuring rise and fall. Death was beginning to seem like a

parlor trick—how long can you hold your breath? I felt myself breathing deeply again, not wanting to participate. I
closed the door, stepping back into the warmth of the autopsy room. "How many can you accommodate?"

"Fifty, maybe, in a pinch. I've never seen more than
eight or so."

"I thought most people went straight to a mortuary."

"They do if they've died of natural causes. We get everything else. Homicide victims, suicides, accidents, any
death of a suspicious or unusual nature. Most of those are
autopsied and then released to a mortuary in a relatively
short period of time. Of the ten we have on hand, some are
indigents. A couple of 'em are John Does we're holding in
hopes we'll get a positive I.D. Sometimes burial arrange-
ments are pending so we hold a body for the next of kin.
Two we've had around for years. Franklin and Eleanor. Like
mascots."

I crossed my arms, feeling chilled, shifting the subject
back to the living. "Do you know Bobby very well?" I asked.
I turned and leaned against the wall, watching him polish
the faucet handles on the stainless-steel sink.

"I hardly know him at all. We worked different shifts."

"How long have you worked out here?"

"Five years."

"What else do you do with your time?"

He paused, looking up at me. He didn't seem to like the
personal questions, but he was too polite to say so. "I'm a
musician. I play jazz guitar."

I stared at him for a minute, hesitating. "Have you ever
heard of Daniel Wade?"

"Sure. He was a local jazz pianist. Everybody's heard of
him. He hasn't been around town in years, though. He a
friend of yours?"

I moved away from the wall, taking up my rounds. "I was
married to him once."

"*Married* to him?"

"That's right." There were some jars filled with a brackish
liquid in which body parts were marinating. I wondered if
there might be a pickled heart tucked in among all the
livers, kidneys, and spleens.

Kelly went back to his work. "Incredible musician," he remarked in a tone of voice that was part caution, part respect.

"That he is," I said, smiling at the irony. I never talked about this stuff and it seemed odd to be doing it in an autopsy room to a morgue attendant in surgical greens.

"What happened to him?" Kelly asked.

"Nothing. He was in New York last I heard. Still playing his music, still on drugs."

He shook his head. "God, the talent that guy has. I never really knew him, but I used to see him every chance I got. I can't understand why he never got anywhere."

"The world is full of talented people."

"Yeah, but he's smarter than most. At least from what I heard."

"Too bad I wasn't as smart as he was. I could have saved myself a lot of grief," I said. Actually, the marriage, though brief, had been the best few months of my life. Daniel had the face of an angel back then . . . clear blue eyes, a cloud of yellow curls. He always reminded me of some artist's rendering of a Catholic saint—lean and beautiful, ascetic-looking, with elegant hands and an unassuming air. He exuded innocence. He just couldn't be faithful, couldn't lay off the drugs, couldn't stay in one place. He was wild and funny and corrupt, and if he came back today, I can't swear I'd turn him down, whatever he asked.

I let the conversation lapse and Kelly, prompted by the silence, finally spoke up.

"What's Bobby doing these days?"

I glanced back at him. He had perched himself on a tall wooden stool, the rag and disinfectant on the counter to his left.

"He's still trying to get his life back together," I said. "He works out every day. I don't know what else he does with his time. I don't suppose you have any idea what was going on back then, do you?"

"What difference does it make at this point?"

"He says he was in some kind of danger, but his memory's shot. Until I fill in the gaps, he's probably still in trouble."

"How come?"

"If somebody tried to kill him once, they may try again."

"Why haven't they done that so far?"

"I don't know. Maybe they think they're safe."

He looked at me. "That's weird."

"He never confided in you?"

Kelly shrugged, his manner ever so slightly guarded again. "We only worked together a couple of times. I was off on vacation for part of the time he was here, and the rest of it, I was on days while he did graveyard shift."

"Is there any chance he might have left a small red leather address book out here?"

"I doubt it. None of us even have lockers for our stuff."

I took a business card out of my wallet. "Will you give me a call if you have any ideas? I'd like to know what was going on back then and I know Bobby'd appreciate some help."

"Sure."

I went in search of Dr. Fraker, passing Nuclear Medicine, the nursing offices, and the offices of a group of local radiologists, all in the basement. I ran into Fraker just as he was coming downstairs again.

"All through?" he said.

"Yes, are you?"

"I've got a 'post' at noon, but we can find an empty office and talk if you like."

I shook my head. "I don't have any other questions for the moment. I may want to check back with you at some point."

"Absolutely. Just give me a call."

"Thanks. I'll do that."

I sat in my car in the parking lot, making notes on some three-by-five index cards I keep in the glove compartment: date, time, and names of the two people I'd talked to. I thought Dr. Fraker was a good resource, even though the interview with him hadn't yielded much. Kelly Borden hadn't been much help either, but at least it was an avenue I'd explored. Sometimes the noes are just as important as the yeses because they represent cul-de-sacs, allowing you to narrow your field of inquiry until you stumble into the heart of the maze. In this case, I had no idea where that might lie or what might be hidden there. I checked my watch. It was 11:45 and I thought about lunch. I have a hard time eating meals when I should. Either I'm not hungry when I'm supposed to be or I'm hungry and not in a place where I can stop and eat. It becomes a weight-control maneuver, but I'm not sure it's good for my health. I started my car and headed toward town.

I went back to the health-food restaurant where Bobby and I had eaten lunch on Monday. I was really hoping to run into him, but he was nowhere in sight. I ordered a longevity salad that was supposed to take care of 100 percent of my nutritional needs for life. What the waitress brought me was a plate piled with weeds and seeds, topped with a zesty pink dressing with specks. It didn't taste nearly as yummy as a Quarter Pounder with cheese, but I did feel virtuous, knowing I had all that chlorophyll coursing through my veins.

When I got back in my car, I checked my teeth in the rearview mirror to make sure they weren't flecked with alfalfa sprouts. I prefer not to interview people looking like I've just been grazing out in some field. I leafed through my notebook for Rick Bergen's parents' address and then I hauled out a city map. I had no idea where Turquesa Road was. I finally spotted it, a street about the size of an ingrown hair, off an equally obscure lane in the foothills that stretch across the back of town.

The house was staunch and plain, all upright lines, with a driveway so steep that I avoided it altogether and squeezed my car in along the ice plant growing below. A bald cinderblock wall prevented the hillside from tumbling into the road and gave the impression of a series of barricades as it zigzagged up to the front. Once I reached the porch, the view was spectacular, a wide-angle shot of Santa Teresa from end to end with the ocean beyond. A hang-glider hovered high up to my right, sailing in lazy circles toward the beach. The day was full of hard sunlight, meager clouds looking like white foam just beginning to evaporate. It was dead quiet. No traffic, no sense of neighbors nearby. I could see a rooftop or two but there was no feeling of people. The landscaping was sparse, composed of drought-tolerant plants: pyracantha, wisteria, and succulents.

I rang the bell. The man who came to the door was short, tense, unshaven.

"Mr. Bergen?"

"That's right."

I handed him my business card. "I'm Kinsey Millhone. Bobby Callahan hired me to look into the accident last—"

"What for?"

I made eye contact. His were small and blue, red-rimmed. His cheeks were prickly with a two-day growth of beard that made him look like a cactus. He was a man in his fifties, radiating the smell of beer and sweat. His hair was thinning and combed straight back from his face. He wore pants that looked like he'd retrieved them from a Salvation Army box and a T-shirt that read "Life's a bitch. Then you die." His arms were soft and shapeless, but his gut protruded like a basketball pumped to maximum pressure per square inch. I wanted to respond in the same rude tone he was using with me, but I curbed my tongue. This man had lost a son. Nobody said he had to be polite.

"He thinks the accident was an attempt on his life," I said.

"Bullshit. I don't mean to be rude to you, lady, but let me fill you in. Bobby Callahan is a rich kid. He's spoiled, irresponsible, and self-indulgent. He fuckin' drank too much and he ran off the road, killing my son, who was incidentally his best friend. Anything else you've heard is horseshit."

"I'm not so sure of that," I said.

"Well, I am and I'm telling you straight. Check the police reports. It's all there. Have you seen 'em?"

"I got copies yesterday from Bobby's attorney," I said.

"No physical evidence, right? You got Bobby's claim someone ran him off the road, but you got nothing to substantiate a word he says, which in my mind makes his story pure crap."

"The police seem to believe him."

"You think they can't be bought off? You think the cops can't be persuaded by a few bucks?"

"Not in this town," I said. This man had really put me on the defensive and I didn't like the way I was handling myself.

"Says who?"

"Mr. Bergen, I know a lot of the local police. I've worked with them—" It sounded lame, but I was sincere.

He interrupted again, saying, "Nuts!" He made a dismissive gesture, turning his head with disgust. "I got no time for this. Maybe my wife'll talk to you."

"I'd rather talk to you," I said. He seemed surprised by that, as though no one ever preferred to talk to him.

"Forget it. Ricky's dead. It's all over with."

"Suppose it's not? What if Bobby's really telling the truth and it wasn't his fault?"

"What's it to me in any event? I don't give a good goddamn about him."

I nearly replied, but I shut my mouth instead, trusting some other instinct. I didn't want to get caught up in endless petty arguments that would only serve to keep this man inflamed. His agitation was profound, but I suspected that there was an ebb and flow to it. "May I have ten minutes of your time?"

He thought about it for a moment and then agreed with an air of annoyance. "Christ, come on in. I'm havin' my lunch. Reva's gone anyway."

He walked away from the door, leaving it up to me to close it after us and follow him through the house, which was drably carpeted and smelled as if it had been closed up. Window shades were drawn against the afternoon sun and the light in the house had an amber cast. I received a brief impression of overscaled furniture: two matching recliners covered in green plastic, and an eight-foot sectional sofa with an afghan on one end, occupied by a big black dog.

The kitchen was done in thirty-year-old linoleum with cabinets painted an intense shade of pink. The appliances made the room look like an illustration from an old issue of *Ladies' Home Journal*. There was a small built-in breakfast nook with newspapers piled up on one bench, and a narrow wooden table with a permanent centerpiece composed of sugar bowl, paper-napkin dispenser, salt and pepper shakers shaped like ducks, a mustard jar, ketchup bottle, and a bottle of A-1 Sauce. I could see his sandwich preparations laid out too: an assortment of processed cheese slices and a lunchmeat laced with olives and ominous chunks of animal snout.

He sat down and motioned me into the bench across from him. I shoved aside some of the newspapers and took a seat.

He was already slathering Miracle Whip on that brand of soft white bread that can double as a foam sponge. I kept my eyes discreetly averted as if he were engaged in pornographic practices. He laid a thin slice of onion on the bread and then peeled the cellophane wrap from the cheese, finishing with layers of lettuce, dill pickles, mustard, and meat. He looked up at me belatedly. "You hungry?"

"Starved," I said. I'd eaten a mere thirty minutes before and it wasn't my fault if I was hungry again. The way I looked at it, the sandwich was filled with preservatives, which might be just what I needed to keep my body from going bad. He cut the first masterpiece diagonally, passing half to me, and then he made a second sandwich more lavish than the first and cut that one, too. I watched him patiently, like a well-trained dog, until he gave the signal to eat.

For three minutes, we sat in silence, wolfing down lunch. He popped open a beer for me and a second one for himself. I despise Miracle Whip but, in this instance, it seemed like a gourmet sauce. The bread was so soft our fingertips left dents near the crust.

Between bites, I dabbed the corners of my mouth with a paper napkin. "I don't know your first name," I said.

"Phil. What kind of name is Kinsey?"

"My mother's maiden name."

And that was the extent of the social niceties until we'd both pushed our plates back with a sigh of relief.

11

After lunch, we sat out on the deck in painted metal porch chairs pockmarked with rust. The deck was actually a shelf of poured concrete, forming the roof of the garage, which had been carved into the hillside. Wooden planters filled with annuals formed a low protective barrier around the perimeter. A mild breeze was picking up, offsetting the heavy blanket of sunshine that settled on my arms. Phil's belligerence was gone. He'd been pacified perhaps by the many chemicals in his lunch, but more likely by the two beers and the prospect of the cigar he was clipping with a pocket guillotine. He plucked a big wooden kitchen match from a can next to his chair and bent down, using the surface of the deck to scratch it into life. He puffed on the cigar until it drew fully, then shook the match out and dropped it in a flat tin ashtray. For a moment, we both sat and stared out at the ocean.

The view was like a mural painted on a blue backdrop. The islands in the channel looked grim and deserted, twenty-six miles out. On the mainland, the small beaches were faintly visible, the surf like a tiny ruffle of white lace. The palm trees looked no bigger than fledgling asparagus. I could pick out a few landmarks: the courthouse, the high school, a big Catholic church, a theater, the one office building downtown over three stories high. From this vantage point, there was no evidence of the Victorian influence or any of the later architectural styles that blended now with the Spanish.

This house, he told me, had been finished in the summer of 1950. He and his wife, Reva, had just bought the place when the Korean War broke out. He'd been drafted and had gone off two days after they moved in, leaving Reva

with stacks of cardboard boxes to unpack, returning four-
teen months later with a service-related disability. He
didn't specify what it was and I didn't ask, but he had apparently only worked sporadically since his medical discharge.
They'd had five children and Rick had been the youngest.
The others were scattered now through the Southwest.

"What was he like?" I asked. I wasn't sure he'd answer.
The silence stretched on and I wondered if perhaps it might
have been the wrong question. I hated to spoil whatever
sense of camaraderie we'd established.

He shook his head finally. "I don't know how to answer
that," he said. "He was one of those kids you think you're
never going to have a minute's trouble with. Always sunny,
did things without being told, good grades in school. Then
when he was sixteen or so—his last year in high school—he
seemed to lose his footing. He graduated all right, but he
didn't seem to know what to do with himself. He was drifting. Had the grades for college and God knows I'd have
found the money someplace, but it didn't interest him.
Nothing did. Oh, he worked, but it never amounted to a
hill of beans."

"Was he doing drugs?"

"I don't think so. At least there was never any sign of it
that I could see. The kid drank a lot. Reva thought it was
that, but I don't know. He did like to party. He was out 'til
all hours, slept the weekends away, hung out with kids like
Bobby Callahan, way above us socially. Then he started dating Bobby's stepsister, Kitty. Christ, that girl was trouble
the day she was born. By then, I was sick of putting up with
him. If he didn't want to be part of the family, fine. Go
somewhere else, though, earn your own keep. Don't think
you can use this place to get meals and laundry done." He
paused, looking over at me. "Was I wrong? I'm asking you."

"I don't know," I said. "How can you answer a question
like that anyway? Kids get off-course and then they
straighten out. Half the time, it doesn't have anything to do
with parents. Who knows what it is?"

He was silent, staring out at the horizon, his lips encircling the cigar like a hose coupling. He sucked in some
nicotine, then blew out a cloud of smoke. "Sometimes I
wonder how bright he was. Maybe he should have seen a

therapist, but how did I know? That's what Reva says now. What's a psychiatrist going to do with a kid who has no ambition?"

I didn't have a response to any of this so I made sympathetic sounds and let it go at that.

Brief silence. He said, "I hear Bobby's all messed up."

His tone was hesitant, a guarded inquiry about a hated rival. He must have wished Bobby dead a hundred times, cursing his good fortune at having survived.

"I'm not sure he wouldn't trade places with Rick if he could," I said, feeling my way. I didn't want to set off a fresh surge of agitation, but I didn't want him harboring the notion that Bobby was somehow "luckier" than Rick. Bobby was working his ass off to make life all right, but it was a struggle.

Below us, an old pale blue Ford rattled into view, spewing exhaust. The driver swung wide around my car and paused, apparently activating an automatic garage door. The car nosed out of sight beneath us and, moments later, I heard the muffled sound of the car door slamming.

"That's my wife," Phil said, as the garage-door mechanism ground under our feet.

Reva Bergen trudged up the steep walk, burdened with grocery sacks. I noted with curiosity that Phil made no move to assist her. She caught sight of us as she reached the porch. She hesitated, her face a perfect blank. Even at that distance, her gaze had an unfocused quality that seemed more pronounced when she finally came out of the back door, moments later, to join us. She was a dishwater blonde with that washed-out look women sometimes acquire in their fifties. Her eyes were small, nearly lashless. Pale eyebrows, pale skin. She was frail and bony, her hands looking as clumsy as gardening gloves on her narrow wrists. The two of them seemed so entirely unsuited to each other that I quickly discarded the unbidden image of their marital bed.

Phil explained who I was and the fact that I was investigating the accident in which Rick had been killed.

Her smile was mean. "Bobby's conscience bothering him?"

Phil interceded before I could frame a response. "Come on, Reva. What harm can it do? You said yourself the police—"

She turned abruptly and went back inside. Phil shoved his hands down in his pockets with embarrassment. "Nuts. She's been like that ever since it happened. Things set her off. I haven't been a joy to live with myself, but this thing has torn her heart out."

"I should be on my way," I said. "But I would like for you to do one thing if you would. I've been trying to figure out what could possibly have been going on back then and I'm not having much luck so far. Did Rick give you any indication that Bobby was in trouble or upset? Or that he might have had some kind of problem himself?"

He shook his head. "Rick's whole life was a problem to me, but it didn't have anything to do with the accident. I'll ask Reva, though, and see if she knows anything."

"Thanks," I said. I shook his hand and then fished a card out of my bag so he'd know how to get in touch with me.

He walked me down to the road and I thanked him again for lunch. As I got in my car, I glanced up. Reva was standing on the porch, staring down at us.

I headed back into town. I stopped by the office to check my answering machine for messages (none) and my mail, which was all junk. I made a fresh pot of coffee and hauled out my portable typewriter, detailing the notes on my investigation to that point. It was painstaking stuff, given the fact that I'd turned up absolutely nothing. Still, Bobby was entitled to know how I'd spent my time and at thirty bucks an hour, he was entitled to know where the money went.

At three o'clock, I locked the office and walked over to the public library, which was two blocks over and two blocks up. I went downstairs to the periodicals room and asked for the previous September's newspapers, now consigned to microfilm. I found a machine and sat down, threading in the first reel. The print was white on black, all of the photographs looking like negatives. I had no idea what I might spot so I was forced to skim every page. Current events, national news, local political issues, fire, crime, storm systems, folks being born and dying and getting divorced. I read the lost-and-found column, the personals, society, sports. The mechanism for advancing the film was somehow out of whack, so that paragraphs jerked onto the nine-by-twelve screen with the focus slightly skewed, generating a motion sickness of sorts. Around me, people were browsing among the magazines or were seated in low chairs, reading newspapers attached to upright wooden lances. The only sounds in the room were the drone of the machine I was using, an occasional cough, and the rustle of newsprint.

I managed to check the papers for the first six days of September before my resolve faltered. I'd have to do this in small doses. My neck felt stiff and my head was starting to ache. A glance at my watch showed that it was nearly five and I was bored to death. I made a note of the last date I'd scanned and then I fled into the late-afternoon sunshine. I walked back to my office building and retrieved my car from the parking lot without going upstairs.

On the way home, I stopped off at the supermarket for milk, bread, and toilet paper, doing a quick tour with my cart. There was so much lyrical music playing overhead, I felt like the heroine in a romantic comedy. Once I'd found what I needed, I moved to the express lane, twelve items or less. There were five of us in line, all surreptitiously counting the contents of each other's carts. The man in front of me had a head too small for the size of his face, like an underinflated balloon. He had a little girl with him, maybe four years old, wearing a brand-new dress several sizes too big. Something about it spelled "poor," but I don't know why. It made her look like a midget; waistline at her hips, the hem down around her ankles. She held the man's hand with perfect trust, giving me a shy smile so filled with pride that I found myself smiling back.

I was tired by the time I got home and my left arm ached. There are days when I scarcely remember the injury, other days when I feel drained by a constant dull pain. I decided to skip my run. To hell with it. I took a couple of Tylenol with codeine, kicked my shoes off, and crawled into the folds of my quilt. I was still there when the phone rang. I awoke with a start, reaching automatically for the receiver. My apartment was dark. The unexpected shrill blast of sound had sent a jolt of adrenaline through me and my heart was pounding. I glanced at the clock with uneasiness. Eleven-fifteen.

I mumbled hello, rubbing a hand across my face and through my hair.

"Kinsey, it's Derek Wenner. Have you heard?"

"Derek, I'm sound asleep."

"Bobby's dead."

"What?"

"I guess he'd been drinking, though we're not even sure of that at this point. His car went off the road and smashed into a tree on West Glen. I thought you'd want to know."

"What?" I knew I was repeating myself, but I couldn't understand what he was talking about.

"Bobby's been killed in a car accident."

"But when?" I don't know why it mattered. I was just asking questions because I couldn't cope with the information any other way.

"A little after ten. He was dead by the time they got him to St. Terry's. I have to go down and identify him, but there doesn't seem to be any doubt."

"Can I do anything?"

He seemed to hesitate. "Well, actually, maybe you could. I tried to reach Sufi, but I guess she's out. Dr. Metcalf's service is tracking him down, so he'll probably be here in a bit. I wonder if you could sit with Glen in the meantime. That way, I can head on over to the hospital and see what's going on."

"I'll be right there," I said and hung up.

I washed my face and brushed my teeth. I was talking to myself the whole time, but I didn't feel anything. All my inner processes seemed to be suspended temporarily while my brain struggled with the facts. The information kept bounding back. No way. Nuh-un. How could Bobby be gone? Not true.

I grabbed a jacket, my handbag, and my keys. I locked up, got in my car, started the engine, pulled out. I felt like a well-programmed robot. When I turned onto West Glen Road, I saw the emergency vehicles and I could feel a chill tickle at the base of my spine. It was just at the big bend, a blind corner near the "slums." The ambulance was already gone, but patrol cars were still there, radios squawking in the night air. Bystanders stood on the side of the road in the dark while the tree he'd hit was washed with high-intensity floodlights, the raw gash in the trunk looking like a fatal wound in itself. His BMW was just being removed by a tow truck. The scene looked, oddly, like a location for a movie being shot. I slowed, turning to peer at the site with an eerie feeling of detachment. I didn't want to add to the confusion and I was worried about Glen, so I drove on. A little voice murmured, "Bobby's dead." A second voice said, "Oh no, let's don't do that. I don't want that to be true, O.K.?"

I pulled into the narrow drive, following it until it opened out into the empty courtyard. The entire house was blazing with lights as if a massive party were in progress, but there was no sound and not a soul in sight, no cars visible. I parked and moved toward the entrance. One of the maids, like an electronic sensing device, opened the door as I approached. She stepped back, admitting me without comment.

"Where's Mrs. Callahan?"

She closed the door and started down the hall. I followed. She tapped at the door to Glen's study and then turned the knob and stepped back again, letting me pass into the room.

Glen was dressed in a pale pink robe, huddled in one of the wing-back chairs, knees drawn up. She raised her face, which was swollen and waterlogged. It looked as if all of her emotional pipes had burst, eyes spilling over, cheeks washed with tears, her nose running. Even her hair was damp. For a moment, still in disbelief, I stood there and looked at her and she looked at me and then she lowered her face again, extending her hand. I crossed and knelt by her chair. I took her hand—small and cold—and pressed it against my cheek.

"Oh Glen, I'm sorry. I'm so sorry," I whispered.

She was nodding acknowledgment, making a low sound in her throat, not even a clearly articulated cry. It was a sound more primitive than that. She started to speak, but she could only manage a sort of dragged-out, stuttering phrase, sub-English, devoid of sense. What difference did it make what she said? It was done and nothing could change it. She began to cry as children cry, deep, shuddering sobs that went on and on. I clung to her hand, offering her a mooring line in that churning sea of grief.

Finally, I could feel the turbulence pass like a battering rain cloud moving on. The spasms subsided. She let go of me and leaned back, taking in a deep breath. She took out a handkerchief and pressed it against her eyes, then blew her nose. She paused, apparently looking inward, much in the way one does at the end of an attack of hiccups.

She sighed. "Oh *God*, how will I get through this?" she said, and the tears welled up again, splashing down her face. She regained control after a moment and went through the mop-up process again, shaking her head. "Jesus. Shit. I don't think I can do this, Kinsey. You know? It's just too hard and I don't have that kind of strength."

"You want me to call anyone?"

"No, not now. It's too late and what's the point? In the morning, I'll have Derek get in touch with Sufi. She'll come."

"What about Kleinert? You want me to let him know?"

She shook her head. "Bobby couldn't stand him. Just let it be. He'll find out soon enough. Is Derek back?" Her tone was anxious now, her face tense.

"I don't think so. You want a drink?"

"No, but help yourself if you like. The liquor's in there."

"Maybe later." I wanted something, but I wasn't sure what it was. Not a drink. I was afraid alcohol would eat through the thin veneer of self-control. The last thing in the world she needed was to have to turn around and comfort me. I sat down in the chair across from her and an image flashed into my mind. I remembered Bobby bending down to say good night to her just two nights ago. He had turned automatically so he could offer her the good side of his face. It had been one of his last night's sleep on this earth, but neither of them had known that, nor had I. I glanced up at her and she was looking at me as if she knew what was going on in my head. I glanced away, but not quickly enough. Something in her face spilled over me like light through a swinging door. Sorrow shot through the gap, catching me off-guard, and I burst into tears.

12

Everything happens for a reason, but that doesn't mean there's a point. The next few days were a nightmare, the more so as mine was only a peripheral role in the pageantry of Bobby's death. Because I'd appeared in the first moments of her grief, Glen Callahan seemed to fix on me, as though I might provide a solace for her pain.

Dr. Kleinert agreed to release Kitty until after the burial, and an attempt was made to reach Bobby's natural father overseas, but he never responded and nobody seemed to care. Meanwhile, hundreds of people streamed through the funeral home: Bobby's friends, old high-school classmates, family friends and business associates, all the town dignitaries, members of the various boards Glen served on. The Who's Who of Santa Teresa. After that first night, Glen was totally composed—calm, gracious, tending to every detail of Bobby's funeral. It would be done properly. It would be done in the best of taste. I would be on hand throughout.

I had thought Derek and Kitty would resent my constant presence, but both seemed relieved. Glen's single-mindedness must have been a frightening prospect to them.

Glen ordered Bobby's casket closed, but I saw him for a moment at the funeral home after his body had been "prepared." In some ways, I needed that glimpse to convince myself that he was really dead. God, the stillness of the flesh when life has gone. Glen stood there beside me, her gaze fixed on Bobby's face, her own expression as blank and inanimate as his. Something had left her with his death. She was unflinching, but her grip on my arm tightened as the lid to the casket was closed.

"Good-bye, baby," she whispered. "I love you."

I turned away quickly.

Derek approached from behind and I saw him move as though to touch her. She didn't turn her head, but she radiated a rage so limitless that he kept his distance, intimidated by the force of it. Kitty stood against the back wall, stony, her face blotchy from tears wept in solitude. Somehow I suspected that she and her father wouldn't remain in Glen's life for long. Bobby's death had accelerated the household decay. Glen seemed impatient to be alone, intolerant of the requirements of ordinary intercourse. They were takers. She had nothing left to give. I scarcely knew the woman, but it seemed clear to me that she was suddenly operating by another set of premises. Derek watched her uneasily, sensing, perhaps, that he wasn't part of this new scheme, whatever it was.

Bobby was buried on Saturday. The church services were mercifully short. Glen had selected the music and a few passages from various non-Biblical sources. I took my cue from her, surviving the eulogy by neatly disconnecting myself from what was said. I wasn't going to deal with Bobby's death today. I wasn't going to lose control in a public setting like this. Even so, there were moments when I could feel my face heat up and my eyes blur with tears. It was more than this loss. It was all death, every loss—my parents, my aunt.

The funeral cortege must have been ten blocks long, cruising across the city at a measured pace. At every intersection, traffic had been forced to stop as we rolled by, and I could see the comments in the faces we passed. "Ooo, a funeral. Wonder whose." "Gorgeous day for it." "God, look at all the cars." "Come on, come on. Get out of the way."

We wound into the cemetery, as green and carefully landscaped as a housing tract. Headstones stretched out in all directions, a varied display, like a stonecutter's yard filled with samples of his work. There were intermittent evergreens, clusters of eucalyptus and sycamore. The cemetery parcels were sectioned off by low walls of shrubbery and on a plot map probably had names like Serenity and Heavenly Meadows.

We parked and everyone trooped across the newly trimmed grass. It felt like an elementary-school outing: everyone on their best behavior, nobody quite sure what to do next. There were occasional murmured conversations, but for the most part, we were silent. Mortuary personnel, in dark suits, escorted us to our seats like ushers at a wedding.

The day was hot, the afternoon sunlight intense. There was a breeze that rustled the treetops and lifted the canvas tent flaps flirtatiously. We sat dutifully while the minister conducted the final rites. I felt better out here and I realized it was the absence of organ music that made the graveside ceremony less potent. Even the most banal of church hymns can rip your heart out at times like this. I preferred the sound of wind.

Bobby's casket was a massive affair of glossy walnut and brass, like an oversized blanket chest too large for the space allotted. Apparently, the casket would fit down into the vault especially purchased to house it underground. There was some kind of complex mechanism set up above the grave site that would eventually be used to lower the casket into the hole, but I gathered that was done at some later time.

Funeral styles had evolved since my parents were buried and I wondered, idly, what had dictated the change. Technology, no doubt. Maybe death was tidier these days and easier to regulate. Graves were dug by machinery, which carved out a neat pit surmounted now by this low-slung contraption on which the casket rested. No more of this horseshit with the loved ones flinging themselves into the grave. With this new apparatus in place, you'd have to get down on your belly and leopard-crawl into the hole, which robbed the gesture of its theatrical effect.

Off to one side among the mourners, I saw Phil and Reva Bergen. He seemed upset, but she was impassive. Her gaze drifted from the minister's face to mine and she stared at me flatly. Behind them, I thought I saw Kelly Borden, but I couldn't be sure. I shifted in my chair, hoping to make eye contact, but the face was gone. The crowd began to disperse and I was startled to realize it was over. The minister, in his black robes, gave Glen a solemn look, but she ignored him and moved toward the limousine. Derek, in a show of good manners, lingered long enough to exchange a few remarks.

Kitty was already in the backseat when we reached the limo. I would have bet money she was high on something. Her cheeks were flushed and her eyes were feverishly bright, her hands restless in her lap, plucking at her black cotton skirt. The outfit she'd elected to wear had an outlandish gypsy air to it, the black cotton top composed of tiers of ruffles, embroidered in garish shades of turquoise and red. Glen had blinked lazily when she'd first set eyes on Kitty and an almost imperceptible smile had hovered on her lips before she turned her attention to something else. She'd apparently decided not to make an issue of it. Kitty's manner had been defiant, but with no resistance on Glen's part the juice had drained out of the drama before she'd even launched into the first art.

I was standing by the limo when I saw Derek approach. He climbed into the backseat and pulled down one of the collapsible camp stools, reaching to pull the door shut.

"Leave it open," Glen murmured.

The limo driver was still nowhere in sight. There was a delay while people took their places in the vehicles parked along the road. Others were milling around on the grass to no apparent purpose.

Derek tried to catch Glen's eye. "Well, I thought that went very well."

Glen turned pointedly and peered out of the far window. When your only child has been killed, who really gives a shit?

Kitty took out a cigarette and lit it. Her hands looked like birds' claws, the skin almost scaly. The elasticized neckline of her blouse revealed a chest so thin that her sternum and costal cartilages were outlined like one of those joke T-shirts.

Derek made a face as the smell of smoke filled the backseat. "Jesus, Kitty, put that out. For Christ's sake!"

"Oh, leave her alone," Glen said, dully. Kitty seemed surprised by the unexpected support, but she stubbed out the cigarette anyway.

The driver appeared and closed the door on Derek's side, then moved around the rear of the limousine and slid in under the steering wheel. I moved on toward my car as he pulled away.

*   *   *

The mood was much lighter once we got to the house. People seemed to shrug death aside, comforted by good wine and lavish hors d'oeuvres. I don't know why death still generates these little têtes-à-têtes. Everything else has been modernized, but some vestige of the wake remains. There must have been two hundred people crowded into the living room and hall, but it all seemed O.K. It was filler, just something to smooth the awkward transition from the funeral to the bone-crushing sleep that was bound to come afterward.

I recognized most of the people who'd been at Derek's birthday gathering that past Monday night: Dr. Fraker and his wife, Nola; Dr. Kleinert and a rather plain woman whom I assumed was Mrs. K.; the other doctor who'd been present, Metcalf, in conversation with Marcy, who had worked with Bobby briefly in the Pathology Department. I snagged a glass of wine and inched my way across the room to Fraker's side. He and Kleinert had their heads bent together and they paused as I approached.

"Hi," I said, suddenly self-conscious. Maybe this wasn't such a hot idea. I took a sip of wine, noting the look that passed between them. I guess they decided I could be privy to their discussion, because Fraker picked up where he'd left off.

"Anyway, I won't be doing the microscopic until Monday, but from the gross, it looks like the immediate cause of death was a ruptured aortic valve."

Kleinert said, "From impact with the steering wheel."

Fraker nodded, taking a sip of wine. The explanation of his findings continued almost as though he were dictating it all over again. "The sternum and multiple ribs were fractured and the ascending aorta was incompletely torn just above the superior border of the valve cusps. Additionally, there was a left hemothorax of eight hundred cc and a massive aortic adventitial hemorrhage."

Kleinert's expression indicated that he was following. The whole thing sounded sickening to me and I didn't even know what it meant.

"What about the blood alcohol?" Kleinert asked.

Fraker shrugged. "That was negative. He wasn't drunk.

We should have the rest of the results this afternoon, but I don't think we're going to find anything. I could be surprised, of course."

"Well, if you're right about the CSF blockage, a seizure was probably inevitable. Bernie warned him to watch for the symptoms," Kleinert said. His face was long and etched with a look of permanent sorrow. If I had emotional problems and needed a shrink, I didn't think it would help me to look at a face like that week after week. I'd want somebody with some energy, pizzazz, somebody with a little hope.

"Bobby had a seizure?" I asked. It was clear by now that they were discussing his autopsy results. Fraker must have realized I didn't have any idea what they were actually saying, because he offered a translation.

"We think Bobby may have been suffering from a complication of the original head injury. Sometimes, a blockage develops in the normal flow of cerebrospinal fluid. Intracranial pressure builds up and part of the brain starts to atrophy, resulting in posttraumatic epilepsy."

"And that's why he ran off the road?"

"In my opinion, yes," Fraker said. "I can't state this categorically, but he'd probably been experiencing headaches, anxiety, irritability perhaps."

Kleinert cut in again. "I saw him at seven, seven fifteen, something like that. He was terribly depressed."

"Maybe he suspected what was going on," Fraker was saying.

"Too bad he didn't speak up then, if that's the case."

The murmuring between them continued while I tried to take in the implications.

"Is there any way a seizure like that could have been drug-induced?" I asked.

"Sure, it's possible. Toxicology reports aren't comprehensive and the analyses' results depend on what's asked for. There are several hundred drugs which could affect a person with a predisposition to seizures. Realistically, it isn't possible to screen for all of them," Fraker said.

Kleinert shifted restlessly. "Actually, after what he went through, it's a wonder he survived as long as he did. We tried to spare Glen, but I think we've all been worried that something like this might occur."

There didn't seem to be anything left to say on the subject.

Kleinert finally turned to Fraker. "Have you eaten yet? Ann and I are going out for supper if you and Nola want to join us."

Fraker declined the invitation, but he did need his wineglass filled and I could see him eyeing the crowd for some sign of his wife. Both doctors excused themselves.

I stood there, unsettled, reviewing the facts. Theoretically, Bobby Callahan had died of natural causes, but in fact, he'd died as a consequence of injuries received in the accident nine months ago, which he, at least, believed was a murder attempt. As nearly as I could remember, California law provides that "a killing is murder or manslaughter if the party dies within three years and a day after the stroke is received or the cause of death is administered." So the truth was, he was murdered and it didn't make any difference at all if he died that night or last week. At the moment, of course, I didn't have any proof. I did still have the bulk of the money Bobby had paid me and a clear set of instructions from him, so I was still in business if I wanted to be.

Mentally, I got up and dusted myself off. It was time to put grief aside and get back to work. I set my wineglass down and had a brief word with Glen to let her know where I'd be and then I went upstairs and systematically searched Bobby's room. I wanted that little red book.

13

I was operating, of course, on the hope that Bobby had hidden the address book somewhere on the premises. He said he remembered giving the book to someone, but that might not be true. There was no way I could search the entire house, but I could certainly comb a couple of places. Glen's study, maybe Kitty's room. It was quiet upstairs and I was glad to be alone for a while. I searched for an hour and a half and came up with nothing. I wasn't discouraged. In some odd way, I was heartened. Maybe Bobby's memory had served him correctly.

At six, I wandered out into the corridor. I leaned my elbows on the balustrade that circled the landing and listened for sounds filtering up from below. Apparently, the crowd had diminished considerably. I heard smatterings of laughter, an occasional light conversational swell, but it sounded like most of the guests had departed. I retraced my steps and tapped on Kitty's door.

Muffled response. "Who is it?"

"It's me. Kinsey," I said to the blank door. After a moment, I heard the lock retracted, but she didn't actually let me in.

Instead, she hollered, "Enter!"

Lord, she was tedious. I entered.

The room had been tidied and the bed was made, I'm sure through no effort of hers. She looked as if she'd been crying. Her nose was reddened, her makeup smeared. She was, of course, doing drugs. She had gotten out a mirror and a razor blade and was laying out a couple of lines of coke. There was a half-filled wineglass on the bed table.

"I feel like shit," she said. She had exchanged her gypsy outfit for a raw silk kimono in a lush shade of green with butterflies embroidered on the back and sleeves. Her arms were so thin she looked like a praying mantis, her green eyes aglitter.

"When are you due back at St. Terry's?" I asked.

She paused to blow her nose, not wanting to screw up her high. "Who knows?" she said, glumly. "Tonight, I guess. At least I'll have a chance to pack some of my own clothes to take with me. Shit, I ended up on the psycho ward with *nothing.*"

"Why do you do this stuff, Kitty? You're playing right into Kleinert's hands."

"Terrific. I didn't know you came up here to lecture me."

"I came up to search Bobby's room. I'm looking for the little red address book he asked you about last Tuesday. I don't suppose you have any idea where it might be."

"Nope." She bent over, using a rolled-up dollar bill like a straw, her nostril forming a little vacuum cleaner. I watched the coke fly up her nose, like a magic trick.

"Can you think who he might have given it to?"

"Nuh-un." She sat back on the bed, pinching her nose shut. She wet her index finger and cleaned the surface of the mirror, running her fingertip across her gums then, like a remedy for teething pains. She reached for her wineglass and settled back against the bed pillows, lighting a cigarette.

"God, that's great," I said. "You're tagging all the bases today. Do a little coke, knock back some wine, cigarettes. They're going to have to run you through Detox before you hit Three South again." I knew I was baiting her, but she got on my nerves and I was spoiling for a fight, which I suspected would feel better than grief.

"Fuck you," she said, bored.

"Mind if I sit down?" I asked.

She gestured permission and I perched on the edge of the bed, looking around with interest.

"What happened to your stash?" I asked.

"What stash?"

"The one you kept in there," I said, indicating the bed table drawer.

She stared. "I never kept a *stash* in there."

I loved the little note of righteous indignation. "That's funny," I said. "I saw Dr. Kleinert pull a whole Ziploc bag full of pills out of there."

"When?" she said in disbelief.

"Monday night when they carted you away. Quaaludes, Placidyls, Tuinals, the works." Actually, I didn't really believe the pills were hers, but I was curious to hear what she had to say.

She stared at me for a moment more, then eased out a mouthful of smoke, which she neatly channeled up her nose. "I don't do any of those," she said.

"What'd you take Monday night?"

"Valium. Prescription."

"Dr. Kleinert gave you a prescription for Valium?" I asked.

She got up with annoyance and started pacing the room. "I don't need your bullshit, Kinsey. My stepbrother was buried today in case your memory's short. I got other things on my mind."

"Were you involved with Bobby?"

"No, I wasn't 'involved' with Bobby. What do you mean, like some kind of sexual thing? Like was I having an *affair*?"

"Yeah, like that."

"God, you are so imaginative. For your information, I didn't even think about him that way."

"Maybe he thought about you that way."

She stopped pacing. "Says who?"

"Just a theory of mine. You know he loved you. Why wouldn't he have sexual feelings as well?"

"Oh come on. Did Bobby say that?"

"No, but I saw his reaction the night you were hospitalized. I didn't think it was strictly brotherly love I was looking at. In fact, I asked Glen about it at the time, but she said she didn't think there was anything going on."

"Well, there wasn't."

"Too bad. Maybe you could have saved each other."

She rolled her eyes, giving me a look—God, adults are such geeks!—but she was restless and distracted. She located an ashtray on the chest of drawers and stubbed out her cigarette. She lifted the lid to a music box and let a few notes of "Lara's Theme" escape before she snapped it shut

again. When she looked at me again, she had tears in her
eyes and she seemed embarrassed by that.

She pushed away from the chest of drawers. "I gotta pack
my stuff."

She went into the closet and hauled out a canvas duffel. She opened her top dresser drawer and snatched up a
stack of underpants, which she shoved into the duffel. She
bumped the drawer shut and opened the next one, grab-
bing T-shirts, jeans, socks.

I got up and moved to the door, turning back with my
hand on the knob. "Nothing lasts, you know. Not even mis-
ery."

"Yeah, sure. Especially not mine. What do you think I do
drugs for, my health?"

"You're tough, right?"

"Shit, why don't you go work in a rescue mission? You got
the line down pat."

"One day some happiness is going to come into your life
in spite of you. You ought to keep yourself alive so you can
enjoy it."

"Sorry. No sale. I'm not interested."

I shrugged. "So die. It won't be that big a deal. It sure
won't be the loss that Bobby's death was. So far, you haven't
given the world a thing."

I opened the door.

I heard her bump a drawer shut. "Hey, Kinsey?"

I looked back at her. Her smirk was almost self-mocking,
but not quite.

"Want to do a line of coke? My treat."

I left the room, closing the door quietly. I felt like slamming it, but what would be the point?

I went down to the living room. I was hungry and I
needed a glass of wine. There were only five or six people
left. Sufi sat next to Glen on one of the sofas. I didn't recognize anybody else. I crossed to the buffet table that had
been set up on the far side of the room. The Chicano maid,
Alicia, was rearranging a platter of shrimp, consolidating
hors d'oeuvres so the plates wouldn't look all ratty and half
eaten. God, there was a lot to this business of being rich. It
had never occurred to me. I thought you just invited people

over and turned 'em loose, but I could see now that entertaining requires all kinds of subtle monitoring.

I filled a plate and picked up a fresh glass of wine. I chose
a seat close enough to the others so I wouldn't seem rude,
but far enough away so I wouldn't have to talk to anyone. I
have a shy streak that surfaces in situations like this. I'd
rather have chatted with some hooker down on lower State
Street than try to exchange pleasantries with this crew.
What could we possibly have discussed? They were talking
about long-term paper. I took a bite of salmon mousse and
tried to keep an interested look on my face, like maybe I
had a lot of long-term paper I was hoping to unloaad. Such a
nuisance, that shit, isn't it?

I felt a light touch on my arm and glanced over to see Sufi
Daniels easing into the chair next to mine.

"Glen tells me Bobby was very fond of you," she said.

"I hope so. I liked him."

Sufi stared at me. I kept eating because I couldn't think
what else to say. She was wearing an odd outfit: a long black
dress of some silky material with a matching jacket over it. I
assumed it was meant to disguise her misshapen form with
its slightly hunched back, but it made her look as if she
were about to perform with some big philharmonic or-
chestra. Her hair was the same lank, pale mess it had been
when I met her the first time and her makeup was inexpert.
She couldn't have been more different from Glen Callahan.
Her manner was faintly patronizing, like she was just on the
verge of slipping me a couple of bucks for my services. I
might have been short with her, but there was always the
chance that she had Bobby's little red book.

"How do you know Glen?" I asked, taking a sip of wine. I
set the glass down on the floor near my chair and forked up
some cold shrimp in a spicy sauce. Sufi's gaze flicked over to
Glen and then back.

"We met in school."

"You've been friends a long time."

"Yes, we have."

I nodded, swallowing. "You must have been around when
Bobby was born," I remarked, just to keep things going.

"Yes."

Shit, this is fun, I thought. "Were you close to him?"

"I liked him, but I can't say we were close. Why?"

I retrieved my wine and took a sip. "He gave someone a little red book. I'm trying to figure out who."

"What sort of book?"

I shrugged. "Addresses, telephone numbers. Small, bound in red leather, from what he said."

She suddenly began to blink at me. "You're not still investigating," she said. It wasn't a question. It was a statement tinged with disbelief.

"Why not?"

"Well, the boy is dead. What difference could any of it possibly make?"

"If he was murdered, it makes a difference to me," I said.

"If he was murdered, it's a matter for the police."

I smiled. "The cops around here love my help."

Sufi looked over at Glen, lowering her voice. "I'm sure she wouldn't want this pursued."

"She didn't hire me. Bobby did. Anyway, why do you care?"

She seemed to catch the danger in my tone, but it didn't worry her much. She smiled thinly, still superior.

"Of course. I didn't mean to interfere," she murmured. "I just wasn't sure what your plans were and I didn't want Glen upset."

I was supposed to make comforting noises back to her, but I just sat there and stared. A bit of color rose in her cheeks.

"Well. It's been nice seeing you again." She got up and wandered over to one of the remaining guests, engaging in conversation with a pointed turning of her back. I shrugged to myself. I wasn't sure what she'd been up to. I didn't care either, unless it pertained to the case. I glanced over at her, speculating.

Soon after, almost at a signal, people started getting into their good-bye behavior. Glen stood by the archway to the living room, being hugged, having her hands pressed in sympathy. Everyone said the same thing. "You know we love you, sweetie. Now you let us know if we can do anything."

She said "I will" and got hugged again.

Sufi was the one who actually walked them to the door.

I was on the verge of following when Glen caught my eye. "I'd like to talk to you if you can stay on for a while."

"Sure," I said. I realized for the first time that I hadn't seen Derek for hours. "Where's Derek?"

"Taking Kitty back to St. Terry's." She sank into one of the couches, slouching down so she could rest her head on the back. "Would you like a drink?"

"Actually, I could use one. Shall I fix you one while I'm at it?"

"God, I'd love it. There's a liquor cabinet in my den if we're low out here. Make it Scotch. Lots of ice, please."

I crossed the hall and went into the den, fetching an old-fashioned glass and the bottle of Cutty Sark. When I reached the living room again, Sufi was back and the house was mantled in that dull quiet that follows too much noise.

There was an ice bucket on the end of the buffet table and I plopped a couple of cubes into the glass with a set of those sterling-silver ice tongs that look somehow like dinosaur claws. It made me feel sophisticated, like I was in a 1940s movie wearing a suit with shoulder pads and stockings with a line up the back.

"You must be exhausted," Sufi was murmuring. "Why don't I get you into bed before I take off?"

Glen smiled wearily. "No, that's all right. You go ahead."

Sufi had no other choice but to bend down and give Glen a buss and then find her purse. I handed Glen the glass with ice, pouring Scotch into it. Sufi made her final farewells and then left the room with a cautionary look at me. A few moments later, I heard the front door shut.

I pulled a chair over and sat down, propping my feet up on the couch, cataloguing my current state. The small of my back ached, my left arm ached. I finished off the wine in my glass and added Cutty Sark.

Glen took a long swallow of hers. "I saw you talking to Jim. What did he have to say?"

"He thinks Bobby had a seizure and that's why he ran off the road. Some kind of epilepsy from his head injuries in the first accident."

"Meaning what?"

"Well, as far as I'm concerned, it means if *that* accident was really a murder attempt, it finally paid dividends."

Her face was blank. She dropped her gaze. "What will you do now?"

"Hey, listen. I still have money left from the retainer Bobby gave me. I'll work 'til I find out who killed him."

She met my eyes and the look she gave me was curious. "Why would you do that?"

"To settle accounts. I believe in clearing the ledger, don't you?"

"Oh yes," she said.

We stared at each other for a moment and then she raised her glass. I lifted mine and we drank.

When Derek came in, the two of them went upstairs and, with Glen's permission, I spent the next three hours in a fruitless search of her den and Kitty's room. Then I let myself out and went home.

14

By Monday morning at eight o'clock I was in the gym again, working out. I felt like I'd been to the moon and back. Without even thinking about it, I looked for Bobby, realizing a millisecond later that he was gone and wasn't ever going to be there again. It didn't sit well with me. Missing someone is a vague, unpleasant sensation, like gnawing anxiety. It isn't as concrete as grief, but it's just as pervasive and there's no escaping it. I kept moving, working out hard, as though physical pain might blot out its emotional counterpart. I filled every minute with activity and I suppose it worked. In some ways, it's like rubbing Ben-Gay on a sore back. You want to believe it's doing you some good, but you can't think why it would. It's better than nothing, but it's no cure.

I showered, got dressed, and headed over to the office. I hadn't been there since Wednesday afternoon. There was several days' mail piled up and I tossed it on the desk. The message light on my answering machine was blinking, but I had other things to attend to first. I opened the French doors and let some fresh air circulate, then made a pot of coffee for myself. I checked the half-and-half in my little refrigerator, sniffing at the carton spout. Borderline. I'd have to replace that soon. When the coffee was done, I found a clean mug and filled it. The half-and-half formed an ominous pattern on the surface, but it tasted O.K. Some days I drink my coffee black, some days with cream for the comfort of it. I sat down in my swivel chair and propped my feet up, punching the replay button on the answering machine.

The tape rewound itself and Bobby came on. I felt a chilly finger touch the nape of my neck when I realized who it was.

"Hi, Kinsey. This is Bobby. I'm sorry I was such a jerk a little while ago. I know you were just trying to cheer me up. One thing came to me. I know this doesn't make much sense, but I thought I'd pass it on anyway. I think the name Blackman ties into this. Somebody Blackman. I don't know if that's who I gave the little red book to or the guy who's after me. Could be it's nothing the way my brain scrambles things. Anyway, we can put our heads together later and see if it means anything. I've got some stuff to do and then I have to see Kleinert. I'll try to get back to you. Maybe we can have a drink or something later tonight. Bye for now, kid. Watch your backside."

I flipped the machine off and stared at it.

I reached in my top drawer for the telephone book and hauled it out. There was one Blackman listed, an S. No address. Probably a woman trying to avoid obscene phone calls. I believe in trying for the obvious first. I mean, why not? Maybe Sarah, or Susan, or Sandra Blackman knew Bobby and had his little red book, or maybe he'd told her exactly what was going on and I could wrap the whole thing up with one phone call. The number was a disconnect. I tried it again, just to double-check. The same recording clicked in again. I made a note. The number might still pertain. Maybe S. Blackman had left town or died mysteriously.

I punched the replay button, just to hear Bobby's voice again. I was feeling restless, wondering how to get down to brass tacks on this thing. I checked back through Bobby's file. I hadn't yet talked to his former girl friend, Carrie St. Cloud, and that seemed like a reasonable possibility. Glen had told me she dropped out of the picture after the accident, but she might remember something from that period. I tried the number Glen had given me and had a brief chat with Carrie's mother, explaining who I was and why I wanted to get in touch with her. Carrie had apparently moved out of the family home a year ago and into a little apartment of her own that she shared with a roommate. She was working full-time now as an aerobics instructor at a studio on Chapel. I made a note of the two addresses, her work and home, and thanked the woman. I set my mug aside, unplugged the coffeepot, locked the office, and trotted down the back stairs.

The day was overcast, the sky a low ceiling of white. A pale gray haze seemed to permeate the streets with chill air. After the insufferable heat of the last few weeks, it seemed odd. The weather in Santa Teresa has been straying from the norm of late. It used to be that you could count on clear sunny skies and a tamed and temperate sea, with maybe a few clouds massing behind the mountains more for the visual effect than anything else. The rains came dutifully in January, two weeks of constant downpour, after which the countryside turned emerald green, bougainvillea and cape honeysuckle exploding across the face of the town like gaudy makeup. Nowadays, there are enexplicable rains in April and October, chilly days like this in August when the temperature should be eighty-five degrees. The shift is baffling, the sort of climatic alteration associated with the eruption of South Sea volcanoes and rumors about the ozone being penetrated by hair sprays.

The studio was only half a block away, housed in a former racquetball club that had gone belly-up once the passion for racquetball had passed. With aerobics coming in, it made perfect sense to convert all those plain narrow rooms with hardwood floors into little fat-burning ovens for women who yearned to be lean and fit. I asked if Carrie was teaching and the woman at the desk pointed mutely toward the source of the deafening music that made further conversation unlikely at best. I followed the end of her finger and rounded the corner. On my right, there was a waist-high wall overlooking an aerobics class in full swing one floor below.

The acoustics were grim. I watched from the observer's gallery while the music blasted. Carrie hollered out encouragement and fifteen of the best-looking female bodies in town exercised with a fanaticism I'd seldom seen. Apparently, I'd caught the class at its apex. They were doing buttocks lifts that looked obscene: women groaning on the floor in frosted, skintight leotards, doing hip thrusts and bun squeezes as if unseen partners were grinding away at them in unison.

Carrie St. Cloud was a surprise. Her name suggested a second runner-up for a Junior Miss pageant, or maybe a budding actress whose real name is Wanda Maxine Smith. I had pictured run-of-the-mill California good looks, the trim surfer's body, blond hair, dazzling white teeth, maybe a little tendency to tap dance. She was none of these things.

She couldn't have been more than twenty-two with a body builder's musculature and dark hair to her waist. Her face was strong, like Greek statuary, with a full mouth, rounded chin. The leotard she wore was a pale yellow Spandex, defining the wide shoulders and lean hips of a gymnast. If she had an ounce of fat on her, I didn't spy it anyplace. She had no breasts to speak of, but the effect was intensely female anyway. This was no beach bunny. She took herself seriously, and she knew what fitness was about, breezing through the exercises without even breathing hard. Every other woman in the place was in pain. It made me grateful that all I have to do is jog three miles a day. I'm never going to look as good as she, but it didn't seem like a bad trade.

Carrie took the class through cool-down, a slow stretch, and a couple of yoga moves and then let them sprawl on the floor like casualties on a battlefield. She turned the music off, grabbed a towel, and buried her face in it, moving out of the room through a doorway just below me. I found the stairs and headed down, catching her at the water fountain just outside the locker rooms. Her hair fell across her shoulders like a nun's veil and she had to gather it in a knot and hold it to one side so she could drink without getting it wet.

"Carrie?"

She straightened up, blotting a trickle of sweat with the sleeve of her leotard, the towel around her neck now, like a fighter just out of the ring. "That's right."

I told her who I was and what I was doing and then asked her if we could talk about Bobby Callahan.

"All right, but we'll have to do it while I clean up. I have to be somewhere at noon."

I followed her through a door and into the locker room. The floor plan was open, with a counter on the right that circled the perimeter about halfway, banks of metal lockers, a line of hair dryers mounted on the wall. The tile was a

pristine white and the place was spotless, with benches an-
chored to the floor, mirrors everywhere. I could hear showers running somewhere out of sight to my left. Women were
beginning to straggle in from the class and the level of
laughter, I knew, would rise as the room filled.

Carrie kicked off her shoes and peeled her leotard down
like a banana skin. I busied myself looking for a place to
perch. As a rule, I don't interview naked ladies in a roomful
of chattering strippers. I noticed that they smelled just like
the guys at Santa Teresa Fitness and I thought that was
nice.

I waited while she tucked her hair up under a plastic cap
and went into the showers. In the meantime, women pa-
raded back and forth in various stages of undress. It was a
comforting sight. So many versions of the female breast, of
buttocks and bellies and pubic nests, endless repetitions of
the same forms. These women seemed to feel good about
themselves and there was a camaraderie among them that I
enjoyed.

Carrie returned from showering, wrapped in a towel. She
pulled her shower cap off and gave her dark mane a toss.
She began to dry herself off, talking to me over her shoulder.

"I thought about coming to the funeral, but I just
couldn't handle it. Did you go?"

"Yeah, I went. I hadn't known Bobby long, but it was
tough. You were dating him when he had the accident,
weren't you?"

"Actually, we'd just broken up. We dated two years and
then things went sour. I got pregnant, among other things,
and that was the end of it. He paid for the abortion, but we
weren't seeing much of each other by then. I did feel terrible when he got hurt, but I stayed away. I know people
thought I was a real cold fish, but what could I do? It was
over. I couldn't see hovering around him loyally just so I'd
look good."

"Did you hear any talk about the accident?"

"Just that someone ran him off the road."

"You have any idea who it might have been or why?"

She sat down on a bench and hauled a foot up, drying
carefully between her toes. "Well, yes and no. Not who

really, but I know something was going on with him. He didn't confide much by then, but he did go with me when I had the abortion and he stayed real close for a couple of days." She switched feet, bending to inspect her toes. "I worry about athlete's foot," she murmured. "Sorry."

She tossed the towel aside and got up, crossing to a locker, taking out clothes. She glanced at me. "I'm just trying to say this right because I don't really have any facts. Just an impression. I remember him saying some friend of his was in trouble and I had the feeling it was blackmail."

"Blackmail?"

"Well, yes, but not in any ordinary sense. I mean, I don't think there was money changing hands or anything like that. It wasn't sinister cloak-and-dagger stuff. Somebody had something on somebody else and it was pretty serious. I gathered he'd been trying to help and he'd just figured out how to do it. . . ." She pulled on her underpants and then an undershirt. I guess she figured her breasts weren't big enough to worry with a bra.

"When was this?" I asked. "Do you remember the date?"

"Well, I know I had the abortion on November sixteenth and he stayed with me that night. The accident was the day after that, I think, the night of the seventeenth, so it was all in that same week."

"I've been going through the newspaper starting in September, thinking maybe he was caught up in something public. Did you get *any* impression of the arena where all this was taking place? I mean, I don't even know what to look for."

She shook her head. "I have no idea. Really. I'm sorry, but I couldn't even make a guess."

"You think Rick Bergen was the friend in trouble?"

"I doubt it. I knew Rick. I think Bobby would have told me if it had been Rick."

"Somebody at work?"

"Look, I just can't help you with that," she said impatiently. "He was being very tight-lipped and I wasn't in a mood to pry. I was just glad the abortion was over with. I was taking pain-killers anyway so I slept a lot and the rest was a blur. He was just talking for the sake of it, to take my mind off things and maybe a little bit from nerves."

"Does the name Blackman mean anything to you?"

"I don't think so."

She pulled on a pair of sweatpants and slipped her feet into some thongs. She bent at the waist, flipped her hair across one shoulder, and gave it a couple of whacks with a hairbrush, then grabbed up her shoulder bag, moving toward the door. I had to do a quick two-step to catch up with her. I didn't think she'd finished dressing but I could see now that this was all she intended to wear. Sweatpants and an undershirt? She was going to freeze once she got outside. I scurried after her, catching the door as she passed into the corridor.

"Who else was he hanging out with back then?" I asked, trotting up the stairs to the main entrance with her. "Just give me a couple of names. I gotta have something to go on."

She paused, glancing back at me. "Try a kid named Gus. I don't know his last name, but he works at that skate-rental place down at the beach. He's an old high-school buddy and I think Bobby trusted him. Maybe he'll know what it's about."

"What were the other things? You said you got pregnant 'among other things.'"

Her smile was tense. "God, you are so persistent. He was in love with someone else. I have no idea who, so don't bother to ask. If I'd known about the other woman I'd have broken off our relationship long before. As it was, I didn't hear about her until I told him I was pregnant. I thought at first he might marry me, but when he told me he was seriously involved with someone else, I knew what I had to do. To his credit, he did feel terrible about the bind I was in and he did as much as he could. There was nothing cheap about Bobby and he really was a sweet guy at heart."

She started to move away and I caught her by the arm, thinking rapidly. "Carrie, is there a chance that the friend in trouble and the woman he was involved with were one and the same person?"

"How do I know?"

"I don't suppose he gave you a little red address book, did he?"

"All he gave me was heartache," she said and walked off without looking back.

15

The skate-rental shack is a dark green box just off a parking lot near the wharf. For three bucks, you can rent roller skates for an hour, with kneepads, elbow pads, and wrist braces thrown in without charge so you won't sue them later for the harm you might do yourself.

Bobby's taste in friends was hard to predict. Gus looked like the sort of fellow if you saw on a street corner, you'd reach over casually and make sure your car doors were locked. He must have been Bobby's age, but he was sunken-chested and frail, and his color was bad. His hair was dark brown and he was struggling to grow a mustache that only made him look like a fugitive. I'd seen mug shots of felons I'd trust before him.

I had introduced myself and ascertained that this was indeed Bobby's friend, when a blonde with flyaway hair and long tanned legs came up to turn in a pair of skates. I watched their interchange. Despite my first impression, Gus had a nice way about him. His manner was mildly flirtatious and he had a tendency to glance in my direction, showing off, I suspect. I waited, looking on while he calculated how much she owed him. He returned her street shoes and I.D. and she hopped over to a bench to put on her tennies. Gus waited until she was gone before he spoke.

"I saw you at the funeral," he said shyly when he turned back to me. "You were sitting near Mrs. Callahan."

"I don't remember seeing you," I said. "Did you come to the house afterwards?"

He shook his head, coloring. "I wasn't feeling too good."

"I don't think there's any way to feel good about that."

"Not when your buddy dies," he said. His voice carried a barely perceptible quaver. He turned away, making a big display of shoving the shoe skates back into the proper slot on the shelf.

"Have you been sick?" I asked.

He seemed to debate for just an instant and then said, "I got Crohn's disease. You know what that is?"

"No."

"Inflammatory bowel disease. Everything goes right through me. I can't keep weight on. Run a fever half the time. Stomach hurts. 'Etiology unknown,' which means they don't know what causes it or where it comes from. I've had it almost two years and it's got me down. I can't keep a real job, so I do this."

"Is that something you recover from?"

"I guess so. In time. That's what they say, at any rate."

"Well, I'm sorry you're suffering. It sounds grim."

"You don't know the half of it. Anyway, Bobby cheered me up. He was in such bad shape himself, we'd get laughin' sometimes. I miss him. When I heard he died, I almost gave up, but then this little voice said, 'Aw Gus, get up off your dead ass and get on with it . . . this isn't the end of the world, so don't be a jerk.'" He shook his head. "It was Bobby, I swear. Sounded just like him. So I got up off my dead ass. Are you looking into his death?"

I nodded, glancing over as a couple of kids approached to rent skates.

Gus conducted some business and came back to me, apologizing for the interruption. It was summer and despite the uncharacteristic chill in the air, the tourists were swarming the beaches. I asked him if he had any idea what Bobby was involved in. He moved uneasily, glancing off across the street.

"I got an idea, but I don't know what to say. I mean, if Bobby didn't tell you, why should I?"

"He couldn't remember. That's what he hired me for. He thought he was in danger and he wanted me to find out what was going on."

"So maybe it's best to just leave it be."

"Leave what be?"

"Look, I don't know anything for sure. Just what Bobby said."

"What are you worried about?"

He shifted his gaze. "I don't know. Let me think about it some. Honest, I don't know much, but I don't want to talk about it unless it feels right. You know what I mean?"

I conceded the point. You can always push people around, but it's not a good idea. Better to let them volunteer information for reasons of their own. You get more that way.

"I hope you'll give me a call," I said. "If I don't hear from you, I might have to come back and make a pest of myself." I took a card out and laid it on the counter.

He smiled, apparently feeling guilty for holding out. "You can skate for nothing if you want. It's good exercise."

"Some other time," I said. "Thanks."

He watched me until I pulled out of the parking lot, turning left. In the rearview mirror, I could see him scratching at his mustache with the corner of my business card. I hoped I'd hear from him.

In the meantime, I decided to see if I could lay my hands on the cardboard box the lab had packed up after Bobby's accident. I drove over to the house. Glen had apparently flown up to San Francisco for the day, but Derek was home and I told him what I needed.

His look was skeptical. "I remember the box, but I'm not sure where it went. Probably out in the garage, if you want to have a look."

He closed the front door behind him and the two of us crossed the courtyard to the three-car garage that stretched out at one end of the house. There were storage bins built into the back wall. None of them was locked, but most were stacked top to bottom with boxes that looked as if they'd been on the premises since the year oughty-ought.

I spotted a carton that seemed to be a good bet. It was shoved against the back wall under a workbench, marked "disposable syringes" with the name of the medical supplier and a torn shipping label addressed to Santa Teresa Hospital Pathology Department. We hauled it out and opened it. The contents looked like Bobby's, but were disappointing nevertheless. No little red book, no reference to anybody named Blackman, no clippings, no cryptic notes, no personal correspondence. There were some medical books, two technical manuals for radiology equipment, and office supplies of the most benign sort. What was I going to do with a box of paper clips and two ballpoint pens?

"It doesn't look like much," Derek remarked.

"It doesn't look like *anything*," I replied. "You mind if I take it with me anyway? I may want to check through it again."

"No, go right ahead. Here let me get that." I stepped back obligingly and let him heft the box up off the floor and carry it to my car. I could have done it, but it seemed important to him, so why hassle? He shoved some stuff aside and we wrestled the box into the backseat. I told him I'd be in touch and then I took off.

I went back to my place and changed into my running clothes. I was just locking up when Henry came around the corner with Lila Sams. They were walking hip to hip, arms entwined. He was a good foot taller than she and lean in all the places she was plump. He looked flushed with happiness, that special aura people take on when they've just fallen in love. He was wearing pale blue brushed denim pants and a pale blue shirt that made his blue eyes look nearly luminous. His hair looked freshly cut and my guess was he'd actually had someone "style" it this time. Lila's smile tensed somewhat when she caught sight of me, but she recovered her composure, laughing girlishly.

"Oh Kinsey, now look what he's gone and done," she said and held her hand out. She was sporting a big square-cut diamond that I hoped was some gaudy fake.

"God, it's gorgeous. What's the occasion?" I asked, heart sinking. Surely, they weren't engaged. She was so wrong for him, so giddy and false, while he was genuine.

"Just celebrating the fact that we met," Henry said with a glance at her. "What was it, a month ago? Six weeks?"

"Well, naughty you," she said with a playful stamp of her little foot. "I have half a mind to make you take this right back. We met June twelfth. It was Moza's birthday and I'd just moved in. You catered that tea she gave and you've spoiled me rotten ever since." She lowered her voice then to its most confidential pitch. "Isn't he awful?"

I don't know how to talk to people this way, exchanging pointless banter. I could feel my smile becoming self-conscious but I couldn't make it go away. "I think he's great," I said, sounding somehow lame and inept.

"Well, of course he's great," she said in a flash. "Why wouldn't he be? He's such an innocent, anyone can take advantage of him."

Her tone was suddenly quarrelsome, as though I'd insulted him. I could feel the warning signals clanging away like crazy, but I still couldn't guess what was coming. She was wagging a finger at me, red painted nails piercing the air near my face. "You, for one, you bad girl. I told Henry and I'll say it right to your face, the rent you pay is a scandal and you know perfectly well you've been robbing him blind."

"What?"

She narrowed her eyes, pushing her face toward mine. "Now don't you play dumb with me. Two hundred dollars a month! My stars. Do you know what studio apartments are renting for in this neighborhood? Three hundred. That's a hundred dollars you take away from him every time you write him a check. Disgraceful. It's just a disgrace!"

"Oh now, Lila," Henry broke in. He seemed nonplussed that she'd launched into this, but it was clearly something they'd discussed. "Let's don't get into this now. She's on her way out."

"You can spare a few minutes, I'm sure," she said with a glittering look at me.

"Sure," I said faintly and then glanced at him. "Have you been unhappy with me?" I felt the same sick combination of heat and cold that Chinese-food syndrome produces. Did he really feel I'd been cheating him?

Lila cut in again, answering before he could even open his mouth. "Let's not put Henry on the spot," she said. "He thinks the world of you, which is why he hasn't had the heart to speak up. You're the one I'd like to spank. How could you take an old softie like Henry and twist him around your finger that way? You should be ashamed."

"I wouldn't take advantage of Henry."

"But you already have. How long have you been living here at that same ridiculous rent? A year? Fifteen months? Don't tell me it never occurred to you that you were getting this place dirt-cheap! Because if you say that, I'll have to call you a liar right to your face and embarrass us both."

I could feel my mouth open, but I couldn't say a word.

"We can talk about this later," Henry murmured, taking her by the arm. He was steering her around me, but her eyes were still fixed on mine and her neck and cheeks were now blotchy with rage. I turned and stared as he moved her toward his back stairs. She was already starting to protest in the same irrational tone I'd heard the other night. Was the woman nuts?

When the door closed behind them, my heart began to thump and I realized I was damp with sweat. I tied my door key to my shoelace and then I took off, breaking into a trot long before I'd had a chance to warm up. I ran, putting distance between us.

I did three miles and then walked back to my place, letting myself in. Henry's back shades were down and his windows were shut. The rear of his house looked blank and uninviting, like a beachfront park after closing time.

I showered and threw some clothes on, and then took off, fleeing the premises. I still felt stung, but I was getting in touch with some anger too. What business was it of hers anyway? And why hadn't Henry leapt to my defense?

When I pushed into Rosie's, it was late afternoon and there wasn't a soul in sight. The restaurant was gloomy and smelled of last night's cigarette smoke. The TV set on the bar was turned off and the chairs were still upside down on the tabletops, like a troupe of acrobats doing tricks. I crossed to the rear and opened the swinging door to the kitchen. Rosie glanced up at me, startled. She was sitting on a tall wooden stool with a cleaver in her hand, chopping leeks. She hated anyone intruding on her kitchen, probably because she violated health codes.

"What happened?" she said when she saw my face.

"I had an encounter with Henry's lady friend," I replied.

"Ah," she said. She whacked a leek with the cleaver, sending hunks flying. "She don't come in here. She knows better."

"Rosie, the woman is crazy as a loon. You should have heard her the other night after you tangled with her. She ranted and raved for hours. Now she's accusing me of cheating Henry on the rent."

"Take a seat. I got some vodka somewhere." She crossed to the cabinet above the sink and stood on tippytoe, tilting a vodka bottle into reach. She broke the seal and poured me a hit in a coffee cup. She shrugged then poured herself one too. We drank and I could feel the blood rush back to my face.

I said, "Woo!" involuntarily. My esophagus felt scorched and I could sense the contours of my stomach outlined in alcohol. I always pictured my stomach much lower down than that. Weird. Rosie placed the chopped leeks in a bowl and rinsed the cleaver at the sink before she turned back to me.

"You got twenty cents? Give me two dimes," she said, holding a hand out. I fished around in my handbag, coming up with some loose change. Rosie took it and crossed to the pay phone on the wall. Everybody has to use that pay phone, even her.

"Who are you calling? You're not calling Henry," I said, with alarm.

"Ssss!" She held a hand up, shushing me, her eyes focusing in the way people do when someone picks up the phone on the other end. Her voice got musical and syrupy.

"Hello, dear. This is Rosie. What are you doing right this minute. Uh-hun, well I think you better get over here. We have a little matter to discuss."

She clunked the receiver down without waiting for a response and then she fixed me with a satisfied look. "Mrs. Lowenstein is coming over for a chat."

Moza Lowenstein sat on the chrome-and-plastic chair that I'd brought in from the bar. She is a large woman with hair the color of a cast-iron skillet, worn in braids wrapped around her head. There are strands of silver threaded through like tinsel, and her face, with its pale powder, has the soft look of a marshmallow. Generally, she likes to hold on to something when she talks to Rosie: a bouquet of pencils, a wooden spoon, any talisman to ward off attack. Today, it was the dish towel she'd brought with her. Apparently, Rosie had interrupted her in the middle of some chore and she'd hurried right over, as bid. She's afraid of Rosie, as anyone with good sense would be. Rosie launched right in, skipping all the niceties.

"Who is this Lila Sams?" Rosie said. She took up her cleaver and began to pound on some veal, making Moza flinch.

Her voice, when she found it, was trembly and soft. "I don't really know. She came to my door, she said in response to an ad in the paper, but it was all a mistake. I didn't have a room for rent and I told her as much. Well, the poor thing burst into tears and what was I to do? I had to ask her in for a cup of tea."

Rosie paused to stare in disbelief. "And then you rented her a room?"

Moza folded the towel, forming a lobster shape like a napkin in a fancy restaurant. "Well, no. I told her she could stay with me until she found a place, but she insisted that she pay her own way. She didn't want to be indebted, she said."

"That's called room rent. That's what that is," Rosie snapped.

"Well, yes. If you want to *put* it that way."

"Where does this woman come from?"

Moza flapped the towel out and dabbed it against her upper lip, blotting sweat. She laid it out on her lap and pressed it with her hand, keeping her fingers together in a wedge like an iron. I saw Rosie's flinty gaze follow every movement and I thought she might give Moza's hand a smack with the cleaver. Moza must have thought so too because she quit fiddling with the towel and looked up at Rosie with guilt. "What?"

Rosie enunciated carefully, as though speaking to an alien. "Where does Lila Sams come from?"

"A little town in Idaho."

"*What* little town?"

"Well, I don't know," Moza said defensively.

"You have a woman living in your house and you don't know what town she comes from?"

"What difference does it make?"

"And you don't know what difference it makes?" Rosie stared at her with exaggerated astonishment. Moza broke eye contact and folded the towel into a bishop's miter.

"You do me a favor and you find out," Rosie said. "Can you manage that?"

"I'll try," Moza said. "But she doesn't like people prying. She told me that and she was quite definite."

"I'm very definite too. I'm definite about I don't like this lady and I want to know what she's up to. You find out where she comes from and Kinsey can take care of the rest. And I don't have to tell you, Moza, I don't want Lila Sams to know. You understand?"

Moza looked cornered. I could see her debate, trying to decide which was worse: infuriating Rosie or getting caught spying on Lila Sams. It was going to be a close contest, but I knew who I was betting on.

16

I went back to my office late in the day and typed up my notes. There wasn't much, but I don't like to get behind. With Bobby dead, I intended to write regular reports and submit itemized bills at intervals, even if it was just to myself. I had tucked his file back in the drawer and I was tidying up my desk when there was a tap at the door and Derek Wenner peered in.

He said, "Oh. Hello. I was hoping I'd catch you here."

"Hi, Derek. Come on in," I said.

He stood for a moment, undecided, his gaze tracing the perimeters of my small office space. "Somehow I didn't picture this," he said. "Nice. I mean, it's small, but efficient. Uh, how'd you do with Bobby's box? Any luck?"

"I haven't had a chance to look closely. I've been doing other things. Have a seat."

He pulled a chair up and sat down, still looking around. He was wearing a golf shirt, white pants, and two-tone shoes. "So this is it, huh?"

This was his version of small talk, I assumed. I sat down and let him ramble briefly. He seemed anxious and I couldn't imagine what had brought him in. We made mouth noises at each other, demonstrating goodwill. I'd just seen him a few hours earlier and we didn't have that much to talk about.

"How's Glen doing?" I asked.

"Good," he nodded. "She's doing pretty well. God, I don't know how she's gotten through, but you know she's made of substantial stuff." He tended to speak in doubtful tones, as if he weren't absolutely certain he was telling the truth.

He cleared his throat and the timbre of his voice changed.

"Say, I'll tell you why I stopped in," he said. "Bobby's attorney gave me a call a little while ago just to talk about the terms of Bobby's will. Do you know Varden Talbot?"

"We've never met. He sent me copies of the reports on Bobby's accident, but that's the extent of it."

"Smart fellow," Derek said. He was stalling. I thought I better goose him along or this could take all day.

"What'd he have to say?"

Derek's expression was a wonderful combination of uneasiness and disbelief. "Well, that's the amazing thing," he said. "From what he indicated, I guess my daughter inherits the bulk of Bobby's money."

It took me a moment to compute the fact that the daughter he referred to was Kitty Wenner, cokehead, currently residing in the psycho ward at St. Terry's. "Kitty?" I said.

He shifted in his seat. "I was surprised too, of course. From what Varden tells me, Bobby made out a will when he came into his inheritance three years ago. At that point, he left everything to Kitty. Then sometime after the accident, he added a codicil, so that a little money would go to Rick's parents as well."

I was about to say "Rick's parents?" as if I were suffering from echolalia, but I clamped my mouth shut and let him continue.

"Glen won't be back until late, so she's not aware of it. I'd imagine she'll want to talk to Varden in the morning. He said he'd make a copy of the will and send it over to the house. He's going to go ahead and file it for probate."

"And this is the first anybody's heard of it?"

"As far as I know." He went on talking while I tried to figure out what it meant. Money, as a motive, always seems so direct. Find out who benefits financially and start from there. Kitty Wenner. Phil and Reva Bergen.

"Excuse me," I said, cutting in. "Just how much money are we talking about?"

Derek paused to run a hand up along his jaw, as though deciding if he was due for a shave. "Well, a hundred grand to Rick's parents and gee, I don't know. Kitty probably stands to gain a couple mill. Now, you're going to have inheritance tax . . ."

All of the little zeros began to dance in my head like sugar plums. "Hundred grand" and "couple mill," as in a hundred thousand dollars and two million of them. I just sat and blinked at him. Why had he come in here to tell me this stuff?

"What's the catch?" I asked.

"What?"

"I'm just wondering why you're telling me about it. Is there some problem?"

"I guess I'm worried about Glen's reaction. You know how she feels about Kitty."

I shrugged. "It was Bobby's money to do with as he saw fit. How could she object?"

"You don't think she'd contest it?"

"Derek, I can't speculate about what Glen might do. Talk to her."

"Well, I guess I will when she gets back."

"I'm assuming the money was put in some kind of trust fund since Kitty's just seventeen. Who was named executor? You?"

"No, no. The bank. I don't think Bobby had a very high opinion of me. To tell you the truth, I'm a little worried about how this might look. Bobby claims someone's trying to kill him and then it turns out Kitty inherits all this money when he dies."

"I'm sure the police will have a chat with her."

"But you don't think she had anything to do with Bobby's accident, do you?"

Ah, the subtext of his visit.

I said, "Frankly, I'd find it hard to believe, but Homicide might see it differently. They might also want to take a look at you while they're at it."

"Me?!" He managed to pack a lot of punctuation into one syllable.

"What if something happens to Kitty? Who gets the money then? She's not exactly in the best of health."

He looked at me uncomfortably, probably wishing he'd never come in. He must have harbored the vague notion that I could reassure him. Instead, I'd only broadened the basis for his anxieties. He wound up the conversation and got up moments later, telling me he'd be in touch. When he turned to go, I could see that the golf shirt was sticking to his back and I could smell the tension in his sweat.

"Oh, Derek," I called after him. "Does the name Blackman mean anything to you?"

"Not that I know. Why?"

"Just curious. I appreciate your coming in," I said. "If you find out anything else, please let me know."

"I will."

Once he was gone, I put in a quick call to a friend of mine at the telephone company and asked about S. Blackman. He said he'd check into it and call me back. I went down to the parking lot and hauled out the cardboard box I'd picked up from Bobby's garage. I went back up to the office and checked the contents, taking the items out one by one. It was all just as I remembered it: a couple of radiology manuals, some medical texts, paper clips, ballpoint pens, scratch pads. Nothing of significance that I could see. I hauled the box back out and shoved it into the backseat again, thinking I'd drop it back at Bobby's house next time I was there.

What to try next? I couldn't think of a thing.

I went home.

As I pulled into a parking place out front, I found myself scanning the walk for signs of Lila Sams. For a woman I'd only seen three or four times in my life, she was looming large, spoiling any sense of serenity I'd come to attach to the notion of "home." I locked my car and went around to the backyard, glancing at the rear of Henry's house to see if he was there. The back door was open and I caught the spicy scent of yeast and cinnamon through the screen. I peered in and spotted Henry sitting at the table with a coffee mug and the afternoon paper in front of him.

"Henry?"

He looked up. "Well, Kinsey. There you are." He came over and unlatched the screen, holding the door open for me. "Come in, come in. Would you like some coffee? I've got a pan of sweet rolls coming out in a minute."

I entered hesitantly, still half expecting Lila Sams to jump out like a tarantula. "I didn't want to interrupt anything," I said. "Is Lila here?"

"No, no. She had some business to take care of, but she should be back by six. I'm taking her out to dinner tonight. We have reservations at the Crystal Palace."

"Oh, wow, impressive," I said. Henry pulled a chair out for me and then poured me some coffee while I looked around. Lila had apparently taken her fine hand to the place. The curtains were new: avocado green cotton with a print of salt and pepper shakers, vegetable clusters, and wooden spoons, tied back with green bows. There were matching placemats and napkins, with accessories in a contrasting pumpkin shade. There was a new trivet on the counter with a homely saying in wrought-iron curlicue. I thought it said, "God Bless Our Biscuits," but that couldn't have been right.

"You've fixed the place up," I said.

His face brightened and he looked around. "You like it? It was Lila's idea. I tell you, the woman has made such a difference in my life."

"Well, that's good. I'm glad to hear that," I said.

"She's made me feel . . . I don't know, *vital* is the word I guess. Ready to start all over again."

I wondered if he was going to pass right over her accusations about my cheating him. He got up and opened the oven door, checking the sweet rolls, which he apparently decided were not quite done. He shoved them back and shut the oven, leaving the pumpkin-colored mitt on his right hand like a boxing glove.

I shifted uncomfortably on the stool where I was perched. "I thought maybe you and I should have a talk about Lila's accusations about the rent."

"Oh, don't worry about it," he said. "She was just in one of her moods."

"But Henry, I don't want you to feel like I'm cheating you. Don't you think we should get that ironed out?"

"No. Piffle. I don't feel you're cheating me."

"But she does."

"No no, not at all. You misunderstood."

"Misunderstood?" I said incredulously.

"Look, this is all my fault and I'm sorry I didn't get it straightened out at the time. Lila flew off the handle and she realizes that. In fact, I'm sure she means to apologize.

She and I had a long talk about it afterwards and I know she felt bad. It had nothing to do with you personally. She's a little high-strung, but she's just the dearest woman you'll ever meet. Once you get to know her, you'll see what a wonderful person she is."

"I hope so," I said. "What worried me is that she and Rosie had that tiff and then she took off after me. I wasn't sure what was going on."

Henry laughed. "Well, I wouldn't take that too seriously. You know Rosie. She gets into tiffs with everyone. Lila's fine. She's got a heart of gold and she's just as loyal as a little pup."

"I just don't want to see you going off the deep end," I said. It was one of those sayings that doesn't really mean anything but somehow it seemed to apply.

"No need to worry about that," he said mildly. "I've been around a long time, you know, and I haven't gone off the deep end yet."

He checked the sweet rolls again, and this time, he took them out and put the pan on the trivet to cool. He glanced over at me. "I haven't had a chance to tell you. She and I are going into a real-estate venture together."

"Oh really?"

"Which is how the subject of your rent came up in the first place. Rental income affects the overall value of the property and that was her main concern. She said she didn't mean to interfere in our relationship at all. She's hard-headed when it comes to business but she didn't want to look like she was butting in."

"What kind of real-estate venture?"

"Well, she owns some property she's going to put up as collateral, and with this place thrown in, we'll just about have the down payment on the property we want."

"Something here in town?"

"I better not say. She swore me to secrecy. I mean, it's not firm yet anyway, but I'll tell you about it when we get the deal put together. It should be happening in the next couple of days. I had to swear I'd keep mum."

"I don't understand," I said. "You're selling your house?"

"I can't even begin to understand the details. Too complicated for me," he said.

"I wasn't aware that she was involved in real estate."

"Oh, she's been doing this sort of thing for years. She was married to some big wheeler-dealer in New Mexico, and when he died, he left her very well off. She's got a bundle. Does real-estate investments almost as a hobby, she says."

"And she's from New Mexico? I thought someone told me it was Idaho."

"Oh, she's lived everywhere. She's a gypsy at heart. She's even talking me into it. You know, just take off into the sunset. Big RV and a map of the States. Go where the road takes us. I feel like she's added twenty years to my life."

I wanted to question him more closely, but I heard Lila's "yoo hoo" at the screen door and her face appeared, wreathed in saucy curls. She put a hand to her cheek when she saw me, turning all sheepish and coy.

"Oh, Kinsey. I bet I know just what you're doing here," she said. She came into the kitchen and paused for a moment, hands clasped in front of her as though she might drop to her knees in prayer. "Now don't say a word until I get this out," she went on. She paused to peer over at Henry. "Oh Henry, you did tell her how sorry I was to fuss at her that way." She was using a special "little" voice.

Henry put an arm around her, giving her a squeeze. "I've already explained and I'm sure she understands," he said. "I don't want you to worry any more about that."

"But I do worry, Puddy, and I won't feel right about it 'til I tell her myself."

Puddy?

She came over to the stool where I was perched and took my right hand, pressing it between her own.

"I am so sorry. I tell you I am so apologetic for what I said to you and I beg your forgiveness." Her tone was contrite and I thought Puddy was going to get all choked up. She was making deep eye contact with me and a couple of her rings were digging into my fingers rather painfully. She had apparently turned the ring around so that the stones were palm inward, producing maximum effect as she tightened her grip.

I said, "Oh, that's all right. Don't think another thing about it. I'm sure I won't."

Just to show her what a brick I was, I got up and put my left arm around her just the way Henry had. I gave her the same little squeeze, easing my foot across the toe of her right shoe and leaning forward slightly. She pulled back from the waist, but I managed to keep my foot where it was so that we were standing hip to hip. We locked eyes for a moment. She gave me a gooey smile and then eased her grip. I shifted my weight from her foot, but not before two coins of color had appeared high up on her cheeks like a cockatiel.

Puddy seemed pleased that we'd come to this new understanding and I was too. I made my excuses and departed soon after that. Lila had stopped looking at me altogether by then and I noticed that she had sat down abruptly, easing off one shoe.

17

I let myself into my apartment and poured a glass of wine and then I made myself a sandwich with creamed cheese and thinly sliced cucumbers and onions on dark bread. I cut it in half and used a piece of paper toweling as a combination napkin and dinner plate, toting sandwich and wineglass into the bathroom. I opened my bathroom window a crack and ate standing in the tub, peering out at intervals to see if Henry and Lila were departing for their dinner date. At 6:45, they came around the corner of the building and Henry unlocked his car, opening the door for her on the passenger side. I eased into an upright position, ducking back out of sight until I heard him start the car and pull away.

I'd finished dinner by then and I had nothing to do in the way of dishes except to wad up my paper towel and throw it in the trash, feeling inordinately pleased with myself. I traded my sandals for tennis shoes, grabbed up my master keys, my key picks, penknife, and a flashlight, then headed down the block to Moza Lowenstein's house, where I rang the bell. She peered out of the side window at me in perplexity, the opened the door.

"I couldn't think who it was at this hour," she said. "I thought Lila must be coming back for something she forgot."

I don't ordinarily visit Moza and I could tell she was wondering what I was doing on her doorstep. She moved back and admitted me, smiling timidly. The television was tuned to a rerun of "M.A.S.H.," helicopters whipping up a cloud of dust.

"I thought I'd do a little background check on Lila Sams," I said, while "Suicide Is Painless" played merrily.

"Oh, but she's just gone out," Moza said in haste. It was already occurring to her that I was up to no good and I guess she thought she could head me off.

"Is this her room back here?" I asked, moving into the corridor. I knew Moza's bedroom was the one at the end of the hall to the left. I figured Lila's must be the former "spare" room.

Moza lumbered after me. She's a big woman, suffering from some condition that makes her feet swell. Her expression was a cross between pain and bewilderment.

I tried the knob. Lila's door was locked.

"You can't go in there."

"Really?"

She was looking fearful by now and she didn't seem reassured by the sight of the master key I was easing into the keyhole. This was a simple house lock requiring only a skeleton key, several styles of which I had on a ring.

"You don't understand," she said again. "That's locked."

"No, it's not. See?" I opened the door and Moza put a hand on her heart.

"She'll come back," she said with a quaking voice.

"Moza, I'm not going to take anything," I said. "I will work with great care and she'll never know I was here. Why don't you sit out there in the living room and keep an eye open, just in case? O.K.?"

"She'll be so angry if she finds out I let you in," she said to me. Her eyes were as mournful now as a basset hound's.

"But she won't find out, so there's nothing to worry about. By the way, did you ever find out what little town in Idaho she's from?"

"Dickey is what she told me."

"Oh good. I appreciate that. She never mentioned living in New Mexico, did she?"

Moza shook her head and began to pat her chest as if she were burping herself. "Please hurry," she said. "I don't know what I'd do if she came back."

I wasn't sure myself.

I eased into the room and closed the door, flipping on the light. On the other side of the door, I heard Moza shuffling back toward the front of the house, murmuring to herself.

The room was furnished with an ancient wood-veneer
bedroom suite that I doubt could be called "antique." The
pieces looked like the ones I've seen out on thrift-shop sidewalks in downtown Los Angeles: creaky, misshapen, smell-
ing oddly of wet ash. There was a chiffonier, matching bed-
tables, a dressing table with a round mirror set between
banks of drawers. The bed frame was iron, painted a flaking
white, and the spread was chenille in a dusty rose with
fringe on the sides. The wallpaper was a tumble of floral
bouquets, mauve and pale rose on a gray background.
There were several sepia photographs of a man whom I
imagined was Mr. Lowenstein; someone, at any rate, who
favored hair slicked down with water and spectacles with
round gold rims. He appeared to be in his twenties, smooth
and pretty with a solemn mouth pulled over slightly pro-
truding teeth. The studio had tinted his cheeks a pinkish
tone, slightly at odds with the rest of the photo, but the
effect was nice. I'd heard that Moza was widowed in 1945. I
would have loved seeing a picture of her in those days. Almost reluctantly, I turned back to the task at hand.

Three narrow windows were locked on the inside, shades
drawn. I moved over and peered out of one, catching a
glimpse of backyard through screens rusted into the old
wooden frames. I checked my watch. It was only seven.
They'd be gone, at the very least, an hour, and I didn't think
I needed to provide myself an emergency exit. On the other
hand, there isn't any point in being dumb about these
things. I went back to the door and opened it, leaving it
ajar. Moza had turned off the TV set and I pictured her
peeking through the front curtain, heart in her throat,
which is about where mine was.

It was still light outside, but the room was gloomy even
with the overhead light on. I started with the chiffonier. I
did a preliminary survey, using my flashlight to check for
any crude attempts at security. Sure enough, Lila had
booby-trapped a couple of drawers by affixing a strand of
hair slyly across the crack. I removed these beauties and
placed them carefully on the hand-crocheted runner on top.

The first drawer contained a jumble of jewelry, several
belts coiled together, embroidered handkerchiefs, a watch
case, hairpins, a few stray buttons, and two pairs of white

cotton gloves. I stared for a long time, without touching anything, wondering why any of it warranted a protective strand of hair. Actually, anybody snooping in Lila's things would probably start here and work down, so maybe it was just a ready reference on her part, a checkpoint each time she returned to her room. I tried the next drawer, which was filled with neat piles of nylon underpants in a quite large old-lady style. I ran an experimental finger down between the stacks, being careful not to disturb the order. I couldn't feel anything significant; no handgun, no unidentifiable boxes or bumps.

On an impulse, I opened the first drawer again and peered up at the underside. Nothing taped to the bottom. I pulled the whole drawer out and checked along the back. Hello! Score one for my team. There was an envelope encased in plastic, sealed flat against the back panel of the drawer and secured by masking tape on all four sides. I took out my penknife and slid the small blade under one corner of the tape, peeling it up so I could remove the envelope from the plastic housing. In it was an Idaho driver's license in the name of Delilah Sampson. The woman had a real biblical sense of humor here. I made a note of the address, date of birth, height, weight, hair and eye color, much of which seemed to apply to the woman I knew as Lila Sams. God, I had really hit pay dirt. I slipped the license back into the envelope, returned the envelope to its hiding place, and pressed the masking tape securely against the wood. I squinted critically at my handiwork. Looked untouched to me, unless she'd powdered everything with some kind of tricky dust that would dye my hands bright red the instant I washed them again. Wouldn't that be a bitch!

The back of the second drawer was also being used as a little safe-deposit box, containing a stack of credit cards and yet another driver's license. The name on this one was Delia Sims, with an address in Las Cruces, New Mexico, and a date of birth that matched the first. Again, I made a note of the details and carefully returned the document to its hiding place. I replaced the drawer, glancing quickly at my watch. Seven thirty-two. I was still O.K., but I had a lot of ground to cover yet. I continued my search, working with delicacy, leaving the contents of each drawer undisturbed.

When I finished with the chiffonier, I retrieved the two hairs and moored them across the drawer cracks again.

The dressing table revealed nothing and the bed-tables were unremarkable. I went through the closet, checking coat pockets, suitcases, handbags, and shoe boxes, one of which still contained the receipt for the red wedgies she'd been wearing the first time we met. There was a credit-card slip stapled to the receipt and I tucked both in my pocket for later inspection. There was nothing under the bed, nothing stashed behind the chiffonier. I was checking back to see if I'd missed anything when I heard a peculiar warbling from the living room.

"Kinsey, they're back!" Moza wailed, her voice hoarse with dread. From out on the street, I caught the muffled thump of a car door slamming.

"Thanks," I said. Adrenaline flooded through me like water through a storm drain and I could have sworn my heart was boinging up against my tank top as in a cartoon. I did a hasty visual canvas. Everything looked O.K. I reached the door to the hallway, eased out, and pulled it shut behind me, snatching the ring of skeleton keys out of my jeans pocket. The flashlight. Shit! I'd left it on the dressing table.

Murmurs at the front door. Lila and Henry. Moza was making nice, asking about dinner. I yanked the door open and did a running tiptoe to the dressing table, snagged the flashlight, and bounded, like a silent gazelle, back to the door again. I tucked the flashlight up under my arm and prayed that I was inserting the proper key into the lock. A twist to the left and I heard the latch slide into the hole. I turned the key back quietly, extracting it with shaking hands, careful not to let the keys jingle together noisily. I glanced back over my shoulder, at the same time looking for an escape route.

The hallway extended about three feet to the right, where the archway to the living room cut through. At the extreme end of the hall was Moza's bedroom. To my left, there was an alcove for the telephone, a closet, the bathroom, and the kitchen, with an archway to the dining room visible beyond that. The dining room, in turn, opened into the living room again. If they were heading back this way, I had to guess they'd come straight through the archway to my right. I took two giant steps to the left and slipped into the bathroom. The minute I did it, I knew I'd made a bad choice. I should have tried the kitchen, with its outside exit. This was a dead end.

There was a separate shower to my immediate left with an opaque glass door, bathtub adjacent. To my right was a pedestal sink, and next to it, the toilet. The only window in the room was small and probably hadn't been opened in years. By now, I could hear voices growing louder as Lila moved into the hall. I stepped into the enclosed shower and pulled the door shut. I didn't dare latch it. I was certain the distinct sound of the metallic click would carry, alerting her to my presence. I set the flashlight down and held on to the door from the inside, bracing my fingers against the tile. I sank down to a crouch, thinking that if someone came in, I'd be less conspicuous if I was hunkered down. The voices in the hall bumbled on and I heard Lila unlock her bedroom door.

The shower was still damp from recent use, scented with Zest soap. A washrag hanging over the cold-water knob dripped intermittently on my shoulder. I listened intently, but I couldn't hear much. In situations like this, you have to get into the Zen of hiding. Otherwise your knees ache, your leg muscles go into spasms, and pretty soon you lose all sense of caution and just want to leap out, shrieking, regardless of the consequence. I leaned my face on my right arm, looking inward. I could still taste the onion from my sandwich. I was longing to clear my throat. Also I needed to pee. I hoped I wouldn't get caught, because I was going to feel like such an ass if Lila or Henry whipped open the shower door and found me crouching there. I didn't even bother to think up an explanation. There wasn't one.

I lifted my head. Voices in the hall. Lila had come out of her room, locking it after her. Maybe she'd gone in to make sure the hairs were in place. I wondered if I should have confiscated the duplicate licenses while I had the chance. No, better that I left them where they were.

Suddenly the bathroom door flew back and Lila's voice echoed against the bathroom walls like a bullhorn. My heart leapt into action so fast it was like being flung in an icy swimming pool. She was right on the other side of the

shower door, her plump form vaguely defined through the
milky glass. I closed my eyes like a kid, willing myself invis-
ible.

"I'll be right there, dearie love," she sang from two feet
away.

She crossed to the john and I heard the rustle of her polyester dress and the snap of her girdle as she struggled with
it.

Please God, I thought, don't let her decide to take an
impromptu shower or a dump. My tension level was so high
that I was bound to sneeze or cough or groan or cackle ma-
niacally. I willed myself into a hypnotic state, feeling my
armpits dampen with sweat.

The toilet flushed. Lila took forever putting herself back
together again. Rustle, pop, snap. I heard her jiggle the
handle when the toilet continued to run. She washed her
hands, the faucet squeaking as she turned it off. How long
could she drag this out? Finally, she moved toward the
bathroom door and opened it, and then she was gone,
footsteps receding toward the living room. Yakety-yak, chit
chat, soft laughter, good-bye sounds, and the front door
closed.

I stayed exactly where I was until I heard Moza in the
hall.

"Kinsey? They're gone. Are you still here?"

I let out the breath I'd been holding and stood up, shoving my flashlight into my back pocket. This is not a dignified
way to make a living, I thought. Hell, I wasn't even getting
paid for this. I peered out of the shower door, making sure I
hadn't been set up in some elaborate ruse. The house felt
quiet except for Moza, who was opening the broom-closet
door, still whispering, "Kinsey?"

"I'm in here," I said, voice booming.

I went out into the hall. Moza was so thrilled we hadn't
been caught that she couldn't even get mad at me. She
leaned against the wall, fanning herself. I figured I better
get out of there before they came back for something else,
taking ten more years off my projected life-span.

"You're terrific," I murmured. "I'm indebted for life. I'll
buy you dinner at Rosie's."

I moved through the kitchen, peering out the back door before I exited. It was fully dark by then, but I made sure the street was deserted before I stepped out of the shadow of Moza's house. Then I walked the half-block toward home laughing to myself. Actually, it's fun to horse around with danger. It's fun to snoop in people's dresser drawers. I might have turned to burgling houses if law enforcement hadn't beckoned to me first. With Lila, I was finally beginning to take control of a situation I didn't like and the surge of power made me feel nearly giddy with relief. I wasn't sure what she was up to, but I intended to find out.

18

When I was safely back in my apartment again, I took out the credit-card receipt I'd lifted from Lila's shoe box. The date on it was May 25 and the store was located in Las Cruces. The credit-card imprint read "Delia Sims." In the box marked "phone number," someone had obligingly penned in a phone number. I hauled out my telephone book and looked up the area code for Las Cruces. Five-oh-five. I picked up the receiver and dialed the number, wondering as I heard it ring on the far end just what I intended to say.

"Hello?" Man's voice. Middle-aged. No accent.

"Oh hello," I said smoothly. "I wonder if I might speak to Delia Sims."

There was a moment of silence. "Hang on."

A palm was secured across the mouthpiece and I could hear muffled conversation in the background.

The receiver was apparently taken over by someone else, because a new voice inquired, "May I help you?"

This one was female and I couldn't classify the age.

"Delia?" I said.

"Who is this, please?" The tone was guarded, as though the call might be obscene.

"Oh, sorry," I said. "This is Lucy Stansbury. That's not you, is it, Delia? It doesn't sound like your voice."

"This is a friend of Delia's. She not here at the moment. Was there something I might help you with?"

"Well, I hope so," I said, mind racing. "Actually, I'm calling from California. I just met Delia recently and she left some of her things in the backseat of my car. I couldn't figure out any other way to reach her except to try this number, which was on a credit-card receipt for a purchase

136

she made in Las Cruces. Is she still in California or is she home again?"

"Just a minute."

Again, a palm across the mouthpiece and the drone of conversation in the background. The woman came back on the line.

"Why don't you give me your name and number and I'll have her get back to you?"

"Oh sure, that's fine," I said. I gave her my name again, spelling it out laboriously and then I made up a telephone number with the area code for Los Angeles. "You want me to mail this stuff back to her or just hang on to it? I'd feel bad if I thought she didn't realize where she'd left it."

"What exactly did she leave?"

"Well, most of it's just clothes. A summer dress I know she's fond of, but I don't guess that matters much. I do have that ring of hers with the square-cut emerald and the little diamond baguettes," I said, describing the ring I'd seen Lila wearing that first afternoon in Henry's garden. "Do you expect her back soon?"

After the barest hesitation, the woman's chill reply came. "Who is this?"

I hung up. So much for trying to fool the folks in Las Cruces. I couldn't imagine what she was up to, but I sure didn't like the notion of this real-estate venture she'd proposed to Henry. He was so smitten, she could probably talk him into anything. She was moving quickly too, and I thought I better come up with some answers before she took him for all he was worth. I reached for a pile of blank index cards in my top desk drawer, and when the phone rang moments later, I jumped. Shit, could someone have put a trace on the call that fast? Surely not.

I lifted the receiver with caution, listening for the white noise of a long-distance connection. There was none.

"Hello?"

"Miss Millhone?" Male. The voice sounded familiar, though I couldn't for the moment figure out who it was. Music blasting in the background was forcing him to yell, and I found myself yelling too.

"This is she."

"This is Gus," he hollered, "Bobby's friend from the skate-rental place."

"Oh, it's you. Hello. I'm glad you called. I hope you have some information for me. I could sure use the help."

"Well, I've been thinking about Bobby and I guess I owe him that much. I should have spoken up this afternoon."

"Don't worry about it. I appreciate your getting back to me. You want to get together or just talk on the phone?"

"Either way is fine. One thing I wanted to mention—and I don't know if this would be a help or not—but Bobby gave me this address book you might want to take a look at. Did he ever talk to you about that?"

"Of course he did. I've been turning the town upside down looking for that thing," I said. "Where are you?"

He gave me an address on Granizo and I said I'd be right there. I hung up the phone and grabbed my handbag and car keys.

Gus's neighborhood was poorly lighted and the yards were flat patches of dirt, graced with occasional palm trees. The cars parked along the curbs were primer-painted low riders with bald tires and ominous dents. My VW fit right in. About every third property boasted a brand-new chain link fence, erected to corral God knows what kind of beast. As I passed one house, I heard something that sounded ugly and snappish scramble forward to the length of its choke chain, whimpering hoarsely when it couldn't quite get to me. I picked up my pace.

Gus lived in a tiny frame cottage in a U-shaped courtyard ringed with cottages. I passed through an ornamental entranceway with the street number in wrought iron arched across it in a rainbow shape. There were eight units altogether, three on each side of a central walkway and two at the end. All were cream-colored and even in the darkness looked drab with soot. I identified Gus's place because the music thundering out was the same stuff I'd heard on the phone. Up close, it didn't sound as good. His front drape consisted of a bedsheet slung over a curtain rod and the knob on his screen was an empty wooden spool on a nail. I had to wait for a brief silence between cuts to pound on the doorframe. The music started up again with a vengeance, but he'd apparently caught my knock.

"Yo!" he called. He opened the door and held the screen for me. I stepped into the room, assaulted by heat, loud rock, and the strong smell of catbox.

"Can you turn that shit down?" I yelled.

He nodded, moving to the stereo, which he flicked off. "Sorry," he said sheepishly. "Have a seat."

His place was about half the size of mine and jammed with twice the furniture. King-sized bed, a big chest of drawers in pecan-wood plastic laminate, the stereo cabinet, sagging brick-and-board bookcases, two upholstered chairs with shredded sides, a space heater, and one of those units the size of a television console, housing sink, stove, and refrigerator. The bathroom was separated from the main room by a panel of material hanging on a length of twine. The room's two lamps were draped with red terry-cloth towels that muted their two-hundred-and-fifty-watt bulbs to a rosy glow. Both chairs were filled with cats, which he seemed to notice about the same time I did.

He gathered one batch of them up by the armload as if they were old clothes and I sat down in the space he had cleared. As soon as he tossed the cats on the bed, they made their way back to their original places. One of them kneaded my lap as if it were a hunk of bread dough and then curled up when he was satisfied with the job he'd done. Another one crowded in beside me and a third one settled on the arm of the chair. They seemed to eye each other, trying to figure out who had the best deal. They appeared to be full-grown and probably from the same litter, as they all sported thick tortoiseshell coats and heads the size of softballs. There were two adolescent cats curled up in the other chair, a buff and a black, tangled together like mismatched socks. A sixth cat emerged from under the bed and paused, pointing each hind foot in turn. Gus watched this feline activity with a shy smile, his face flushed with pride.

"Aren't they great?" he said. "I just never get tired of these little peckerheads. At night, they pile on the bed with me like a quilt. I got one sleeps on my pillow with his feet in my hair. I can kiss their little faces anytime I want." He

snatched one up and cradled it like a baby, an indignity the
cat endured with surprising passivity.

"How many do you have?"

"Six right now, but Luci Baines and Lynda Bird are both
pregnant. I don't know what I'm gonna do about that."

"Maybe you could get them fixed," I said helpfully.

"Well, after this batch is born, I guess I should. I'm real
good at finding homes for the kittens, though, and they're
always so sweet."

I wanted to mention how good they smelled too, but I
didn't have the heart for sarcasm when he was clearly so
crazy about his brood. There he was, looking like a police
artist's composite of a sex killer, making a fool of himself over
this collection of domesticated furs.

"I guess I should have spoken up sooner about this stuff,"
he was saying. "I don't know what got into me." He crossed
to the bookshelf and sorted through the mess on top, coming up with an address book about the size of a playing card,
which he held out to me.

I took it, leafing through. "What's the significance? Did
Bobby fill you in?"

"Well no. He told me to keep it and he said it was important, but he didn't explain. I just assumed it must be a list
or a code, *some* kind of information he had, but I don't know
what."

"When did he give you this?"

"I don't remember exactly. It was sometime before the
accident. He stopped over one day and gave it to me and
asked me if I'd just hold on to it for him, so I said sure. I'd
forgotten all about it until you brought it up."

I checked the index tab for *B*. There wasn't a Blackman
listed there, but I did find the name penciled inside the
back cover, with a seven-digit number beside it. No area
code indicated, so it was probably local, though I didn't
think it matched the number for S. Blackman I'd found in
the telephone book.

"What did he actually say at the time?" I asked. I knew I
was repeating myself, but I kept hoping to solicit some indication of Bobby's intent.

"Nothing really. He wanted me to hang on to it is all. He
didn't tell you either, huh?"

I shook my head. "He couldn't remember. He knew it was important, but he had no idea why. Have you ever heard the name Blackman? S. Blackman? Anybody Blackman?"

"Nope." The cat was squirming and he put it down.

"I understand Bobby had fallen in love with someone. I wonder if it might have been this S. Blackman."

"If it was, he didn't tell me. A couple of times he did meet some woman down at the beach. Right out in that parking lot by the skate shack."

"Before the accident or afterwards?"

"Before. He'd sit in his Porsche and wait and she'd pull in and then they'd talk."

"He never introduced you or mentioned who she was?"

"I know what she looked like but not her name. I saw 'em go in the coffee shop once and she was built odd, you know? Kind of like a Munchkin. I couldn't figure that out. Bobby was a good-lookin' guy and he always hung out with these real foxy chicks, but she was a dog."

"Blond wispy hair? Maybe forty-five?"

"I never saw her up close so I don't know about her age, but the hair sounds right. She drives this Mercedes I see around now and then. Dark green with a beige interior. Looks like a 'fifty-five or 'fifty-six, but it's in great shape."

I glanced through the address book again. Sufi's address and telephone number were listed under the D's.

Had he been having an affair with *her*? It seemed so unlikely. Bobby had been twenty-three years old and, as Gus said, a good-looking kid. Carrie St. Cloud had mentioned a blackmailing scheme, but if Sufi was being blackmailed by someone, why would she turn to him for help? Surely it wasn't a matter of her blackmailing *him*. Whatever it was, it gave me a lead and I was grateful for that. I tucked the book in my handbag and looked up. Gus was watching me with amusement.

"God, you should see your face. I could really watch the old wheels turn," he said.

"Things are beginning to happen and I like that," I said. "Listen, this has been a big help. I don't know what it means yet, but believe me, I'll figure it out."

"I hope so. I'm just sorry I didn't speak up when you asked. If there's anything else I can do, just let me know."

"Thanks," I said. I shifted the cat off my lap and got up, shaking hands with him.

I went out to my car, brushing at my jeans, picking cat hair off my lip. It was now ten o'clock at night and I should have headed home, but I was feeling wired. The episode at Moza's and the sudden appearance of Bobby's address book were acting on me like a stimulant. I wanted to talk to Sufi. Maybe I'd stop by her place. If she was up, we could have a little chat. She'd tried once to steer me away from this investigation and I wondered now what that was about.

19

I pulled into the shadows across the street from Sufi's place on Haughland Road in the heart of Santa Teresa. For the most part, the houses I had passed were two-story frame-and-stone on large lots complete with junipers and oaks. Many lawns sported the ubiquitous California crop of alarm-company signs, warning of silent surveillance and armed patrols.

Sufi's yard was darkened by the interlacing tree branches overhead, the property stretching back in a tangle of shrubs and surrounded by a picket fence with wide pales. The house was done in a dark shingle siding, possibly a muted brown or green, though it was hard to tell which at this hour of the night. The side porch was narrow and deeply recessed with no exterior light visible. A dark green Mercedes was parked in the drive to the left.

It was a quiet neighborhood. The sidewalks were deserted and there was no traffic. I got out of my car and crossed to the front of the house. Up close, I could see that the place was massive, the kind being converted now to bed-and-breakfast establishments with odd names: The Gull and Satchel, The Blue Tern, The Quackery. They're all over town these days: renovated Victorian mansions impossibly quaint, where for ninety bucks a night, you can sleep in a bed with a fake brass frame and struggle, the next morning, with a freshly baked croissant that will drop pastry flakes in your lap like dandruff.

From the look of it, Sufi's was still a single-family dwelling, but it had a shabby air. Maybe, like many single women her age, she'd reached that point where the absence of a man translates out to dripping faucets and rain gutters in need of repair. A single woman my age would haul out a

143

crescent wrench or shinny up the down spout, feeling that odd joyousness that comes with self-sufficiency. Sufi had let her property decline to a state of lingering disrepair and it made me wonder what she did with her salary. I thought surgical nurses made good money.

At the rear of the house, there was a glass-enclosed porch, the windows flickering with the blue/gray reflections of a television set. I fumbled my way up several crumbling concrete steps and tapped on the door. After a moment, the porch light came on and Sufi looked through the curtain.

"Hi, it's me," I said. "Can I talk to you?"

She leaned closer to the glass, peering around, apparently checking to see whether I was accompanied by roving bands of thugs.

She opened the door in her robe and slippers, clutching the lapels together at her throat, one arm circling her waist. "Oh my God, you scared me to death," she said. "What are you doing here at this hour? Is something wrong?"

"Not at all. Sorry to alarm you. I was in the neighborhood and I needed to talk to you. Can I come in?"

"I was on my way to bed."

"We can talk out here on the porch, then."

She gave me a grudging look, stepping back reluctantly so I could enter. She was half a head shorter than I and her blond hair was so thin, I could see stretches of scalp underneath. I hadn't pegged her as the type who'd lounge around in a slinky peach satin wrapper and matching mules with dandelion fuzz across the instep. This was hotsy-totsy stuff. I wanted to say, "Hubba-hubba" but I was afraid she'd take offense.

Once inside, I took a quick mental picture and stored it away for future assessment. The room was cluttered, disorganized, and probably unclean judging from the used dishes piled here and there, the dead flowers in a vase, and the wastebasket spilling trash out onto the floor. The water in the bottom of the vase was cloudy with bacteria and probably smelled like the last stages of some disease. There was a crumpled cellophane packet on the arm of the easy chair and I saw that she'd been sneaking Ding Dongs. A *Reader's Digest* condensed book was open facedown on the ottoman. The place smelled like pepperoni pizza, some of which I spied sitting in a box on top of the television set. The heat from the circuitry was keeping it warm, the scent of oregano and mozzarella cheese mingling with the odor of hot cardboard. God, I thought, when did I last eat?

"You live alone?" I asked.

She looked at me as if I were casing the joint. "What of it?"

"I've been assuming you were single. I just realized no one had ever really said as much."

"It's very late to be doing a survey," she said tartly. "What did you want?"

I find it so liberating when other people are rude. It makes me feel mild and lazy and mean. I smiled at her. "I found Bobby's address book."

"Why tell me?"

"I was curious about your relationship with him."

"I didn't have a relationship with him."

"That's not what I hear."

"Well, you heard wrong. Of course I *knew* him. He was Glen's only child and she and I are best friends and have been for years. Aside from that, Bobby and I didn't have that much to say to one another."

"Why'd you need to meet him down at the beach, then?"

"I never 'met' Bobby at the beach," she snapped.

"Somebody saw you with him on more than one occasion."

She hesitated. "Maybe I ran into him once or twice. What's wrong with that? I used to see him at the hospital, too."

"I wondered what you talked about, that's all."

"I'm sure we talked about lots of things," she said. I could see her shifting gears, trying another tack. Some of the huffiness dropped away. She'd apparently decided to roll out the charm. "God, I don't know what's the matter with me. I'm sorry if I sounded rude. As long as you're here, you might as well sit down. I have wine chilled if you want some."

"I'd like that. Thanks."

She left the room, probably grateful for the chance to stall while she figured out how to cover her tracks. For my part, I was delighted with the opportunity to nose around. I crossed in haste to the easy chair, checking the table beside it. The top was littered with things I didn't want to touch. I eased the drawer open. The interior looked like a catchall for household fallout. Batteries, candles, an extension cord, receipts, rubber bands, packets of matches, two buttons, a sewing kit, pencils, junk mail, a dinner fork, a stapler gun— all of it surrounded by accumulated grit. I ran a hand down along the chair cushion and came up with a nickel, which I left there. I heard the chirp of a wine cork in the kitchen and the tinkle of wineglasses as she removed them from a cabinet. The glass rims began to clink together as she moved back toward the TV room. I abandoned my search and perched myself casually on the arm of the couch.

I was trying to think of something nice to say about her house, but I was secretly worried about my tetanus shots being out of date. This was the kind of place if you had to use the john, you'd want to put paper down on the seat. "Quite a house," I remarked.

Sufi made a face. "The cleaning lady comes tomorrow," she said. "Not that she does much. She worked for my parents for years and I don't have the heart to let her go."

"Do they live with you?"

She shook her head. "Dead. Cancer."

"Both of them?"

"That's the way it goes," she said with a shrug.

So much for family sentiment.

She poured a glass of wine and handed it to me. I could tell from the label, it was the same ultra-crummy stuff I drank before I got into the boxed brand with the picture of a phony-looking vineyard on the front. Clearly, neither of us had the budget or the palate for anything decent.

She settled into the easy chair, wineglass in hand. The change in her manner was conspicuous. She must have come up with a good one while she was gone.

She took a sip of wine, staring at me over the rim of her glass. "Have you talked to Derek lately?" she asked.

"He stopped by my office this afternoon."

"He moved out. When Glen got back from San Francisco this evening, she had the maid pack his bags and put them out in the driveway. Then she changed the locks."

"My, my," I said, "I wonder what brought that on."

"You'd be smart to talk to him before you worry about me."

"Why's that?"

"He had a motive for killing Bobby. I didn't, if that's what you're getting at."

"What motive are you referring to?"

"Glen discovered he'd taken out a big life-insurance policy on Bobby eighteen months ago."

"What?" My wineglass tipped and wine slopped out on my hand. I couldn't disguise the fact that I was startled, but I didn't like the smug look that crossed her face in response.

"Oh yes. The insurance company tracked her down to ask for a copy of the death certificate. I guess the agent read about Bobby in the paper and remembered the name. That's how Glen found out."

"I thought you couldn't take out a policy on someone without their signature."

"Technically, that's true, but it can be done."

I busied myself wiping up spilled wine with a tissue. In the midst of the mop-up procedure, I realized, like a cartoon light bulb going on overhead, that she felt an intense dislike for Derek. "What's the story?" I asked.

"Derek got caught with his pants down," she said. "His claim is that he got the policy ages ago after Bobby'd totaled his car a couple of times. He thought Bobby would self-destruct. You know the type. One accident after another until the kid winds up dead. It becomes a socially acceptable form of suicide. Personally, I'm not sure Derek was that far off. Bobby drank like a fish and I'm sure he did drugs. He and Kitty were both a mess. Rich and spoiled and self-indulgent—"

"Be careful what you say here, Sufi. I liked Bobby Callahan. I think he had guts."

"I think we're all aware of that," she said. She was using that superior tone of voice that drove me mad, but I couldn't afford to react at this point. She crossed her legs, swinging one foot. The dandelion fuzz on that slipper undulated as the air passed over it. "You may not like it, but it *is* the truth. And that's not all of it. Word has it that Derek took out a policy on Kitty too."

"For how much?"

"Half a million bucks on each."

"Come on, Sufi. That doesn't make any sense. Derek wouldn't kill his own daughter."

"Kitty isn't dead, though, is she?"

"But why would he kill Bobby? He'd have to be nuts. The first thing the cops are going to do is turn around and look at him."

"Kinsey," she said patiently. "Nobody ever said Derek had brains. He's an idiot. A fool."

"He's not that big a fool," I said. "How could he hope to get away with it?"

"Nobody's got any proof that he did anything. There never was any evidence from the first accident and Jim Fraker seems to think this one came about because Bobby had a seizure first. How can they pin that on Derek?"

"But why would he do it? He's got money."

"*Glen's* got money. Derek doesn't have a dime. He'd go for anything that would get him out from under her. Don't you know that?"

All I could do was stare at her, running the information through my mental computer. She took another sip of wine and smiled at me, loving the effect she'd produced.

Finally, I said, "I just don't believe it."

"You can believe anything you like. All I'm saying is you better check that out before you do anything else."

"You don't like Derek, do you?"

"Of course not. I think he's the biggest ass who ever lived. I don't know what Glen saw in him in the first place. He's poor. He's dumb. He's pompous. And those are his *good* qualities," she said with energy. "Aside from all that, he's ruthless."

"He doesn't seem ruthless to me," I said.

"You haven't known him as long as I have. He's a man who'd do anything for money and I suspect he's got lots he's not anxious to discuss. Doesn't he strike you as a man with a past?"

"Like what?"

"I'm not sure. But I'd be willing to bet you his buffoonery is just a cover for something else."

"Are you saying Glen's been hoodwinked? She seems smarter than that."

"She's smart about everything but men. This is her third time around, you know, and Bobby's father was a mess. Husband number two I don't know about. She was living in Europe when she married him and it didn't last long."

"Let's get back to you for a minute. The day of Bobby's funeral, I got the impression you were trying to steer me away from the investigation. Now you're giving me leads. Why the switch?"

She had to stop and pay attention to the tie on her robe, though she was talking to me the whole time. "I guess I thought you'd be prolonging Glen's pain and heartache," she said, looking up at me then. "It's clear now that nothing I say is going to dissuade you in any event, so I might as well tell you what I know."

"Why'd you meet Bobby down at the beach? What was going on?"

"Oh, poo. Nothing," she said. "I ran into him a couple of times and he wanted to bitch about Derek. Bobby couldn't stand him either and he knew I made a good audience. That's all it amounted to."

"Why didn't you say that in the first place?"

"I'm not accountable to you. You show up at my door uninvited and quiz me about all this bullshit. It's none of your business so why should I answer to you? I don't think you know how you come off sometimes."

I felt myself flush at the well-placed insult. I drank the last of my wine. I was having trouble believing her story about meeting Bobby, but it was clear I wasn't going to get much more out of her. I decided to drop it for the moment, but it didn't sit well with me. If she'd only been listening to his complaints, why not just say so to begin with?

A glance at my watch showed that it was just after eleven and I decided to try to catch Glen at home. I excused myself abruptly and got out. I'm sure the haste of my departure wasn't lost on her.

There are times when things begin to break by sheer dint of dumb luck. I don't pretend to take credit for what happened next. By the time I got to my little VW, I realized how chilly it was. I hopped in and shut the door, locking it as is my habit, and then I turned and started rooting around in my junky backseat for a sweatshirt I'd tossed back there.

I'd just laid my hands on it and I was in the process of hauling it out from under a pile of books when I heard a car start up. I glanced to my right. Sufi's Mercedes was being backed out of the driveway. I did a quick surface dive, disappearing from view. I wasn't sure if she knew my car or not, but she must have assumed I was gone because she pulled straight off. As soon as she did, I rolled into the driver's seat, fumbling for my keys. I started the car and did a quick U-turn, catching a glimpse of her taillights as she hung a right, heading toward State Street.

She couldn't have had time enough to change her clothes. At best, she might have thrown a coat over her satin lounging outfit. Who did she know well enough to visit unannounced in a Jean Harlow getup at this hour of the night? I couldn't wait to see.

20

In Santa Teresa, the rich are divided into two cliques: half live in Montebello, half in Horton Ravine. Montebello is the old money, Horton Ravine, the new. Both communities have acres of old trees, bridle paths, and country clubs requiring proper sponsorship and entrance fees of twenty-five grand. Both communities discourage fundamentalist churches, tacky yard ornaments, and door-to-door sales. Sufi was headed for Horton Ravine.

As she passed through the main gates on Los Piratas, she slowed to thirty miles an hour, reluctant perhaps to get picked up for speeding while dressed like a call girl on her way to a john. I slowed my car at a pace with hers, hanging back as far as I could. I was worried about having to pursue her along miles of winding road, but she surprised me by turning into one of the first driveways on the right. The house was set back about a hundred yards, a one-story California "bungalow": maybe five bedrooms, four thousand square feet, not remarkable to look at, but expensive nevertheless. The property was probably five acres all told, surrounded by an ornamental split-rail fence, with rambling roses laid along its length. Exterior lights had come on when Sufi's Mercedes reached the house. She got out of the car in a blur of peach satin and mink, moving toward the front door, which opened and swallowed her up.

I had passed the house by then. I drove on as far as the first road on the right, where I did a turnaround, dousing my headlights as I drifted back. I parked my car on the berm on the left-hand side, hugging some shrubs. The area was shrouded in darkness, no streetlights at all. Across from me, the tag end of the golf course was visible and the narrow artificial lake that served as a water hazard. Moonlight glimmered on the surface of the lake, making it as glossy as a remnant of gray silk.

I removed the flashlight from the glove compartment and got out of my car, picking my way carefully through the tall grass growing by the road. It was thick and wet, soaking my tennis shoes and the legs of my jeans.

I reached the driveway. There wasn't any name on the mailbox, but I noted the numbers. I could always stop by my office and check my crisscross directory if I needed to. I had gone about halfway up the drive when I heard a dog barking at the house. I had no idea what kind it was, but it sounded big—one of those dogs that knows how to bark from its balls—deep, businesslike barks, suggestive of sharp teeth and a bad attitude. Furthermore, that sucker had picked up my scent and was anxious to make contact. There was no way I could creep any closer without alerting the occupants of the house. They were probably already wondering what was making Old Dog Tray wet himself with excitement. For all I knew, they'd release him from his three-eighths-inch chain and send him flying down the driveway after me, toenails scratching along the blacktop. I've been chased by dogs before and it's not that much fun.

I reversed my course and got back in the car. Common sense is no disgrace in the private-eye trade. I watched the house for an hour, but there was no sign of activity. I was getting tired and this felt like a waste of time. Finally, I started the engine and eased the car into gear, not flipping on my headlights until I was out through the gate again.

By the time I got home, I was exhausted. I made a few quick notes and packed it in for the night. It was nearly one o'clock when I finally turned out the light. I got up at six and did a three-mile run just to get my head on straight. Then I sped through my morning ablutions, grabbed an apple, and arrived at the office by seven. It was Tuesday and I was thankful I wasn't scheduled for physical therapy that day. Now that I thought about it, my arm was feeling pretty good, or maybe the fact that I was involved in an investigation distracted me from whatever pain or immobility remained.

There were no messages on my answering machine and no mail that needed dealing with from the day before. I hauled out my crisscross and checked the house numbers on Los Piratas. Well, well. I should have guessed. Fraker, James and Nola. I wondered which of them Sufi had gone to see and why the rush. It was possible, of course, that she'd consulted with both, but I couldn't quite picture that. Could Nola be the woman Bobby'd fallen in love with? I couldn't see how Dr. Fraker tied into this, but something was sure going on.

I took out Bobby's address book and tried the number for Blackman. I got a recorded message from that woman who sounds like the fairy godmother in a Walt Disney cartoon. "We're sorry, but the number you've dialed cannot be connected in the eight-oh-five area code. Please check the number and dial again. Thank you." I tried the codes for surrounding areas. No luck. I spent a long time looking through the other entries in the book. If all else failed, I'd have to sit here and contact each person in turn, but it seemed like a tiresome prospect and not necessarily productive. In the meantime, what?

It was too early in the morning to make house calls, but it occurred to me that a visit to Kitty might make sense. She was still at St. Terry's and, given hospital routine, she'd probably been rousted out of bed at dawn. I hadn't seen her for days anyway and she might be of help.

The chill of the day before was gone. The air was clear and the sun was already intense. I slid my VW into the last available space in the vistors' lot and went around to the front entrance. The information desk in the lobby was deserted but the hospital itself was in full swing. The coffee shop was jammed, the scent of cholesterol and caffeine wafting irresistibly through the open doorway. Lights were on in the gift shop. The cashier's office was busy, filled with young female clerks preparing final bills as if this were some grand hotel nearing check-out time. There was an aura of excitement—medical personnel gearing up for birth and death and complex surgeries, cracked bones and breakdowns and drug overdoses . . . a hundred life-threatening episodes any given day of the week. And through it all the insidious sexuality that made it the stuff of soaps.

I went up to the third floor, turning left when I got off the elevators near 3 South. The big double doors were locked, as usual. I pushed the buzzer. After a moment, a heavyset black woman in jeans and a royal blue T-shirt rattled some keys and opened the door a crack. She wore a nursy no-nonsense watch and those shoes with two-inch crepe soles designed to offset fallen arches and varicose veins. She had startling hazel eyes and a face that radiated competence. Her white plastic tag indicated that her name was Natalie Jacks, LVN. I showed Ms. Jacks the photostat of my license and asked if I could talk to Kitty Wenner, explaining that I was a friend of the family.

She looked my I.D. over carefully and finally stepped back to let me in.

She locked the door behind me and led the way down the corridor to a room near the end. I was sneaking peeks into rooms along the way. I don't know what I anticipated— women writhing and babbling to themselves, men imitating ex-Presidents and jungle beasts. Or the lot of them in a drug-induced stupor that would swell their tongues and make their eyes roll back in their heads. Instead, as I passed each door, I saw faces raised in curiosity toward mine, as if I were a new admission who might shriek or do birdcalls while I tore off my clothes. I couldn't see any difference between them and me, which I thought was worrisome.

Kitty was up and dressed, her hair still wet from a shower. She was stretched out on her bed, pillows propped up behind her, a breakfast tray on the bed-table next to her. She wore a silk caftan that drooped on her frame as if she were a coat hanger. Her breasts were no bigger than buttons on a couch and her arms were bare bones fleshed out with skin as thin as tissue paper. Her eyes were enormous and haunted, the shape of her skull so pronounced that she looked as if she were seventy. Sally Struthers could have used her picture in an ad for foster parenting.

"You got a visitor," Natalie said.

Kitty's eyes flicked to me, and for a moment, I could see how scared she was. She was dying. She had to know that. The energy was seeping out of her pores like sweat.

Natalie inspected the breakfast tray. "You know they're going to put you on an I.V. if you don't do better than this. I thought you had a contract with Dr. Kleinert."

"I *ate* some," Kitty said.

"Well, I'm not supposed to pester you, but he'll be doing rounds soon. Try picking away at this while you talk to her, O.K.? We're on your team, baby. Honestly."

Natalie gave us both a brief smile and left, moving into the room next door, where we could hear her talking to someone else.

Kitty's face was suffused with pink and she was fighting back tears. She reached for a cigarette and lit it, coughing some against the back of her bony hand. She shook her head, conjuring up a smile that had some sweetness to it. "God, I can't believe I got myself into this," she said, and then wistfully, "You think Glen might come see me?"

"I don't know. I may go over there after I talk to you. I'll mention it to her if you like."

"She kicked Daddy out."

"So I heard."

"She'll probably kick me out next."

I couldn't look at her anymore. Her longing for Glen was so tangible it hurt me to see it. I studied the breakfast tray: a fresh fruit cup, a blueberry muffin, a carton of strawberry yogurt, granola, orange juice, tea. There was no indication that she'd eaten any of it.

"You want some of that?" she asked.

"No way. You'll tell Kleinert you ate it."

Kitty had the good grace to blush, laughing uneasily.

"I don't understand why you don't eat," I said.

She made a face. "Everything just looks so gross. There's this girl two doors down and she was suffering from anorexia, you know? So they brought her in here and she finally started to eat? Now she looks like she's pregnant. She's still thin. She's just got half a basketball for a stomach. It's disgusting."

"So what? She's alive, isn't she?"

"I don't want to look like that. Nothing tastes good anyway and it just makes me throw up."

There was no point in pursuing the subject so I let it go, shifting over to something else instead. "Have you talked to your father since Glen kicked him out?"

Kitty shrugged. "He's here every day in the afternoon. He's moved into the Edgewater Hotel until he finds a place."

"Did he tell you about Bobby's will?"

"Some. He says Bobby left me all this money. Is that true?" Her tone was one of dismay as much as anything.

"As far as I know, it is."

"But why would he do that?"

"Maybe he felt like he messed up your life and wanted to do right by you. Derek tells me he left some money to Rick's parents too. Or maybe he considered it a little incentive for you to get your shit together for a change."

"I never made any deals with him."

"I don't think he meant to make a 'deal.'"

"Well, I don't like to feel controlled."

"Kitty, I think you've demonstrated the fact that you can't be controlled. We're all getting that message loud and clear. Bobby loved you."

"Who asked him to? Sometimes I wasn't even nice to him. And I didn't exactly have his best interests at heart."

"Meaning what?"

"Nothing. Skip it. I wish he hadn't left me anything is all. It makes me feel crummy."

"I don't know what to tell you," I said.

"Well, I never asked him for a thing." Her tone was argumentative, but I couldn't understand what her position was.

"What's bothering you?"

"Nothing."

"What's all the fretting about, then?"

"I'm not fretting! God. Why should I fret? He did it so he'd feel good, right? It had nothing to do with me."

"It had *something* to do with you or he'd have left the money to someone else."

She started gnawing on her thumbnail, temporarily abandoning the cigarette, which sat on the lip of the ashtray and sent up a tiny trail of smoke like an Indian signal on a distant mountaintop. Her mood was getting dark. I wasn't sure why she was so upset at the notion of two million dollars being dumped in her lap, but I didn't want to alienate her. I wanted information. I shifted the subject again. "What about the insurance your father took out on Bobby's life? Did he mention that?"

"Yeah. That's weird. He does stuff like that, and later, he can't understand why people get upset. He doesn't see anything wrong with it at all. To him, it just makes sense. Bobby'd cracked up his car once or twice so Daddy just figured if he died, somebody might as well benefit. I guess that's why Glen threw him out, huh?"

"I think that's a safe bet. She'd never tolerate his profiting from Bobby's death. My God, it was the worst possible move he could have made as far as she's concerned. Besides which, it sets him up as a murder suspect."

"My father wouldn't kill anyone!"

"That's what he says about you."

"Well, it's true. I didn't have any reason to want Bobby dead. Neither of us did. I didn't even know about the money and I don't want it anyway."

"Money might not be the motive," I said. "It's an obvious place to start, but it doesn't necessarily go anywhere."

"But you don't think Daddy did it, do you?"

"I haven't made up my mind about that yet. I'm still trying to figure out what Bobby was up to and I need to fill in some gaps. Something was going on back then and I can't get a line on it. What was his relationship to Sufi? You have any idea?"

Kitty picked up her cigarette, averting her gaze. She took a moment to tap the ash from the end, and then she took a last, deep drag and put it out. Her nails were bitten down so far the pads of the fingers seemed like little round balls.

She was debating something with herself. I kept my mouth shut and gave her some room. "She was a contact," she said finally, her voice low. "Bobby was doing this investigation or something for somebody else."

"Who?"

"I don't know."

"It had to be the Frakers, right? I talked to Sufi last night, and the minute I left, she hightailed it over to their place. She was in there so long, I finally had to go home."

Kitty's eyes came up to mine. "I don't know for sure what it was."

"But how'd he get into it? What was it about?"

"All I know is he told me he was looking for something and he got the job out at the morgue so he could search at night."

"Medical records? Something stored out there?"

Her face closed down again and she shrugged.

"But Kitty, when you realized someone was trying to kill him, didn't you figure it was connected to that?"

She was chewing on her thumbnail in earnest by now. I saw her eyes flick and I turned around. Dr. Kleinert was standing in the doorway, staring at her. When he realized I'd seen him, he looked over at me. His smile seemed forced and it was not full of merriment.

"Well. I didn't know you were entertaining this morning," he said to her. Then briefly to me, "What brings you in so bright and early?"

"I just stopped by on my way to Glen's. I've been trying to persuade Kitty to eat," I said.

"No need for that," he said easily. "This young lady has an agreement with me." He gave a practiced glance at his watch, adjusting the face of it on his wrist before it disappeared up his cuff again. "I hope you'll excuse us. I have other patients to see and my time is limited."

"I'm on my way out," I said. I glanced at Kitty. "I may give you a call in a little while. I'll see if Glen can stop in to visit you."

"Great," she said. "Thanks."

I waved and moved out of the room, wondering how long he'd been standing there and how much he'd heard. I was trying to remember what Carrie St. Cloud had said. She'd told me Bobby was involved in some kind of blackmail scheme, but not the usual kind with money changing hands. Something else. "Somebody had something on some friend of his and he was trying to help out," was the way she'd put it as nearly as I could remember. If it was extortion, why didn't he go to the police? And why was it up to him to do anything?

I got back in my car and headed out to Glen's place.

21

It was just after nine when I pulled into Glen's driveway. The courtyard was deserted. The fountain sent up a column of water fifteen feet high, cascading back on itself in a tumble of pale green and white. I could hear a power mower whining from one of the terraces in the rear and rainbirds were jetting a fine spray into the giant fern, dappled with sunlight, that bordered the gravel walks. The air seemed tropical, scented with jasmine.

I rang the bell and one of the maids admitted me. I asked for Glen and she murmured something in Spanish, raising her eyes to the second floor. I gathered that Glen was upstairs.

The door to Bobby's room was open and she was seated in one of his easy chairs, hands in her lap, her face impassive. When she caught sight of me, she smiled almost imperceptibly. She was looking drawn, dark lines etched under her eyes. Her makeup was subtle, but it only seemed to emphasize the pallor in her cheeks. She wore a knit dress in a shade of red too harsh for her. "Hello, Kinsey. Come sit down," she said.

I sat in the matching plaid chair. "How are you doing?"

"Not that well. I find myself spending much of the day up here. Just sitting. Waiting for Bobby."

Her eyes strayed to mine. "I don't mean that literally, of course. I'm far too rational a person to believe the dead return. I keep thinking there's something more, that it can't be over yet. Do you know what I mean?"

"No. Not quite."

She stared at the floor, apparently consulting her inner voices. "Part of it is a feeling of betrayal, I think. I was brave and I did everything I was supposed to. I was a trouper and now I want the payoff. But the only reward that interests me is having Bobby back. So I wait." Her gaze moved around the room as if she were taking a series of photographs. Her manner seemed very flat to me, despite the emotional content of her speech. It was curious, like talking to a robot. She said human things, but mechanically. "You see that?"

I followed her eyes. Bobby's footprints were still visible on the white carpeting.

"I won't let them vacuum in here," she said. "I know it's stupid. I don't want to turn into one of those dreadful women who erect a shrine for the dead, keeping everything just as it was. But I don't want him erased. I don't want him wiped out like that. I don't even want to go through his belongings."

"There's no need to do anything yet, is there?"

"No. I guess not. I don't know what I'll do with the room anyway. I have dozens and they're all empty. It's not like I need to convert it into a sewing room or a studio."

"Are you taking care of yourself otherwise?"

"Oh, yes. I know enough to do that. I feel like grief is an illness I can't recover from. What worries me is I notice there's a certain attraction to the process that's hard to give up. It's painful, but at least it allows me to feel close to him. Once in a while, I catch myself thinking of something else and then I feel guilty. It seems disloyal not to hurt, disloyal to forget even for a moment that he's gone."

"Don't get mean with yourself and suffer more than you have to," I said.

"I know. I'm trying to wean myself. Every day I mourn a little less. Like giving up cigarettes. In the meantime, I pretend to be a whole person, but I'm not. I wish I could think of something that would heal me. Ah, God, I shouldn't go on and on about it. It's like someone who's had a heart attack or major surgery. It's all I can talk about. So self-centered."

Again, she paused and then she seemed to remember polite behavior. She looked at me. "What have you been doing?"

"I went over to St. Terry's this morning to see Kitty."

"Oh?" Glen's expression was devoid of interest.

"Is there any chance you might stop by to see her?"

"Absolutely none. For one thing, I'm furious that she's alive while Bobby's not. I hate it that he left her all that money. As far as I'm concerned, she's grasping, self-destructive, manipulative—" She broke off, closing her mouth. She was silent for a moment. "Sorry. I don't mean to be so vehement. I never liked her. Just because she's in trouble now doesn't change anything. She's done it to herself. She thought there'd always be someone who'd bail her out, but it won't be me. And Derek's not capable of it."

"I heard he left."

She stirred restlessly. "We had a terrible fight. I didn't think I'd ever get him out of here. I finally had to call one of the gardeners. I despise him. Truly. It makes me sick to think he was ever in my bed. I don't know which is worse . . . the fact that he took out that ghoulish policy on Bobby's life or the fact that he hadn't the faintest sense how despicable it was."

"Can he collect?"

"He seems to think so, but I intend to fight him every step of the way. I've put the insurance company on notice and I've contacted a firm of lawyers in L.A. I want him out of my life. I don't really care what it costs, though the less of mine he gets the better. Fortunately, we signed premarital agreements, though he swears he'll challenge me on that if I thwart his insurance claim."

"Jesus, you're really drawing up battle lines."

She rubbed her forehead wearily. "God, it was horrible. I called Varden to see if I can get a restraining order out on him. It's lucky there wasn't a gun in the house or one of us would be dead."

I was silent.

After a moment, she seemed to collect herself. "I don't mean to sound so crazy. Everything I say comes out so manic somehow. Anyway. Enough of that. I'm sure you didn't come here to listen to me rave. Would you like some coffee?"

"No thanks. I just wanted to touch base with you and bring you up to date. Most of this has to do with Bobby, so if you don't want to talk about it now, I can stop back another time."

"No, no. That's fine. Maybe it will give me something new to think about. I do want you to find out who killed him. It may be the only form of relief I can look forward to. What have you come up with so far?"

"Not a lot. I'm putting it together piece by piece and I'm not really sure of my facts. For one thing, I may have people lying to me, but since I don't really know the truth, I can't be sure," I said.

"I understand."

I hestitated, oddly reluctant to pass on my conjecture. It felt intrusive to speculate about his past, in poor taste somehow to discuss the intimate details of his life with the woman who was trying so hard to cope with his death. "I think Bobby was having an affair."

"That's not surprising. I think I mentioned that he was dating someone."

"Not her. Nola."

She stared at me as though waiting for the punch line. Finally, she said, "You can't be serious."

"From what I've heard, Bobby was having an affair with someone and he fell in love. That's why he broke up with Carrie St. Cloud in the first place. I have reason to believe it was Nola Fraker, though I haven't confirmed it yet."

"I don't like that. I hope that's not true."

"I don't know what to tell you. It seems to fit the facts."

"I thought you said he was in love with Kitty."

"Maybe not 'in love.' I think he loved her a lot. That doesn't mean he acted on it. She claims there was nothing going on between them and I tend to believe her. If they'd had a sexual relationship, I'm sure you'd have been the first to know—for the shock value if nothing else. You know how she is. She's obviously immature and confused and he was certainly aware of your attitude toward her. Anyway, whatever he felt for her wouldn't have precluded an involvement with someone else."

"But Nola's happily married. She and Jim have been here dozens of times. There was never even a hint of anything between her and Bobby."

"I hear what you're saying, Glen, but that's the way the game is played. You're having a clandestine affair. You and your lover end up at the same social event and walk around

chatting politely, ignoring each other . . . but not too pointedly because that would be conspicuous. Sly little hand
touches by the punch bowl, secret glances across the room.
It's a big hot joke and later you giggle about it in bed like a
couple of kids because you put one over on the grown-ups."

"But why Nola? The whole idea is ludicrous."

"Not at all. She's a beautiful woman. Maybe they ran into
each other and suddenly the spark was there. Or maybe
they'd been eyeing each other for years. Actually, it must
have started last summer because I don't think his relationship to her could have overlapped his to Carrie by
much. He didn't strike me as the type who'd have two af-
fairs running at the same time."

Glenn's expression changed and she glanced at me with
apparent discomfort.

"What?"

"I just remembered. Derek and I were in Europe for two
months last summer. When we got back, I noticed we were
suddenly seeing more of the Frakers, but I shrugged it off.
You know how it is. Sometimes you see a lot of another
couple and then they drop out of your life for a while. I just
can't believe she'd do that to me or to Jim. It makes me feel
like a jealous spouse. Like I've been duped."

"But Glen, come on. Maybe it was the best thing that
ever happened to him. Maybe it helped him grow up some.
Who knows? Bobby was a good kid. What difference could
it possibly make at this point anyway?" I said. It felt mean
but I didn't want her getting into this bullshit of denying
who he was and what he did.

Her cheeks had taken on a tint of pink and she turned a
cold eye toward me. "I get the message. I still don't understand why you're telling me this."

"Because it's not up to me to shield you from the truth."

"It's not up to you to carry tales either."

"Yes. All right. You're right about that. I'm not into gossip
for the sake of it. There's a chance that it's tied up with
Bobby's death."

"How?"

"I'll get to that, but I have to have your assurances first
that this won't go any further."

"What's the connection?"

"Glen, you're not listening. I'll tell you as much as I can, but I can't tell you everything and I don't want you flying off the handle. If you turn around and repeat this to anyone, you could be putting both of us in jeopardy."

Her eyes came into focus and I felt she was finally taking in what I was saying. "I'm sorry. Of course. I won't say a word to anyone."

I told her briefly about Bobby's last message on my answering machine, and about the blackmail scheme, which I still didn't understand. I deleted mention of Sufi's part in all of this because I was still worried Glen would take matters into her own hands and do something dumb. She seemed volatile right now, unstable, like a vial of nitroglycerin. One minor bump and she might blow.

"I do need your help," I said when I finished.

"Doing what?"

"I want to talk to Nola. So far I still don't have confirmation on this and if I call or stop by out of a clear blue sky, it's going to scare the shit out of her. I'd like you to call her and see if you can set something up."

"For when?"

"This morning if possible."

"What would you want me to say to her?"

"Tell her the truth. Tell her I'm looking into Bobby's death, that we think he may have been involved with some woman last summer, and since you were gone, you thought maybe she might have seen him around with someone. Ask her if she'd mind talking to me."

"Won't she suspect? Surely, she'll figure out that you're onto her."

"Well, for starters, I could be wrong. Maybe it's not her. That's what I'm trying to determine. If she's innocent, she won't care one way or the other. And if she's not, let her cook up a cover so she'll feel secure. I don't care. The point is, she won't have the balls to shut the door in my face, which is what she'd probably do if I went over there unannounced."

She considered briefly. "All right."

She got up and crossed to the telephone on the night stand, punching in Nola's number from memory. She handled the request as deftly as anything I'd ever heard, and I could see how good she must be at fund raising. Nola couldn't have been nicer or more cooperative and in fifteen minutes I was on my way back to Horton Ravine.

By day, I could see that the Frakers' house was pale yellow with a shake roof. I went up the driveway and pulled onto the parking pad to the left of the house, where a dark maroon BMW and a silver Mercedes were parked. As I was not feeling suicidal, I leaned out of my car window, looking for the dog. Rover or Fido, whatever his name was, turned out to be a great dane with rubbery black-rimmed lips, complete with strings of slobber hanging down. From that distance, I swear it looked like his collar was studded with spikes. His food dish was a wide aluminum bowl with bite marks around the rim.

I got out of the car cautiously. He ran up to the fence and started barking bad breath in my direction. He stood up on his hind legs, his front paws tucked over the gate. His dick looked like a hot dog in a long, furry bun and he wagged it at me like a guy who's just stepped out of a phone booth to open his raincoat.

I was just on the verge of insulting him when I realized that Nola had come out on the porch behind me.

"Don't mind him," she said. She was wearing another jump suit, this one black, with spike heels that made her half a head taller than me.

"Nice pup," I remarked. People always love it when you say their dogs are nice. Just shows you how out of touch they are.

"Thanks. Come on in. I have something to do first, but you can wait in the den."

22

The interior of the Fraker house was cool and spare; gleaming dark wood floors, white walls, bare windows, fresh flowers. The furniture was upholstered in white linen and the den into which Nola ushered me was lined with books. She excused herself and I heard her high heels tap-tap-tapping away down the hall.

It's never a good idea to leave me in a room by myself. I'm an incurable snoop and I search automatically. Having been raised from the age of five by an unmarried aunt, I spent a lot of time as a child in the homes of her friends, most of whom had no children of their own. I was told to keep quiet and amuse myself, which I managed in the first five minutes with the latest in an endless series of coloring books we brought with us when visiting. The problem was that I was terrible at keeping in the lines and the pictures always seemed dumb to me—little children frolicking with dogs and visiting farms. I didn't like to color chickens or hogs, so I learned to search. In this manner, I discovered people's hidden lives—the prescriptions in the medicine cabinets, tubes of jelly in bed-table drawers, cash reserves in the back of coat closets, startling sex manuals and marital artifacts between the mattress and box springs. Of course, I could never quiz my aunt afterward about the extraordinary-looking objects I came across because I wasn't supposed to know about them in the first place. Fascinated, I would wander into the kitchen, where the adults in those days seemed to congregate, drinking highballs and talking about achingly dull things like politics and sports, and I would stare at women named Bernice and Mildred whose husbands were named Stanley and Edgar, and I would wonder who did what with the long doodad with the battery

stuck in one end. It was not a flashlight. That much I knew.
Early on, I discerned the sometimes remarkable distinction
between public appearances and private tastes. These were
the people my aunt forbade me to swear in front of no matter how we talked at home. Some of the phrases she used, I
thought might have application here, but I could never con-
firm this. The whole process of education for me was learning the proper words to attach to things I already knew.

The Frakers' den exhibited a shocking lack of hiding
places. No drawers, no cabinets, no end tables with cup-
boards underneath. The two chairs were chrome with
leather straps. The coffee table was glass with narrow
chrome legs, sporting a decanter of brandy and two snifters
on a tray. There wasn't even a carpet to peek under. Jesus,
what kind of people were they? I was reduced to touring the
bookshelves, trying to divine their hobbies and avocations
from the volumes on hand.

People do tend to hang on to hardbacked books, and I
could see that Nola had gone through interior design,
gourmet cooking, gardening, needlework, and personal
beauty hints. What caught my attention, however, were the
two shelves lined with books on architecture. What was that
about? Surely, neither she nor Dr. Fraker was commis-
sioned to design buildings in their spare time. I took out an
oversized volume called *Architectural Graphic Standards*
and checked the flyleaf. The engraved bookplate showed a
lithograph of a seated cat staring at a fish in a bowl. Under
the Ex Libris, the name Dwight Costigan was scratched in a
masculine hand. A reminder bell tinkled at the back of my
brain. I thought he was the architect who designed Glen's
house. A borrowed book? I checked three more in rapid
succession. All of them were "from the library of" Dwight
Costigan. That was odd. Why here?

I heard Nola tapping back in my direction and I slipped
the book into place, then eased over to the window and
acted as though I'd occupied my time by looking out. She
came into the den with a smile that went on and off again
like a loose connection. "Sorry you had to wait. Have a
seat."

I hadn't really given a lot of thought to how I was going to
handle this. Every time I rehearse these little playlets in

advance, I'm brilliant and the other characters say exactly what I want to hear. In reality, nobody gets it right, including me, so why worry about it before the fact?

I sat down in one of the chrome-and-leather chairs, hoping I wouldn't get lodged in the straps. She sat down on the edge of a white linen love seat, resting one hand gracefully on the surface of the glass coffee table in an attitude that suggested serenity, except that she was leaving little pads of perspiration at her fingertips. I took in the sight of her at a quick glance. Slim, long-legged, with those perfect apple-sized breasts. Her hair was a paid-for shade of red, framing her face in a tumble of soft waves. Blue eyes, flawless skin. She had that clear ageless look that comes with first-rate cosmetic surgery, and the black jumpsuit she wore emphasized her lush body without being vulgar or crass. Her manner was solemn and sincere, and struck me as false.

"What can I help you with?" she asked.

I had a split second in which to make a judgment. Could Bobby Callahan *truly* have gotten involved with a woman as phony as this? Oh hell, who was I trying to kid? Of course!

I gave her a fifteen-watt smile, resting my chin on my fist. "Well, I have a little problem, Nola. May I call you Nola?"

"Certainly. Glen mentioned you were investigating Bobby's death."

"That's true. Actually Bobby just hired me a week ago and I feel like I ought to give him his money's worth."

"Oh. I thought maybe there was something wrong and that was why you were looking into it."

"There might be. I don't know yet."

"But shouldn't the police be doing that?"

"I'm sure they are. I'm conducting a . . . you know, an auxiliary investigation, just in case they're on the wrong track."

"Well, I hope somebody figures it out. Poor kid. We all feel so bad for Glen. Are you having any luck?"

"As a matter of fact, I am. Somebody told me half the story and all I have to do is figure out the rest."

"It sounds like you're doing pretty well, then." She hesitated delicately. "What kind of story?"

I suspect she didn't really want to ask, but the nature of the conversation dictated that she must. She was pretending to cooperate so, of course, she had to feign interest in a subject she'd probably prefer to ignore.

I let a moment pass while I stared down at the tabletop. I thought it lent a note of credibility to the lie I was about to tell. I looked back at her, making significant eye contact. "Bobby told me he was in love with you."

"With me?"

"That's what he said."

The eyes blinked. The smile went off and on. "Well, I'm astonished. I mean, it's very flattering and I always thought he was a sweet kid, but really!"

"I didn't find it that astonishing."

Her laugh conveyed a wonderful combination of innocence and disbelief. "Oh, for heaven's sake. I'm married. And I'm twelve years older than he is."

Shit, she was quick—shaving years off her age without pausing to count on her fingers or anything. I'm not that fast at subtraction so it's probably fortunate that I don't lie about how old I am.

I smiled slightly. She was pissing me off and I found myself using a mild, deadly tone. "Age doesn't matter. Bobby's dead now. He's older than God. He's as old as anybody's ever going to get."

She stared at me, cuing in to the fact that I was mad. "You don't have to get nasty about it. I can't help it if Bobby Callahan decided he was in love with me. So the kid had a crush on me. So what?"

"So the kid had an *affair* with you, Nola. That's what. You got your tit in a wringer and the kid was helping you out. The *kid* was murdered because of you, ass eyes. Now, shall we quit bullshitting each other and get down to business on this or shall I call Lieutenant Dolan down at Homicide and let him have a chat with you?"

"I don't know what you're talking about," she snapped. She got up, but I was already on my feet and I clamped a hand around that dainty wrist so fast she gasped. She gave a little jerk and I released her, but I could feel myself expand with anger like a hot-air balloon.

"I'm telling you, Nola. You've got a choice. You tell me what was going on or I'm going to start leaning on you. In fact, I may do that anyway. I'll whip on down to the

courthouse and I'll start going through public records and
newspaper accounts and police files until I get a little background information on you and then I'm going to figure out
what you're hiding and *then* I'm going to find a way to stick
it to you so bad you'll wish you'd blabbed the whole story
out right here."

That's when I got the jolt. In the back of my brain, I
heard a sound like a parachute catching air. Thwunk . . . it
opened up. It was one of those extraordinary moments
when automatic recall clicks in and a piece of information
pops up like a flash card. It must have been the adrenaline
pumping through my head because I suddenly retrieved
some data from my memory bank and it appeared on my
mental screen just as clear as could be . . . not the whole of
it, but enough. "Wait a minute. I know who you are. You
were married to Dwight Costigan. I knew I'd seen you
somewhere. Your picture was in all the papers."

Her face drained of color. "That has nothing to do with
this," she said.

I laughed, primarily because sudden recollection does
that to me. A mental leap has a little chemical component to
it that gives a quick rush.

"Oh come on," I said. "It does connect. I don't know how
yet, but it's all the same tale, isn't it?"

She sank back down on the love seat, one hand reaching
for the glass tabletop to steady herself. She breathed
deeply, trying to relax. "You would do well to let this pass,"
she said, not looking at me.

"Are you nuts?" I said. "Are you out of your tiny mind?
Bobby Callahan hired me because he thought somebody
was trying to kill him and he was right. He's dead now and
he's got no way to rectify the situation, but *I* do and if you
think I'll back off this sucker, you don't know me."

She was shaking her head. All the beauty was gone and
what remained seemed drab. She looked, then, like we all
look in fluorescent lighting—tired, sallow, shopworn. Her
voice was low. "I'll tell you what I can. And then I beg you
to drop the investigation. I mean that. For your own good. I
did have an affair with Bobby." She paused, searching for
the path she wanted to take. "He was a wonderful person.
He really was. I was crazy about him. He was so uncompli-

cated and he had no history. He was just young and healthy, vigorous. God. He was twenty-three. Even the sight of his *skin*. He was like a—" Her eyes came up to mine and she broke off with embarrassment, a smile forming and faltering, this time from some emotion I couldn't read . . . pain or tenderness, perhaps.

I eased into the chair carefully, hoping I wouldn't spoil the mood.

"When you're that age," she said, "you still think things can be made right. You still think you can have anything you want. You think life's simple, that you only have to do one or two little things and it will all turn around. I told him it wasn't like that for me, but he had a streak of gallantry in him. Sweet fool."

She was silent for a long time.

"'Sweet fool,' what?" I said quietly.

"Well, he died for it, of course. I can't tell you the guilt I've felt. . . ." She trailed off and she looked away.

"Tell me the front end. How does Dwight fit in? He was shot, right?"

"Dwight was much older than I. Forty-five when we were married. I was twenty-two. It was a good marriage . . . up to a point at any rate. He adored me. I admired him. He did incredible things for this town."

"He designed Glen's house, didn't he?"

"Not really. His father was the original architect when the house was built back in the twenties. Dwight did the restoration," she said. "I think I need a drink. Do you want one?"

"Sure, that's fine," I said.

She reached for the brandy decanter, removing the heavy glass stopper. She laid the neck of the decanter against the edge of one of the snifters, but her hands were shaking so badly I thought she'd crack the glass. I reached over and took the bottle from her, pouring her a stiff shot. I poured myself one too, though at ten in the morning, it was the last thing I wanted. She gave hers a perfunctory swirl and we both drank. I swallowed and my mouth came open automatically as if I'd just risen to the surface of a swimming pool. This was clearly fine stuff, but I didn't think I'd need my teeth cleaned for a *year*. I watched her calm herself, taking a deep breath or two.

I was trying desperately to recall the accounts I'd read of the incident in which Costigan was killed. It must have been five or six years ago. As nearly as I could remember, someone had broken into their Montebello house one night and had shot Dwight to death after a struggle in the bedroom. I'd been off in Houston for a client so I hadn't followed the events very closely, but as far as I knew, it was still sitting on the books as an unsolved homicide.

"What happened?" I asked.

"Don't ask and don't interfere. I pleaded with Bobby to let it go, but he wouldn't listen and it cost him his life. The past is the past. It's over and done with and I'm the only one paying for it now. Forget it. I don't care, and if you're smart, you won't either."

"You know I can't do that. Tell me what went on."

"What for? It won't change anything."

"Nola, I'm going to find out whether you tell me or not. If you lay it out for me maybe it won't have to go any further than this. Maybe I'll understand and agree to drop the whole thing. I'm not unreasonable, but you've gotta play fair."

I could see the indecision written in her face. She said, "Oh God," and put her head down for a moment. She looked at me with anxiety. "We're talking about a lunatic. Someone so crazy. You'd have to swear . . . you'd have to promise to back off."

"I can't make a promise like that and you know it. Tell me the story and then we'll figure out what has to be done."

"I've never told anyone except Bobby and look what happened to him."

"What about Sufi? She knows, doesn't she?"

She blinked at me, momentarily startled at the mention of Sufi's name. She looked away from me. "No, not at all. I'm sure she doesn't know what's going on. Why would she?" The answer seemed too hesitant to be convincing, but I let it pass for the time being. Could Sufi be blackmailing her?

"Well, *somebody* else knows," I said. "From what I gather, you're being blackmailed and that's what Bobby was trying to stop. What's the deal? What does this person have on you? What kind of leverage?"

I let the silence stretch, watching as she struggled with her need to unload.

Finally, she started talking, her voice so low I was forced to lean forward so I could hear her. "We'd been married nearly fifteen years. Dwight was on medication for high blood pressure and it made him impotent. We'd never had a highly charged sex life anyway. I got restless and found . . . someone else."

"A lover."

She nodded, eyes closed as if the recollection hurt her. "Dwight walked in on us one night in bed. He was crazed. He got a gun from the study and came back and there was a struggle."

I caught the sound of footsteps coming down the hall. I glanced toward the door and she did too, her voice becoming urgent.

"Don't breathe a word of this. Please."

"Trust me, I won't. What's the rest?"

She hesitated. "I shot Dwight. It was an accident, but somebody has the gun with my fingerprints on it."

"And that's what Bobby was searching for?"

She nodded almost imperceptibly.

"But who has it? Your ex-lover?"

Nola raised a finger to her lips. There was a tap at the door and Dr. Fraker stuck his head in, apparently surprised to see me sitting there. "Oh, hi, Kinsey. Is that your car in the drive? I was just about to take off, and I couldn't figure out who was here."

"I stopped by to talk to Nola about Glen," I said. "I don't think she's doing too well and I was wondering if we shouldn't work out some arrangement to take turns spending time with her now that Derek's gone."

He shook his head regretfully. "Dr. Kleinert told me she'd kicked him out. Damn shame. Not that I have any use for him myself, but she's got her share of trouble right now. I hate to see her saddled with something else."

"Me, too," I said. "Do you need me to move my car?"

"No, that's fine," he said, looking over at Nola. "I've got some work to do at the hospital, but I shouldn't be back too late. Do we have dinner plans?"

She smiled pleasantly, though she had to clear her throat before she could speak. "I thought we'd eat here if that's all right with you."

"Sure, it's fine. Well. I'll let you two hatch your little schemes. Nice to see you, Kinsey."

"Actually we're finished," Nola said, getting up.

"Oh, well good," he said, "I'll walk you out."

I knew she was just using his appearance as a way to terminate the conversation, but I couldn't think of any delaying tactics, especially with the two of them standing there looking at me.

We exchanged brief good-byes and then Dr. Fraker held the door for me and I left the den. As I glanced back, I could see that Nola's expression was tinged with anxiety, and I suspected she was wishing she'd kept her secret to herself. She had a lot at stake: freedom, money, status, respectability. She was vulnerable to anyone who knew what I now knew. I wondered how desperate she was to hang on to what she had and what kind of payment had been extracted from her as a result.

23

I went into the office. There was a pile of mail on the floor under the door slot. I gathered that up and tossed it on my desk, opening the French doors to let in some fresh air. The message light on my answering machine was blinking. I sat down and pressed the playback button.

The message was from my friend at the telephone company with a report on the disconnect for S. Blackman, whose full name was Sebastian S., male, age sixty-six, with a forwarding address in Tempe, Arizona. Well, that didn't sound very promising. If all else failed, I could double back and check that out to see if there was any tie to Bobby. Somehow I doubted it. I made a note in his file. There was a certain security in having it all committed to paper. At least that way, if anything happened to me, someone could come along afterward and pick up the thread—a grim notion, but not unrealistic given Bobby's fate.

I spent the next hour and a half going through my mail, catching up on my bookkeeping. A couple of checks had come in and I entered those in accounts receivable, making out a deposit slip. One statement had been shipped back to me unopened, marked "Addressee Unknown. Return to Sender" with a big purple finger pointing right at me. God, a deadbeat. I hated getting stung for services rendered. I'd done some good work for that guy, too. I'd known he was a slow pay, but I didn't think he'd actually stiff me for my fee. I set it aside. I'd have to track him down when I had some time.

It was almost noon by then and I glanced at the phone. I knew there was a call I should make and I picked up the receiver, punching in the number before I lost my nerve.

"Santa Teresa Police Department. Deputy Collins."

"I'd like to speak to Sergeant Robb in Missing Persons."

"Just a moment. I'll connect you."

My heart was thudding in a way that made my armpits damp.

I'd run into Jonah while I was investigating the disappearance of a woman named Elaine Boldt. He was a nice guy with a bland face, maybe twenty pounds overweight, amusing, direct, a bit of a rebel, pirating copies of some homicide reports for me against all the rules. He'd been married for years to his junior-high-school sweetheart, who'd abandoned him a year ago, departing with his two daughters, and leaving him with a freezer full of crappy dinners that she'd done up herself. He hadn't been flashy but I don't look for that anyway and I'd liked him a lot. We'd never been lovers, but he'd exhibited a bit of healthy male interest and I'd taken a dim view of it when he went back to his wife. Face it, I was miffed, and I'd kept my distance from him ever since.

"Robb here."

"Jesus," I said, "I haven't even talked to you yet and I'm already pissed."

I could hear him hesitate. "Kinsey, is that you?"

I laughed. "Yes, it's me and I just figured out how frosted I am."

He knew exactly what I was talking about. "God. I know, babe. What a load of pig swill that was. I've thought about you so often."

I was saying "uh-hun, uh-hun" in what I hoped was my most skeptical tone. "How's Camilla?"

He sighed and I could almost see him run a hand through his hair. "About the same. She treats me like dirt. I don't know why I let her back in my life."

"Must be nice to have the girls home though, isn't it?"

"Well, yeah, that's true," he said. "And we're seeing a counselor. Not them. Me and her."

"Maybe that will help."

"Maybe it won't." He caught himself and changed his tone. "Ah. Well. I shouldn't complain. I guess I did it to myself. I'm just sorry it ended up affecting you."

"Don't worry about it. I'm a big girl. Besides, I've got a way for you to redeem yourself. I thought maybe I could buy you lunch today and pick your brain."

"Sure. I'd love it, only lunch is on me. It'll help assuage my guilt. How you like that 'assuage' stuff? That's the word of the day on my vocabulary calendar. Yesterday was 'ineluctable.' I never did figure out how to sneak that one in. Where do you want to go? You name the place."

"Oh, let's keep it simple. I don't want to spend a lot of time on social niceties."

"How about the courthouse? I'll pick up some sandwiches and we can eat on the lawn."

"God, right out in public. Won't the department talk?"

"I hope so. Maybe Camilla will get wind of it and leave me again."

"See you at twelve-thirty."

"Is there something you want me to research in the meantime?"

"Oh right. Good point." I gave him a quick synopsis of the Costigan shooting, leaving Nola Fraker out of it. I'd decide later how much of the story I could trust him with. For now, I fed him the public version and asked if he could take a peek at the files.

"I have a vague recollection of that one. Let me see what I can dig up."

"And one more thing if you would," I said. "Could you run a check through NCIC on a woman named Lila Sams?" I gave him her two a.k.a.'s, Delia Sims and Delilah Sampson, the birthdate I'd taken off the driver's license, and the additional information I had in my notes.

"Right. Got it. I'll do what I can. See you shortly," he said and hung up.

It had occurred to me that if Lila was running some kind of scam on Henry, she might well have a prior record. There was no way I'd have access to the National Crime Information Center except through an authorized law-enforcement agency. Jonah could have the name run through the computer and get feedback in minutes and at least then I'd know if my instincts were accurate.

I tidied up my office, grabbed the bank deposit, and locked up, going next door for a few minutes to chat with Vera Lipton, one of the claims adjusters for California Fidelity Insurance. I stopped off at the bank on the way over to the courthouse, depositing most of the money to savings, with enough to my checking account to cover current expenses.

The day, which had started out on preheat, was cranked up to broil by now. The sidewalks shimmered and the palms looked bleached out by the sun. Where occasional potholes in the street had been filled, the asphalt was as soft and grainy as cookie dough.

The Santa Teresa Courthouse looks like a Moorish castle: hand-carved wooden doors, towers, and wrought-iron balconies. Inside, there's so much mosaic tile on the walls, it looks like someone's covered them with patchwork quilts. One courtroom sports a cycloramic mural that depicts the settling of Santa Teresa by the early Spanish missionaries. It's sort of the Walt Disney version of what really went on as the artist has omitted the introduction of syphilis and the corruption of the Indians. I prefer it myself, if the truth be known. It would be hard to concentrate on justice if you had to stare up at some poor bunch of Indians in the last stages of paresis.

I cut through the great archway toward the sunken gardens in the rear. There were about two dozen people scattered across the lawn, some eating lunch, some napping or taking in the sun. Idly, I catalogued the merits of a good-looking man coming toward me in a pale blue short-sleeved shirt. I was doing one of those visual surveys that starts at the bottom and moves up. Uh-hun, nice hips, dressing left . . . uh-hun, flat belly, great arms, I thought. He'd almost reached me when I checked out the face and realized it was Jonah.

I hadn't seen him since June. Apparently the diet and his weight-lifting regimen had worked like a charm. His face, which in the past I'd labeled "harmless," was now nicely honed. His dark hair was longer and he'd picked up a tan so that his blue eyes now blazed in a face the color of maple sugar.

"Oh, God," I said, stopping dead in my tracks. "You look great."

He flashed me a smile, loving it. "You think so? Thanks. I must have lost twenty pounds since I saw you last."

"How'd you do it? Hard work?"

"Yeah, I did a little work."

He stood and stared at me and I stared back. He was exuding pheromones like a musky aftershave and I could feel my body chemistry start to shift. Mentally, I shook myself. I didn't need this. The only thing worse than a man just out of a marriage is a man who's still *in* one.

"I heard you got shot," he said.

"A mere .22, which hardly counts. I got beat up too, and that's what hurt. I don't know how guys put up with that shit," I said. I rubbed at the bridge of my nose ruefully. "Broke my schnoz."

He reached out impulsively and ran a finger down my nose. "Looks O.K. to me."

"Thanks," I said. "It still blows pretty good."

We endured one of those awkward pauses that had always punctuated our relationship.

I shifted my bag from one shoulder to the other, just for something to do. "What'd you bring?" I said, indicating the paper sack he held.

He glanced down. "Oh, yeah. I forgot. Uh, subs and Pepsis and Famous Amos cookies."

"We could even eat," I said.

He didn't move. He shook his head. "Kinsey, I don't remember going through this before," he said. "Why don't we fuckin' skip lunch and go over there behind that bush?"

I laughed, because I'd just had this quick flash of something hot and nasty that I don't care to repeat. I tucked my hand through his arm. "You're cute."

"I don't want to hear about cute."

We went down the wide stone steps and headed toward the far side of the courthouse lawn, where shaggy evergreens shade the grass. We sat down, distracted by the business of eating lunch. Pepsis were opened and lettuce fell out of sandwiches and we exchanged paper napkins and murmured about how good it all was. By the time we finished eating, we'd recovered some professional composure and conducted most of our remaining conversation like adults instead of sex-starved kids.

He shoved his empty Pepsi can in the sack. "I'll tell you the scuttlebutt on that Costigan shooting. The guy I talked to used to work Homicide and he says he always thought it was the wife. It was one of those situations where the whole story stank, you know? She claimed some guy broke in, husband gets a gun, big struggle, boom! The gun goes off and hubby's dead. Intruder runs away and she calls the cops, distraught victim of a random burglary attempt. Well, it didn't look right, but she stuck to her guns. Hired some hotshot lawyer right off the bat and wouldn't say a word until he got there. You know how it goes. 'Sorry my client can't answer this.' 'Sorry I won't let her respond to that.' Nobody believed a word she said, but she never broke down and in the end there wasn't any proof. No evidence, no informant, no weapon, no witness. End of tale. I hope you're not working for her because if you are, you're screwed."

I shook my head. "I'm looking into Bobby Callahan's death," I said. "I think he was murdered and I think it connects back to Dwight Costigan." I sketched the whole story out for him, avoiding his gaze. We were stretched out in the grass by then and I kept having these images of sexual misbehavior that I didn't think would serve. I plowed right ahead, talking more than I should have just to create a diversion.

"God, you come up with something on the Costigan killing and Lieutenant Dolan's gonna crochet you a watch," he said.

"What about Lila Sams?"

He held a finger up. "I was saving the best for last," he said. "I ran a field check on her and came up with a hit. This lady has a string of wants and warrants as long as your arm. Priors going back to 1968."

"What for?"

"Fraud, obtaining property by false pretenses, larceny by trick and device. She's been passing bad paper, too. She's got six outstanding warrants on her even as we speak. Well, wait. Take a look for yourself. I brought the print-out."

He held out the computer print-out and I took it. Why didn't I feel more elated at the notion of nailing her? Because it would break Henry's heart and I didn't want to take responsibility for that. I ran an eye down the sheet. "Can I keep this?"

"Sure, but don't jump up and down like that. Calm yourself," he said. "I take it you know where she is."

I looked over at him with a weak smile. "Probably sitting in my backyard drinking iced tea," I said. "My landlord is head over heels in love with her and I suspect she's on the verge of taking him for everything he's worth."

"Talk to Whiteside in Fraud and he'll have her picked up."

"I think I better talk to Rosie first."

"That old bag who runs the dive down the street from you? What's she got to do with it?"

"Oh, neither one of us can stand Lila. Rosie wanted me to do the background check for the aggravation if nothing else. We needed to know where she was coming from."

"So now you know. What's the problem?"

"I don't know. It just feels crummy somehow, but I'll figure it out. I don't want to rush into anything I'll regret."

There was a momentary silence and then Jonah gave my shirt a tug. "You been up to the shooting range lately?"

"Not since we were there together," I said.

"You want to go up there sometime?"

"Jonah, we can't do that."

"Why not?"

"Because it might feel like a date and confuse us both."

"Come on. I thought we were friends."

"We are. We just can't hang out together."

"Why not?"

"Because you're too good-looking and I'm too smart," I said tartly.

"We're back to Camilla again, right?"

"Right. I'm not going to interfere with that. You've been with her a long time."

"I tell you something. I'm still kicking myself. I could have gone to the other junior high school, you know? Seventh grade. How did I know I was making a decision that would haunt me in middle-age?"

I laughed. "Life is full of that stuff. You had to choose between metal or woodshop, right? You could have turned out to be an auto mechanic. Instead you're a cop. You know what my choices were? Child psychology or home ec. I didn't give a shit about either one."

"I wish I hadn't seen you again."

I could feel my smile fade. "Well, I'm sorry for that. It was my fault." I could tell we'd been looking at each other too long, so I got up, brushing grass off my jeans. "I have to go."

He got up too and we said some good-bye things. We parted company shortly thereafter. I walked backward for a few steps, watching him head back to the station. Then I continued on toward my office, turning my attention back to the matter of Henry Pitts. I realized then that there wasn't any point in talking to Rosie about it. Of course I'd have to tell the cops where Lila was. She'd been a con for nearly twenty years and she wasn't going to reform and make Henry a happy man in the twilight of their days. She was going to cheat him silly, thus breaking his heart anyway. What difference did it make how she got caught or who turned her in? Better to do it now before she took every cent he had.

I'd been walking rapidly, head down, but when I got to the corner of Floresta and Anaconda, I did an abrupt left and headed for the police station.

24

I was at the police station for an hour and forty-five minutes. Fortunately, the Missing Persons Department and Fraud were nowhere near each other so I didn't have to worry about running into Jonah again. First, Whiteside was at lunch and then he had a quick meeting to attend. Then when I explained the situation to him, he had to place a call to a county in northern New Mexico where three of the warrants had been issued. While he was waiting for a response to that inquiry, he contacted the county sheriff in some little town up near San Francisco, trying to get confirmation on a no-bail warrant that originated in Marin. The charge on the fifth warrant in Boise, Idaho, turned out to be a misdemeanor and the fraud detective said he couldn't afford to come get her in any event. The sixth warrant, in Twin Falls, had been recalled for reasons unspecified. So far, Lila Sams was home free.

At 3:20, Marin County finally returned Whiteside's call, confirming the no-bail warrant and indicating that they'd have someone pick her up once they knew she was actually in custody. Their cooperation was largely due to the fact that one of their deputies was vacationing in Santa Teresa anyway and had agreed to accompany her back to Marin. Whiteside said as soon as a telexed copy of the warrant came through, he'd send the beat officer over to make the arrest. He didn't really have to have the warrant in hand, but I think he'd sensed by now that she was slippery. I gave him Moza's address, my address, and a thorough description of Lila Sams.

It was 3:40 by the time I got home. Henry was sitting on a chaise in the backyard, surrounded by books. He looked up from his legal pad as I came around the corner.

"Oh, it's you," he said. "I thought it might be Lila. She said she'd stop in and say good-bye before she took off."

That caught me by surprise. "She's leaving?"

"Well, she's not really 'leaving.' She's going to Las Cruces for a few days, but she hopes to be back by the end of the week. I guess a little problem came up on some property she owns and she has to get things squared away. It's a darn nuisance, but what can you do?"

"She's not gone already, though, is she?"

He checked his watch. "I can't imagine she would be. Her plane takes off about five. She said she had to go to the title company and then she'd toss a few things in a suitcase. Did you want to talk to her?"

I shook my head, unable to say yet what needed to be said. I could see that he was mapping out a new crossword puzzle, jotting down preliminary notes. At the top of the page, he'd written two titles, "Elementary, Dear Watson!" and "Home Sweet Holmes."

He smiled shyly when he saw me take note. "This one's for the Sherlockeans in the crowd," he said. He set the legal pad aside, as though self-conscious at having someone watch him work. "Well, now, how are things with you?"

He seemed so innocent, nothing more on his mind than his passion for words. How could she deceive a man like that?

"Something's come up I think you ought to know about," I said. I unfolded the computer print-out and handed it to him.

He looked down at it. "What's this?"

Lila's name apparently caught his eye then, because his gaze settled on the page. His face lost animation as he assimilated the facts. When he finished reading, he gestured aimlessly. He was silent for a moment and then he glanced up at me. "Well. Makes me look like a fool, doesn't it?"

"Come on, Henry. Don't talk like that. I don't think so at all. You took a risk and she brought you some happiness. Hey, so later it turns out she's a crook. That's not your fault."

He stared at the paper like a kid just learning to sound out words. "What made you check into it?"

I thought there might be a tactful explanation, but nothing occurred to me. "I didn't like her much, to tell you the truth. I guess I felt protective, especially when you talked about doing business with her. I just didn't think she was on the level and it turns out she's not. You haven't given her any money, have you?"

He folded the print-out. "I closed out one of my accounts this morning."

"How much?"

"Twenty thousand in cash," he said. "Lila said she'd deposit it to an escrow account at the title company. The bank manager urged me to reconsider, but I thought he was simply being conservative. I see now, he was not." His manner had become very formal and it nearly broke my heart.

"I'm going down to Moza's to see if I can intercept her before she takes off. You want to come?"

He shook his head, his eyes bright. I turned on my heel and moved off at a quick clip.

I trotted the half-block to Moza's. A taxicab was cruising at half speed, the driver scanning house numbers. The two of us reached Moza's at just about the same time. He pulled over to the curb. I crossed to the passenger side, peering into the open window. He had a face like a beachball made of flesh.

"You the one wanted a cab?"

"Uh, sure. Lila Sams?"

He checked his trip sheet. "Right. You got any bags you need help with?"

"Actually, I don't need the cab. A neighbor said she'd run me out to the airport. I called back, but I guess the dispatcher didn't head you off in time. Sorry."

He gave me a look, then heaved an exasperated sigh, making a big display of crossing the address off his sheet. He shifted gears with annoyance, pulling away from the curb with a shake of his head. God, he could go on stage with an act like that.

I crossed Moza's yard at an angle and took the porch steps two at a time. She was holding the screen door open, looking out anxiously at the departing taxi. "What did you say to him? That was Lila's cab. She has to get to the airport."

"Really? He told me he had the wrong address. He was looking for Zollinger, one street over, I think."

"I better try another company. She ordered a cab thirty minutes ago. She's going to miss her plane."

"Maybe I can help," I said. "Is she in here?"

"You're not going to cause any trouble, Kinsey. I won't have that."

"I'm not causing trouble," I said. I moved through the living room and into the hall. The door to Lila's room was open.

The place had been stripped of personal possessions. One of the drawers where she'd concealed a phony I.D. was sitting on top of the chest of drawers, its back panel bare. She'd left the masking tape in a wad like a hunk of chewing gum. One suitcase was packed and sat near the door. Another was open on the bed, half filled, and beside it was a white plastic purse.

Lila had her back to me, bending over to remove a stack of folded clothes from one of the dressing-table drawers. The polyester pantsuit she wore was not very flattering. From the rear, her ass looked like two hanging foam-rubber hams. She caught sight of me as she turned. "Oh! You scared me. I thought it was Moza. What can I do for you?"

"I heard you were leaving. I thought maybe I could help."

Uncertainty flickered in her eyes. Her abrupt departure was probably at the urging of her cohorts in Las Cruces, alerted by my phone call of the night before. She might have suspected it was me, but she couldn't be sure. For my part, I was just hoping to stall until the cops showed up. I had no intention of confronting her. For all I knew, she might whip out a little two-shot Derringer or fly at me with some kind of old-lady karate-type move that would take me right out.

She checked her watch. It was now almost 4:00. It took twenty minutes to get to the airport and she'd have to be there by 4:30 or risk losing her seat. That gave her ten minutes. "Oh dear. Well, I don't know why my taxi isn't here. I might need a ride to the airport, if you could do that," she said.

"No problem," I said. "My car's right down the street. Henry said you'd be stopping by his place anyway to say good-bye."

"Of course I am, if I have time. He's such a sweetie." She finished laying in the armload of clothes and I could see her look around the room to see if she'd missed anything.

"Did you leave anything in the bathroom? Shampoo? Hand laundry?"

"Oh, I believe I did. I'll be right back." She moved past me, heading for the bathroom.

I waited until she rounded the corner and then reached over and opened her purse. Inside was a fat manila envelope with Henry's name penciled on the front. I took off the rubber band and checked the contents. Cash. I closed her purse again and tucked the envelope into the waistband of my jeans at the small of my back. I figured Henry was never going to press charges and I hated to see his savings confiscated and itemized as police property. No telling when he'd get it back. I was just adjusting my T-shirt over the bulge when she returned, toting shampoo, shower cap, hand lotion. She tucked them in around the sides of her folded clothes and closed up the suitcase, snapping the locks shut.

"Here, I'll get it," I said. I hauled that suitcase off the bed and picked up the other one, moving out into the hall like a pack mule. Moza was standing there, wringing out an imaginary dish towel in her anxiety.

"I can take one of those," she said.

"I got it."

I headed for the door, with Moza and Lila bringing up the rear. I certainly hoped the cops would show. Lila and Moza were saying those last-minute things to one another, Lila faking it out the whole time. She was taking off. She was gone. She had no intention of coming back.

As we reached the front, Moza moved ahead so she could hold the screen door open for me. A black-and-white patrol car had just pulled up in front. I was afraid if Lila spotted them too soon, she'd bolt for the rear.

"Did you get that pair of shoes under the bed?" I asked over my shoulder. I paused in the doorway, blocking her view.

"I don't know. I just looked and I didn't see any."

"You probably got them, then," I said.

"No, no. I better check." She hurried toward the bedroom while I set the two suitcases on the porch.

Moza, meanwhile, was staring at the street with puzzlement. Two uniformed officers were coming up the walk, one male, one female, both bareheaded, in short-sleeved shirts. In Santa Teresa, there's been a move afoot to divest the police of their authoritarian images, but these two managed to seem ominous anyway. Moza probably thought she'd violated some civil code—grass too long, TV too loud.

I left her to have a little conversation with them while I herded Lila up this way, so she wouldn't spot the cops and try slipping out the back. "Lila, your ride's here," I called.

"Well thank heaven for that," she said, as she came through the living room. "I didn't find anything under the bed, but I'd left my ticket right up on the chest, so it's lucky I went back."

As she reached the front door, I eased behind her. She glanced up, catching sight of the officers.

The guy, according to his name tag, was G. Pettigrew. He was black, maybe in his thirties, with big arms and a barrel chest. His partner, M. Gutierrez, looked almost as hefty as he.

Pettigrew's eyes settled on Lila. "Are you Lila Sams?"

"Yes." She loaded that one syllable with puzzlement, blinking at him. Her body seemed to change so that she looked older and more squat.

"Could you step out onto the porch, please?"

"Of course, but I can't think what this is about." Lila made a move toward her purse, but Gutierrez intercepted, checking the contents quickly for weapons.

Pettigrew told Lila she was under arrest, reciting her rights to her from a card he held. I could tell he'd done it all a hundred times and didn't really need the cue, but he read it anyway so there wouldn't be any question later.

"Could you turn around and face the wall, please?"

Lila did as she was told and Gutierrez did a pat-down, then snapped on a pair of handcuffs. Lila was starting to wail pitifully. "But what have I done? I haven't done anything. This is all a terrible mistake." Her desperation seemed to set Moza off.

"What's going on, officer?" Moza said. "This woman is my tenant. She hasn't done anything wrong."

"Ma'am, we'd appreciate it if you'd step back, please. Mrs. Sams is entitled to contact an attorney when we get downtown." Pettigrew touched at Lila's elbow, but she pulled away, her voice rising to a shrill pitch.

"Help! Oh no! Let go of me. Help!"

The two officers took control of her, one on either side, moving her off the porch at a businesslike pace, but Lila's shrieks were beginning to bring curious neighbors out onto their porches. She went limp, sagging heavily between them, craning her face toward Moza with a piteous cry. They hustled her into the squad car, picking her feet up to deposit her in the rear. Lila somehow conveyed the impression that this was a Gestapo arrest, that she was being hauled off by the Nazis and might never be heard from again. Shaking his head, Officer Pettigrew gathered up her belongings, which were now strewn along the walk. He tucked her suitcases in the trunk.

The man next door apparently felt called upon to intercede and I saw him in conversation with Pettigrew while Gutierrez called in to the station and Lila thrashed about, flinging herself at the mesh that separated her from Gutierrez in the front seat. Finally Pettigrew got in the car on the driver's side, slamming the door shut, and they pulled away.

Moza was dead white and she turned a stricken face to me. "This was your doing! What in heaven's name were you thinking of? The poor woman."

But I'd caught sight of Henry half a block away. Even at that distance, his face seemed blank with disbelief, his body tense. "I'll talk to you later, Moza," I said and headed toward him.

25

By the time I reached my place, Henry was nowhere in sight. I pulled the envelope out of my waistband and knocked on his back door. He opened it. I held the envelope up and he took it, glancing at the contents. He gave me a searching look, but I didn't explain how I'd come by it and he didn't ask.

"Thank you."

"We'll talk later," I said, and he closed the door again, but not before I caught a glimpse of his kitchen counter. He had gotten out the sugar canister and a new blue-and-white sack of flour, turning to the activity he knew best while he worked through his pain. I felt awful for him but I had to let him sort it out for himself. God, it was all so unpleasant. In the meantime, I had to get back to work.

I let myself into my apartment and got out the telephone book, looking for Kelly Borden. If Bobby'd been searching for the gun out at the old county building, I wanted to have a crack at it too and I thought maybe Kelly could tell me where to start. No sign of him in the telephone book. I tried to find the number for the former medical facility, but there wasn't a listing for it and the information operator was being obtuse, pretending she had no idea what I was talking about. If he worked a seven-to-three shift, he'd be gone anyway. Shit. I looked up the number of Santa Teresa Hospital and put a call in to Dr. Fraker. His secretary, Marcy, told me he was "away from his desk" (meaning in the men's room), but would be back shortly. I told her I needed to talk to Kelly Borden and asked for his address and telephone number.

"Gee, I don't know," she said. "Dr. Fraker probably wouldn't mind my giving you the information, but I'm not really supposed to do it without his O.K."

"Look, I've got some errands to run anyway so why don't I stop by. It'll take me ten minutes," I said. "Just make sure he doesn't leave work before I get there."

I drove over to St. Terry's. Parking turned out to be a trick and I had to leave my car three blocks away, which was okay with me because I had to stop at a drugstore. I went in through the back entrance, following varicolored lines on the floor, as though on my way to Oz. Finally, I reached a set of elevators and took one down to the basement.

By the time I reached Pathology, Dr. Fraker was off again, but Marcy had told him I was coming and he'd instructed her to forward me, like a piece of mail. I trailed after her through the lab and finally came across him in surgical greens, standing at a stainless-steel counter with a sink, disposal, and hanging scales. He was apparently about to launch into some procedure and I was sorry I had to interrupt.

"I really didn't mean to disturb you," I said. "All I need is Kelly Borden's address and telephone number."

"Pull up a chair," he said, indicating a wooden stool at one end of the counter. And then to Marcy, "Why don't you look up the information for Kinsey and I'll keep her amused in the meantime."

As soon as she departed, I pulled the stool over and perched.

For the first time, I cued in to what Fraker was actually doing. He was wearing surgical gloves, scalpel in hand. There was a white plastic carton on the counter, a one-pint size, like the kind used for chicken livers in the meat section of the supermarket. As I watched, he dumped out a glistening blob of organs, which he began to sort through with a pair of long tweezers. Against my will, I felt my gaze fix on this small pile of human flesh. Our entire conversation was conducted while he trimmed off snippets from each of several organs.

I could feel my lips purse in distaste. "What are those?"

His expression was mild, impersonal, and amused. He used the tweezers to point, touching each of several hunks in turn. I half expected the little morsels to draw away from his probing, like live slugs, but none of them moved. "Well, let's see. That's a heart. Liver. Lung. Spleen. Gall bladder.

This fella died suddenly during surgery and nobody can figure out what his problem was."

"And you can? Just from doing that?"

"Well, not always, but I think we'll come up with something in this case," he said.

I didn't think I'd ever look at stew meat in quite the same
way. I couldn't take my eyes away from his dicing process
and I couldn't get it through my head that these had once
been functioning parts of a human being. If he was aware of
my fascination, he didn't give any indication of it and I tried
to be as nonchalant about the whole deal as he was.

He glanced over at me. "How does Kelly Borden figure
into this?"

"I'm not sure," I said. "Sometimes I have to look at things
that end up having no connection whatever to a case.
Maybe it's the same as what you do—inspecting all the
pieces of the puzzle until you come up with a theory."

"I suspect this is a lot more scientific than what you do,"
he remarked.

"Oh, no doubt about it," I said. "But I'll tell you one
advantage I have."

He paused, looking over at me again, but with the first
genuine interest I'd seen.

"I know the man whose death I'm dealing with and I have
a personal stake in the outcome. I think he was murdered
and it pisses me off. Disease is neutral. Homicide's not."

"I think your feeling for Bobby is coloring your judgment.
His death was accidental."

"Maybe. Or maybe I can persuade Homicide that he died
as a result of a murder attempt nine months ago."

"If you can prove that," he said. "So far I gather you don't
have much to go on, which is where your work differs from
mine. I can probably come up with something conclusive
here and I won't have to leave the room."

"I do envy you that," I said. "I mean, I don't doubt Bobby
was killed, but I don't have any idea who did it and I may
never have any evidence."

"Then I have it all over you," he said. "For the most part,
I deal in certainty. Once in a while, I'm stumped, but not
often."

"You're lucky."

Marcy returned with Kelly's address and telephone number on a slip of paper, which she handed to me.

"I prefer to think I'm talented," he was saying wryly. "I better not keep you in any case. Let me know how it comes out."

"I'll do that. Thanks for this," I said, holding up the slip of paper.

It was now five o'clock. I found a pay phone in an offshoot of one of the hospital corridors and tried Kelly's number.

He picked up on the third ring. I identified myself, reminding him of Dr. Fraker's introduction.

"I know who you are."

"Listen," I said, "could I stop by and talk to you? There's something I need to check out."

He seemed to hesitate at first. "Sure, O.K. You know where I am?"

Kelly's apartment was on the west side of town, not far from St. Terry's. I trotted back to my car and drove over to an address on Castle. I parked in front of a frame duplex and walked down a long driveway to a small wooden outbuilding at the rear of the property. His place, like mine, had probably been a garage at one time.

As I rounded some shrubs, I spotted him sitting on his front step, smoking a joint. He wore jeans and a leather vest over a plaid shirt, feet bare. His hair was pulled back in the same neat braid, beard and mustache looking grayer somehow than I remembered. He seemed very mellow, except for his eyes, which were aquamarine and impossible to read. He held the joint out to me, but I declined with a shake of my head.

"Didn't I see you at Bobby's funeral?" I asked.

"Might have. I saw you." His eyes settled on me with a disconcerting gaze. Where had I seen that color before? In a swimming pool where a dead man was floating like a lily pad. That had been four years ago, one of the first investigations I ever did.

"Chair over there if you have time to sit." He managed to get this sentence out while holding his breath, dope smoke locked in his lungs.

I glanced around and spotted an old wooden lawn chair, which I dragged over to the step. Then I took the address book out of my handbag and passed it to him, open to the back cover. "Any idea who this is? It's not a local number."

He glanced at the penciled entry and then gave me a quick look. "You tried calling?"

"Sure. I also tried the only Blackman listed in the book. It's a disconnect. Why? Do you know who it is?"

"I know the number, but it's not a telephone listing. Bobby moved the hyphen over."

"What's it for? I don't understand."

"These first two digits indicate Santa Teresa County. Last five are the morgue code. This is the I.D. number on a body we got in storage. I told you we had two that had been out there for years. This is Franklin."

"But why list it under Blackman?"

Kelly smiled at me, taking a long pull off his joint before he spoke. "Franklin's black. He's a black man. Must have been Bobby's joke."

"Are you sure?"

"Reasonably sure. You can check it yourself if you don't believe me."

"I think he was searching for a handgun out there. Would you have any idea where he might have started?"

"Nope. Place is big. They must have eighty, ninety rooms out there that haven't been used in years. Could be anywhere. Bobby would have worked his shift by himself. He had the run of the building as long as no one found out he was away from his work."

"Well. I guess I'll just have to wing it. I appreciate your help."

"No problem."

I went back to my office. Kelly Borden had told me that a kid named Alfie Leadbetter would be working the three-to-eleven shift at the morgue. The guy was a friend of his and he said he'd call ahead and let him know I was coming out.

I hauled out my typewriter again and made some notes. What was this? What did the corpse of a black man have to do with the murder of Dwight Costigan and the blackmailing of his former wife?

The phone rang and I picked it up like an automaton, my mind on the problem at hand. "Yes?"

"Kinsey?"

"Speaking."

"I wasn't sure that was you. This is Jonah. You always answer that way?"

I focused. "God, sorry. What can I do for you?"

"I heard about something I thought might interest you. You know that Callahan accident?"

"Sure. What about it?"

"I just ran into the guy who works Traffic and he says the lab boys went over the car this afternoon. The brake lines were cut just as clean as you please. They transferred the whole case to Homicide."

I could feel myself doing the same kind of mental double take I'd done just minutes before when I finally heard what the name Blackman meant. "What?"

"Your friend Bobby Callahan was murdered," Jonah said patiently. "The brake lines on his car had been cut, which means all the brake fluid ran out, which means he crashed into that tree because he rounded the curve with no way to slow down."

"I thought the autopsy showed he had a stroke."

"Maybe he did when he realized what was happening. That's not inconsistent as far as I can tell."

"Oh, you're right." For a moment I just breathed in Jonah's ear. "How long would that take?"

"What, cutting the brake lines or the fluid running out?"

"Both, now that you mention it."

"Oh, probably five minutes to cut the lines. That's no big deal if you know where to look. The other depends. He probably could have driven the car for a little while, pumped the brakes once or twice. Next thing he knew, he'd have tried 'em and boom, gone."

"So it happened that night? Whoever cut the lines?"

"Had to. The kid couldn't have driven far."

I was dead silent, thinking of the message Bobby'd left on my machine. He'd seen Kleinert the night he died. I remember Kleinert mentioning it too.

"You there?"

"I don't know what it means, Jonah," I said. "This case is starting to break and I just can't figure out what's going on."

"You want me to come over and we'll talk it out?"

"Not, not yet. I need to be by myself. Let me call you later when I have more to go on."

"Sure. You've got my home number, haven't you?"

"Better give it to me again," I said and jotted it down.

"Now, listen," he said to me. "Swear to me you won't do anything stupid."

"How can I do anything stupid? I don't even know what's going on," I said. "Besides, 'stupid' is after the fact. I always feel smart when I think things up."

"God damn it, you know what I'm talking about."

I laughed. "You're right. I know. And believe me, I'll call you if anything comes up. Honestly, my sole object in life is to protect my own ass."

"Well," he said grudgingly. "That's good to hear, but I doubt it."

We said our good-byes and he hung up. I left my hand on the receiver.

I tried Glen's number. I felt she should have the information and I couldn't be sure the cops would bring her up to date, especially since, at this point, they probably didn't have any more answers than I did.

She picked up the phone and I told her what was going on, including the business about Blackman in Bobby's address book. Of necessity, I told her as much as I knew about the blackmailing business. Hell, why not? This was no time to keep secrets. She already knew that Nola and Bobby were lovers. She might as well understand what he had undertaken in Nola's behalf. I even took the liberty of mentioning Sufi's involvement, though I still wasn't sure about that. I suspected that she was a go-between, ferrying messages between Nola and Bobby, counseling Bobby, perhaps, when his passion clashed with his youthful impatience.

She was quiet for a moment in the same way I had been. "What happens now?"

"I'll talk to Homicide tomorrow and tell them everything I know. They can handle it after that."

"Be careful in the meantime," she said.

"No sweat."

26

There was still an hour and a half of daylight left when I reached the old county medical complex. From the number of parking spaces available, it was clear that most of the offices were closed, personnel gone for the day. Kelly had told me there was a second parking lot around the side that was used by the janitorial staff at night. I didn't see any reason to park that far away. I pulled into a slot as close to the entrance as I could get, noting with interest that there was a bicycle chained to a rack just off to my left. It was a banged-up old Schwinn with fat tires and a fake license plate wired onto the rear, reading "Alfie." Kelly had told me the building was generally locked up by seven, but that I could buzz in and Alfie would buzz back to admit me.

I grabbed my flashlight and my key picks, pausing to pull a sweatshirt over my tank top. I remembered the building as chilly, even more so, I imagined, if I was there after sunset. I locked my car and headed for the entrance.

I paused at the double doors in front and pressed a bell to my right. After a moment, the door buzzed back, releasing the lock, and I went in. The lobby was already accumulating shadows and reminded me vaguely of an abandoned train station in a futuristic movie. It had that same air of vintage elegance: inlaid marble floors, high ceilings, beautiful woodwork of buffed oak. The few remaining fixtures must have been there since the twenties, when the place was built.

I crossed the lobby, glancing idly at the wall directory as I passed. Almost subliminally, a name caught my eye. I paused and looked again. Leo Kleinert had an office out here, which I hadn't realized before. Had Bobby driven this far for weekly psychiatric sessions? Seemed a bit out of the way. I went downstairs, footsteps scratching on the tile steps. As before, I could feel the temperature dropping, like a descent into the waters of a lake. Down here, it was gloomier, but the glass door to the morgue was lighted, a bright rectangle in the gathering darkness of the hall. I checked my watch. It wasn't even 7:15.

I tapped on the glass for form's sake and then tried the knob. It was unlocked. I opened the door and peered in.

"Hello?"

There was no one in evidence, but that had happened to me before when Dr. Fraker and I had visited. Maybe Alfie was in the refrigerated storage room where the bodies were kept.

"Heellloo!"

No response. He'd buzzed me in, so he had to be around here someplace.

I closed the door behind me. The fluorescent lighting was harsh, giving the illusion of winter sunlight. There was a door to my left. I crossed and knocked before I opened it to find an empty office with a dark brown Naugahyde couch. Maybe the guy on the graveyard shift snagged some shut-eye in here when nothing else was going on. There was a desk and a swivel chair. The outside of the window was covered with ornamental wrought-iron burglar bars, the daylight blocked out by a mass of unruly shrubs. I closed the door and moved over to the refrigerated room where the bodies were kept, peering in.

No Alfie in sight. Inside, the light was constant, occupants laid out on blue fiberglass berths, engaged in their eternal, motionless naps, some wrapped in sheets, some in plastic, necks and ankles wound with what looked like masking tape. Somehow, it reminded me of quiet time at summer camp.

I returned to the main room and sat for a while, staring at the autopsy table. My customary procedure would have been to snoop into every cabinet, drawer, and storage bin, but it felt disrespectful here. Or maybe I was afraid I'd stumble onto something grotesque: trays of dentures, a Mason jar chock-full of floating eyeballs. I don't know what I thought I'd see. I shifted restlessly. I felt as if I were wasting time. I went to the door and looked out into the hall, tilting my head to listen. Nothing.

"Alfie?" I called. I listened again, then shrugged and closed the door. It occurred to me that as long as I was there, I could at least verify that the number Bobby'd written down was, in fact, the same as the number on Franklin's toe tag. That wouldn't do any harm. I took the address book out of my handbag and turned to the penciled entry on the back cover. I went into the cold-storage room again, moving from body to body, checking I.D. tags. This was like some kind of bargain-basement sale only nothing was marked down.

When I got to the third body, the numbers matched. Kelly was right. Bobby'd shifted the hyphen over so the seven-digit code looked like a telephone number. I stared at the body, or what I could see of it. The plastic that Franklin was wrapped in was transparent but yellowing, as though stained with nicotine. Through the swaddling, I could see that he was a middle-aged black man of medium height, slim, with a face of stone. Why was this corpse significant? I was feeling anxious. I figured Alfie would be back shortly and I really didn't want to be caught nosing around in here. I went back to my chair.

Coming out of the cold-storage room was like leaving an air-conditioned theater. It made the autopsy room feel balmy by comparison. I was getting itchy to explore. I couldn't help myself. I was irritated that no one was there to help me and feeling edgy from the quiet. This was not a fun place. Ordinarily, I don't hang out in morgues and it was making me tense.

Just to soothe my nerves, I peered into a drawer, testing the contents against the grisly images I'd conjured up. This one contained scratch pads, order blanks, and miscellaneous paper supplies. Reassured, I tried the next drawer: small vials of several drugs, the names of which I did not recognize. I was warming up here and I checked on down the line. Everything appeared to be related to the business of dissecting the dead; not surprising, given the locale, but not very enlightening.

I straightened up and looked around the room. Where were the files? Didn't anybody keep records around this

place? Somebody had mentioned that there were medical
charts stored out here, but where? This floor? Somewhere
on one of the floors above? I didn't relish the idea of creep-
ing through the empty building by myself. I'd been picturing Alfie Leadbetter at my side, telling me what was
accessible and where I might start. I'd even pictured slipping him a twenty-dollar bill if that's what it took to enlist
his aid.

I glanced at my watch. I'd now been here forty-five minutes and I wanted some results. I grabbed my handbag and
went out in the hall, looking in both directions. It was getting darker down here, although I could see through a window at the end of the hall that it was still light outside. I
found a wall switch and flipped on the lights and then I
wandered along the corridor, reading the small white signs
mounted above each office door. The radiology offices were
right next to the morgue. Beyond that, Nuclear Medicine,
and nursing offices. I wondered if Sufi Daniels had occasion
to come out here.

Something was beginning to stir at the back of my brain.
I was thinking about the cardboard box full of Bobby's belongings. What was in it? Medical texts and office supplies
and two radiology manuals. What was he actually doing
with those? He hadn't even been a medical student and I
couldn't think why he'd need the manuals for equipment he
might not be using for years, if ever. He'd indicated no particular interest in radiology.

I went upstairs. It wouldn't hurt to look at that stuff
again. When I reached the front entrance, I slipped off my
sweatshirt and wedged it in the opening. I could push the
door open with no problem, but I didn't want the lock snapping shut behind me as I went out. I crossed to my car and
unlocked it, wrestling the carton out the backseat. I removed the two radiology books and leafed through them
quickly. These were technical manuals for specific equipment, information about the various gauges and dials and
switches, with a lot of esoteric talk about exposures, rads,
and roentgens. At the top of one page was a penciled
number, like a doodle, surrounded by curlicues. Franklin's
again. The sight of the now familiar seven-digit code

seemed eerie, like the sound of Bobby's voice on my answering machine five days after he died.

I tucked the two manuals under my arm and locked my car again, leaving the box on the front seat. Slowly, I returned to the building. I let myself in, pausing to pull on my sweatshirt. As long as I was on the first floor, I did a superficial survey. I kept thinking it was medical records I was looking for, the handgun tucked down in a banker's box packed with old charts. This had been a working hospital at one time and there had to be a records department somewhere. Where else would old charts be kept? If my memory of St. Terry's served me, the Medical Records Department was fairly centrally located so that doctors and other authorized personnel would have easy access.

Not many offices on this floor appeared to be occupied. I tried door handles randomly. Most were locked. I rounded the corner at the end of the hall and there it was, "Medical Records" painted above a set of double doors in a faded scrawl. I could see now that many of the old departments were similarly marked: florid lettering on a painted scroll, as though by declaration of the conquistadors.

I tried the knob, expecting to have to experiment with my key picks. Instead, the door swung open with a low-pitched creak that might have been contrived by a special-effects man. Waning daylight filtered in. The room yawned before me, barren, stripped of everything. No file cabinets, no furniture, no fixtures. A crumpled cigarette pack, some loose boards, and a couple of bent nails were scattered across the floor. This department had literally been dismantled at some point and God only knew where the old records were now. It was possible they were somewhere in one of the abandoned hospital rooms above, but I really didn't want to go up there by myself. I'd promised Jonah I wouldn't be stupid and I was trying to be a good scout on that score. Besides, something else was nagging at me.

I returned to the stairs, descending. What was that little voice in the back of my head murmuring? It was like a radio playing in the next room. I could pick up only a faint phrase now and then.

When I reached the basement, I crossed to the radiology office and tried the knob. Locked. I got out my key picks and played around for a while. This was one of those "burglar-proof" locks that *can* be picked, but it really is a pain in the ass. Still, I wanted to see what was in there and I worked patiently. I was using a set of rocker picks, with random depth cuts spaced along the top, the back side of each pick ground to an oval. The whole idea is that with enough different cut combinations, together with an applied rocking motion, somewhere along the way all the pins will, by chance, be raised to the shear line at the same time, popping the lock.

Like hiding, the only way to approach the whole process is to give oneself up to it. I stood there for maybe twenty minutes, easing the pick forward, rocking it, applying slight pressure when I felt movement of any sort. Lo and behold, the sucker gave way and I let out a little exclamation of delight. "Oh, wow. Hey, that's great." It's this sort of shit that makes my job fun. Also illegal, but who was going to tell?

I eased into the office. I flipped the overhead light on. It looked like ordinary office space. Typewriters and telephones and file cabinets, plants on the desks, pictures on the walls. There was a small reception area where I imagined patients seated, waiting to be called for their X rays. I wandered through some of the rooms in the rear, picturing the procedures for chest X rays and mammograms, upper G.I. series. I stood in front of the machines and opened one of the manuals I'd brought in from the car.

I checked the diagrams against the various dials and gauges on the X-ray equipment itself. It was a match, more or less. Maybe some variation according to year, make, or model of the actual machinery installed. Some of it looked like the stuff of science fiction. Massive nose cone on a swinging arm. I stood there, manual open in my arms, pages pressed to my chest while I stared at the table and the lead apron that looked like a baby bib for a giant. I thought about the X rays I'd had taken of my left arm two months ago, just after I'd been shot.

It wasn't as if the idea came to me all at once. It formed around me, like fairy dust, gradually taking shape. Bobby had been out here all by himself, just like this. Night after night, searching for the handgun that had Nola's fingerprints on it. He knew who had hidden it, so he must have formed some kind of theory about the hiding place. I had to guess that he'd found the gun and that's why he was killed. Maybe he'd actually retrieved it, but I didn't think so. I'd been operating on the assumption that it was still hidden out here and that still seemed like a good bet. He'd made some little notes to himself, doodling the I.D. number of a corpse in his little red book and again in the pages of a radiology manual he'd acquired.

The phrases running through my head began to connect. Maybe you should X-ray the corpse, said I to myself. Maybe that's what Bobby did and maybe that's why he made the penciled notation in the radiology book. Maybe the gun is *inside* the corpse. I thought about it briefly, but I couldn't see why I shouldn't give it a try. The worst that could happen (aside from my getting caught) was that I'd be wasting time and making a colossal fool of myself. This would not be a first.

I left my handbag and the manuals on one of the X-ray tables and went next door to the morgue. In the refrigerated storage room, I spotted a gurney against the right wall. I was on automatic pilot by now, simply doing what I knew had to be done. There was still no sign of Alfie Leadbetter and no one was going to help me. I might be wrong, so maybe it was just as well that no one knew what I was up to. The building was deserted. It was early yet. Even if I fumbled the X-ray procedure, it couldn't hurt the dead man.

I rolled the gurney over to the fiberglass bunk where the body lay. I pretended I was a morgue attendant. I pretended I was an X-ray technician or a nurse, some thoroughly professional person with a job to do.

"Sorry to disturb you, Frank," I said, "but you have to go next door for some tests. You're not looking so good."

Tentatively, I reached out and eased a hand under Franklin's neck and knees and pulled, slipping him from his resting place onto the gurney. He was surprisingly light, and cold to the touch, about the consistency of a package of raw chicken breasts just out of the fridge. God, I thought, why do I plague myself with these domestic images? I'd never be motivated to learn to cook at this rate.

It took incredible maneuvering to get the gurney through
the morgue and out into the corridor, then into the reception area of the radiology offices and into one of the X-ray
rooms in the rear. I lined the gurney up parallel to the X-ray
table and shoved the body into place. I raised and lowered
the nose cone a couple of times experimentally, sliding it
along its overhead track until it was right over Franklin's
abdomen. At some point, I was going to have to figure out
how far away from the body it should be. Meanwhile, since
I intended to take some pictures, I thought I better find
some film of some kind.

I looked through the four cabinets in the room and found
nothing. I circled the room. There was a shallow cupboard
mounted on the wall, like a fuse box with double doors. A
strip of masking tape was pasted on one side, with the word
exposed printed on it in ballpoint pen. A second strip of
tape said *unexposed*. I opened that door. There were film
cassettes of varying sizes lined up like serving trays. I took
one out.

I went over to the table and studied the layout of the
machinery. I didn't see any way to slide the cassette into the
apparatus above the table, but there was a sliding tray in the
table itself, just under the padded edge. I pulled it out and
inserted the cassette. I hoped I had guessed right about
which side should be up. Looked right to me. Maybe I
could fashion a whole new career out of this.

I figured Franklin didn't need protecting, so I picked up
the full-length lead apron and put it on myself, feeling
somehow like the goalie in a hockey match. Actually, I'd
never seen an X-ray technician running around in one of
these things, but it made me feel secure. I pointed the nose
cone at Franklin's belly, about three feet up, and then went
behind the screen in one corner of the room.

I checked the manual again, leafing through until I found
diagrams that seemed relevant. There were numerous
gauges with little arrow-shaped pointers at rest, ready to
whip into the green zone, the yellow, or the red at the flick
of a switch. There was a lever on the right marked "power
supply," which I flipped to the "on" position. Nothing went
on. A puzzlement. I flipped it off and then checked the wall
to my left. There were two breaker boxes with big switches

that I shifted from "off" to "on." There was a murmur of power being generated. I flipped the power supply lever to "on" again. The machine came on. I smiled. That was great.

I studied the panel in front of me. There was a timer that would apparently have to be set on a scale from 1/120 of a second to six seconds. A gauge for kilovolts. One marked "milliamperes." God, three rows of lighted green squares to choose from. I started with a midrange setting on everything, figuring I could use one gauge as a control and adjust the other two in some sort of rotating system. In between, I would check my results on the finished film and see what kind of picture I was getting.

I peered around the screen. "O.K., Frank, take a deep breath and hold."

Well, at least he got the "holding" part right.

I pressed the switch on the handgrip. I heard a brief bzzt. Cautiously, I came out from behind the screen as though X rays might still be flying around the room. I crossed to the table and removed the cassette. Now what? There had to be some kind of developing process, but it didn't appear to be in here. I left the machine on and carried the cassette with me, checking into rooms nearby.

Two doors away, I found what looked right to me. On the wall was a flow chart, giving the step-by-step procedure for developing plates. I could get a job out here after this.

Again, it was necessary to switch the power on. After that, I worked in the dull red glow of the safelights, squinting my way through the process slowly. I filled the wall-mounted tank with water as specified. I flipped the cassette over and unlatched the back, removing the film, which I eased into the tray. It disappeared into the machine with a sound.

Shoot, where'd it go? I couldn't see anything in the room that looked like it would produce a piece of processed film. I felt like a puppy learning what happens when a ball rolls under the couch. I left the room and went next door. The hind end of the automatic developer was there, looking like a big Xerox machine with a slot. I waited. A minute and a half later, a finished piece of film slid out. I looked at it. Pitch black. Shit. What had I done wrong? How could it be overexposed when I'd been so careful? I stared at the developer. The lid was open a crack. I peered at it. Experimentally, I gave it a push. It snapped shut. Maybe that would do it.

I went back into the other room and got a second cassette out and went through the entire process again. Two rounds later, I found what I was looking for. The overall quality of the picture was poor, but the image was distinct. In the center of Franklin's belly was the solid white silhouette of a handgun. It looked like a large-frame automatic, arranged at an angle, maybe to accommodate his skeletal structure or internal organs. There was something unnerving about the sight. I rolled up the X ray and put a rubber band around it. Time to get out of here.

Hastily, I shut down the machinery and shifted Franklin onto the cart for the ride back to the morgue, turning off lights and locking up the office in my wake.

I navigated the gurney back through the hall and into the morgue. I was easing Franklin onto his berth again when something caught my eye. I glanced over at the next tier of bunks. A man's hand was resting just about at eye level and it didn't look right. The bodies I'd seen had been deadly pale, the flesh like a doll's skin, rubbery and unreal. This hand seemed too pink. I could see now that the body itself was only loosely covered with plastic sheeting. Had it been there before? I moved closer, reaching out hesitantly. I think I made that little humming sound you make when you're close to a shriek, but haven't yet committed yourself.

Tentatively, I lifted the plastic away from the face. Male, white, in his twenties. There was no pulse evident but that was probably because there was a ligature wound around his neck so tightly that it had all but disappeared, sinking into the flesh until his tongue bugged out. The body was cool, but not cold. I stopped breathing. I thought my heart would stop as well. I was reasonably sure I'd just made the acquaintance of Alfie Leadbetter, newly deceased. At that instant I wasn't as worried about who had killed him as who had buzzed the door open to let me in. I didn't think it was Alf. I suddenly suspected that I'd been cruising around that deserted building in the company of a killer who was undoubtedly still there, waiting to see what I was up to, waiting to do to me what had been done to the hapless morgue attendant who'd gotten in the way.

I backed out of the room as fast as I could, my heart banging away, sending sick spurts of fear through my electrified frame. The morgue was reassuringly bright, but so deadly still.

Mentally, I traced an escape route, wondering what choices I had. The windows down here were covered with burglar bars too narrow to slip through. The exterior doors were heavy glass, embedded with wire that I might or might not be able to penetrate. I certainly wasn't going to smash through them without calling attention to myself. I'd have to try for the stairs, pushing out of the same double doors I'd come through in the first place, though the idea of even going out into the *hall* at this point was nearly more than I could bear.

Somewhere above me, a door slammed and I jumped. I heard someone coming down the stairs, whistling aimlessly. A security guard? Someone coming back after work? I absolutely could not move. It was too late for action, too late for escape, and there was no place to hide. Transfixed, I stared at the door as footsteps approached. Someone paused in the corridor, singing the first few snatches of "Someone to Watch over Me." The knob turned and Dr. Fraker came in, glancing up, startled, at the sight of me.

"Oh! Hello. I didn't expect to see you here," he said. "I thought you were off talking to Kelly."

I let out a breath and found my voice. "I did that. A little while ago."

"Jesus, what's wrong? You're as white as a ghost."

I shook my head. "I was just on my way out when I heard the door slam. You scared the shit out of me." My voice cracked in the middle of the sentence as if I'd just reached puberty.

"Sorry. I didn't mean to spook you like that." He had on his surgical greens. I watched him cross the counter and open a drawer, taking out instruments. From the next drawer down, he took out a vial and a syringe.

"Listen, we've got a problem," I said.

"Oh really. What's that?" Dr. Fraker turned to smile at me and Nola's line popped into my head. "We're talking about a lunatic. Someone so crazy," she had whispered. Dr. Fraker's eyes were fixed on mine as he filled the syringe. The penny dropped. She hadn't wanted to stay *in* the marriage. She had wanted *out*. Bobby Callahan in his naïveté had thought he could help.

It was there in his face and the lazy way he moved. This man meant to kill me. Judging from the tools he'd assembled, he had all of the equipment he needed—nice table with a drain, hacksaws, scalpels, a working disposal just under the sink. He knew anatomy too, all the tendons and ligaments. I pictured a turkey wing, how you have to bend it backward to ease the blade into that joint.

I usually cry when I'm scared and I could feel tears well up. Not sorrow, but horror. Given all the lies I'd told in my life, right then I couldn't think of one. My mind was empty of thought. There I stood with the X ray in my hand, the truth, I'm sure, written all over my face. My only hope was to act before he did and move twice as fast.

I dove for the door, fumbling with the knob. I yanked it open and ran for the stairs, taking two at a time, then three, looking back with a moan of raw fear. He was coming out of the door, syringe held loosely in one hand. What scared me was that he was moving slowly, as if he had all the time in the world. He'd taken up the song lyric where he left off, a sort of tuneless rendition that didn't do the Gershwins justice.

"Like a little lamb who's lost in the wood . . . I know I could always be good . . . to one who'll watch over me . . ."

I reached the top of the stairs. What did he know that I didn't know? Why did he feel that this leisurely pace would suit when I was flying toward the entrance? I lowered a shoulder and slammed up against the double doors, but neither gave way. I rammed them again. The entranceway, locked like this, formed a small cul-de-sac. If I gave him time to reach the corridor, I'd have no way out. I reached the hall just as he got to the top of the stairs.

Chit, chit. I could hear his footsteps scratch on the tile while he sang on.

"Although he may not be the man some girls think of as handsome, to my heart he'll carry the key . . ."

Still taking his time. I wanted to scream, but what was the point? The building was empty. It was locked up tight. Dark except for the pale light filtering in from the parking lot. I needed a weapon. Dr. Fraker had his little syringe filled with whatever he meant to pop me with. He was a big guy too, and once he made contact, I was in trouble.

I flew down the hall to the old medical-records room and slammed the door back on its hinge. I snatched up a two-by-four, still running, and headed back out into the corridor, racing for the far end. There had to be stairs. There had to be windows to smash, *some* way out.

Behind me, from a man who couldn't even carry a tune, I heard . . . *"Won't you tell him please to put on some speed, follow my lead, oh how I need, someone to watch over me . . ."*

I reached the stairwell and headed up, beginning to analyze the situation as I ran. At this rate, he could chase me all over the building. I'd soon be exhausted and he wouldn't even be breaking a sweat. Not a good idea, this form of pursuit. I reached the landing and snatched for the door. Locked. There was just one more floor. Was I being trapped or herded? In either case, I had the feeling he was in charge, that he'd set this all up in advance.

He was just coming into the stairwell below me as I took to the stairs again, heading toward the third floor, the two-by-four clutched in my hot little hand. I didn't like this. The door at the third floor flew back at a touch and I stepped into the darkened hall. I took off to my right, forcing myself to slow my pace. I was out of breath from climbing the stairs, bathed in sweat. I considered searching out a place to hide, but my choices were limited. There were rooms opening off on either side of me, but I was afraid I was going to get cornered in one. All he had to do was check each one in turn and pretty soon he'd figure out where I was. Also I hate hiding. It turns me into a six-year-old and I'm sick of that. I wanted to be on my feet, in motion, taking action instead of crouching down with my hands held over my face hoping God had rendered me transparent.

I made another right-hand turn. Behind me, I heard the door to the third-floor landing slam shut. I spotted an elevator halfway down the corridor on the right-hand side. I sprinted, and when I reached it, pounded on the "down" button with my palm.

Dr. Fraker had just taken up a new tune, this time whistling the first few bars of "I Don't Stand a Ghost of a Chance with You." Was this man sick or what?

I banged on the button again, listening fervently as the elevator cable whirred softly on the other side of the door. I looked to my right. There he came, his surgical greens showing up as a pale glow in the shadows. I heard the mechanism stop. He seemed to be moving faster, but he was still twenty yards away from me. The elevator doors slid open. Oh fuck!

I stepped forward just as I flashed on the fact that there was nothing there except a yawning shaft and a gust of cold air wafting up from below. I caught myself half a second from tumbling into that pitch-black hole. A low cry escaped me as I caught at the doorframe, swinging out over the pit for an instant before I managed to right myself. I stumbled backward to safety but I'd lost my purchase. I was down and the two-by-four flew out of my hand, skittering off. I flipped over on my hands and knees scrambling toward it.

He had caught up to me by then and he grabbed me by the hair, hauling me upright just as my hand closed around the board. I swung it up, whacking at him. I made contact but the angle was awkward and there was no force behind the blow. I felt the sting of the needle in my left thigh. Both of us barked out a sound at the same time. Mine was a shrill yelp of pain and surprise, his the low grunt as the impact from the two-by-four registered. I had the advantage of a split second and I took it, lashing out with a side kick that caught him in the shin. No good, too low. The wisdom of self-defense would have it that there's no point in simply inflecting pain on your attacker. It'll just piss him off. Unless I could disable him, I didn't have a chance.

He grabbed at me from behind. I snapped my left elbow back, but again I was slightly off the mark. I pushed at him, kicking repeatedly at his shin until he backed off, breathing hard. I cracked him one across the shoulder with the two-by-four and ran, pounding down the hall. I stumbled briefly, but regained my footing. I felt as if I'd stepped in a hole, and it occurred to me belatedly that whatever he'd injected me with was taking effect. My left leg was feeling wobbly, my kneecap loose, both feet going numb. The same fear that had sent adrenaline coursing through my body was speeding some drug on its way. Like snakebite. They say you shouldn't run.

I glanced back. He was clutching his shoulder, just beginning to move in my direction, coming slowly again. He didn't seem worried that I'd get away, so I had to guess that he had jammed the door to the stairwell as he came through. Either that or he knew that the shit he'd popped me with would soon knock me out. I was losing contact with my extremities and I could scarcely sense my own grip on the board. A chill was seeping from my skin toward my core as if I were being put through a quick-freeze process for shipping to God knows where. I was working as hard as I could, but the darkness had become gelatinous and I felt slow. Time was grinding down too as my body labored against the drug. My mind was working, but I felt myself distracted by the odd sensations I experienced.

Oh, the bothersome details that finally fall into place like a little right-brain joke. It did come to me, in a flash, like a bubble through my veins, that Fraker was the one supplying Kitty with drugs, probably in exchange for information about Bobby's search for the gun. The stash in her bed-table drawer was a plant. He'd been there that night. Maybe he thought it was time to take her out, lest she in her guilt admit to her own duplicity where Bobby was concerned.

The distance to the corner of the hallway had been extended. I'd been running forever. The simple commands I was managing to send to my body were taking too long and I was losing the feedback system that records a response. Was I, in fact, running? Was I going anywhere? Sound was being stretched out, the echo of my own footsteps coming belatedly. I felt as if I were bounding down a corridor with a floor like a trampoline. Flash number two. Fraker had rigged the autopsy report. No seizure. He'd cut the brake lines. Too bad I hadn't figured it out before now. God, what a dummy I was.

I reached the corner slowing, and I could feel my body folding down on itself. As I rounded the corner, I had to pause. I propped myself against the wall, working to breathe. I had to clear my head. Stay upright. I had to lift my arms if I could. Time had begun to stretch out like taffy, long strands, sticky, hard to manage.

He was singing again, treating me to some oldies but goodies in his own private hit parade. He'd moved on now to "Accentuate the positive . . . eliminate the negative" . . . vowels dragged out like a phonograph record slowing when the power shuts off.

Even the voice in my own brain got hollow and remote. Crouch, Kinsey, it said.

I thought I might be crouching but I couldn't tell anymore where my legs were or my hips or much of my spine. My arms were feeling heavy and I wondered if my elbows were bent.

Batter up, the voice said and I believed, but couldn't have sworn to the fact, that I was drawing the two-by-four back, elbow crooked as my aunt had taught me long long ago.

Day was passing into night, life into death.

Fraker's voice droned out the song. "*Acceeennntuate the poooosssitive, eeeelllliiiimindaate the neeegatiiiive . . .*"

When he came around the corner, I stepped into the swing, the two-by-four aimed straight at his face. I could see the board begin its march through space, like a series of time-lapse photographs, light against dark, closing down the distance. I felt the board connect with a sweet popping sound.

It was out of the ball park and I went down with the roar of the crowd in my ears.

Epilogue

They told me later, though I remember little of it, that I managed to make my way down to the morgue, where I dialed 911, mumbling a message that brought the cops. What comes back to me most clearly is the hangover I endured after the cocktail of barbiturates I was injected with. I woke in a hospital bed, as sick as a dog. But even with a pounding head, retching into a kidney-shaped plastic basin, I was glad to be among the living.

Glen spoiled me silly and everyone came to see me, including Jonah, Rosie, Gus, and Henry, bearing hot cross buns. Lila, he said, had written to him from a jail up north, but he didn't bother to reply. Glen never relented in her determination to reject both Derek and Kitty, but I introduced Kitty Wenner to Gus. Last I heard, they were dating and Kitty was cleaning up her act. Both had gained weight.

Dr. Fraker is currently out on bail, awaiting trial on charges of attempted murder and two counts of first-degree murder. Nola pleaded guilty to voluntary manslaughter, but served no time. When I got back to the office, I typed up my report, submitting a bill for thirty-three hours, plus mileage; a total I rounded off to an even $1000. The balance of Bobby's advance I returned to Varden Talbot's office to be factored into his estate. The rest of the report is a personal letter. Much of my last message to Bobby is devoted to the simple fact that I miss him. I hope, wherever he may be, that he sails among the angels, untethered and at peace.

—Respectfully submitted,
Kinsey Millhone

ABOUT THE AUTHOR

SUE GRAFTON was already a successful screenwriter and the author of two novels when she launched the Kinsey Millhone series in 1983. She is currently at work on *"D" Is for Deadbeat*, which is set to appear in 1987.

from Sue Grafton
author of "A" IS FOR ALIBI

"B" IS FOR BURGLAR
A Kinsey Millhone Mystery

KINSEY MILLHONE IS ...

"The best new private eye."　　　　　*—The Detroit News*

"A woman we feel we know, a tough cookie with a soft center, a gregarious loner."　　　　*—Newsweek*

"Smart, sexual, likable, and a very modern operator."
　　　　　　　　　　　—Dorothy Salisbury Davis

"A stand-out specimen of the new female operatives."
　　　　　　　　　　　—Philadelphia Inquirer

"Thirty-two, twice divorced, and lives in a fifteen-foot-square room in a converted garage ... On the road she stays in crummy motels because she's cheap. She likes people for good reasons. She's smart but she makes mistakes ... I like Millhone."　　　　　　*—The Detroit Free Press*

Finding wealthy Elaine Boldt seems like a quickie case to Kinsey Millhone. The flashy widow was last seen wearing a $12,000 lynx coat, leaving her condo in Santa Teresa for her condo in Boca Raton. But somewhere in between, she vanished. Kinsey's case goes from puzzling to sinister when a house is torched, an apartment is burgled of worthless papers, the lynx coat comes back without Elaine, and her bridge partner is found dead. Soon Kinsey's clues begin to form a capital M—not for missing, but for murder. And plenty of it.

Look for "B" IS FOR BURGLAR in your bookstore or use this coupon:

50 YEARS OF GREAT AMERICAN MYSTERIES FROM BANTAM BOOKS

Stuart Palmer

"Those who have not already made the acquaintance of Hildegarde Withers should make haste to do so, for she is one of the world's shrewdest and most amusing detectives."
—*New York Times*
May 6, 1934

☐ 25934-2 THE PUZZLE OF THE SILVER PERSIAN (1934) $2.95
☐ 26024-3 THE PUZZLE OF THE HAPPY HOOLIGAN
(1941) $2.95

Featuring spinster detective Hildegarde Withers

Craig Rice

"Why can't all murders be as funny as those concocted by Craig Rice? —*New York Times*
☐ 26345-5 HAVING WONDERFUL CRIME $2.95
"Miss Rice at her best, writing about her 3 favorite characters against a delirious New York background."
—*New Yorker*
☐ 26222-X MY KINGDOM FOR A HEARSE $2.95
"Pretty damn wonderful!" —*New York Times*

Barbara Paul

☐ 26234-3 RENEWABLE VIRGIN (1985) $2.95
"The talk crackles, the characters are bouncy, and New York's media world is caught with all its vitality and vulgarity." —*Washington Post Book World*
☐ 26225-4 KILL FEE (1985) $2.95
"A desperately treacherous game of cat-and-mouse (whose well-wrought tension is heightened by a freakish twist that culminates in a particularly chilling conclusion." —*Booklist*

For your ordering convenience, use the handy coupon below: